DOWN & DIRTY: CROW

Dirty Angels MC, book 10

JEANNE ST. JAMES

Editor: Proofreading by the Page
Cover Art: Susan Garwood of Wicked Women Designs
Beta Readers: Author Whitley Cox, Krisztina Hollo, Andi Babcock and Sharon Abrams

www.jeannestjames.com

Sign up for my newsletter for insider information, author news, and new releases:
www.jeannestjames.com/newslettersignup

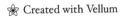 Created with Vellum

Keep an eye on her website at http://www.jeannestjames.com/ or sign up for her newsletter to learn about her upcoming releases: http://www.jeannestjames.com/newslettersignup

Down & Dirty 'til Dead

CHAPTER ONE

C row heard the front door buzzer sound over the whine of his tattoo machine. He glanced up and his heart skipped a beat. Quickly pulling his boot off the foot pedal, he put the gun down on the tray before the straight line he was drawing became a wavy mess.

Holy fuck.

She was the last person he ever expected to walk into his shop.

He almost didn't recognize her. She'd changed.

This was not the girl he knew. The person who stood just inside In the Shadows Ink was not the same woman he knew all those years ago.

Recognizable, but not.

He pushed to his feet and, before he could stop himself, took long strides across the shop floor, ignoring the complaints from the customer abandoned in his tattoo chair.

Crow never slowed as he approached her, even as her green eyes darkened, slightly widened and quickly filled with a little bit of uncertainty.

He ignored that, too.

When he got to her, he gathered her in his arms, crushing her against him tightly. She stiffened, her spine becoming ramrod straight, her arms hanging like metal poles at her side. But he wasn't letting her go.

Not yet.

He needed to hold her, make sure she was real.

He needed proof that she still existed, since he'd wondered if she'd disappeared forever.

Finally, a whimper came from the woman whose face he had shoved into his chest, inside his cut. His arms and black leather vest surrounded her slight body like the wings of a bird protecting its young.

Though, she was no baby bird.

Hell no, she wasn't.

She was a survivor.

Her rigid body suddenly went soft, melted against him and she began to tremble. Her thin arms snaked around his waist under his cut and she squeezed him just as tightly as he did her, her fingers fisting in his T-shirt at his back. He pressed his face into her hair and closed his eyes.

He didn't know why she was here. He didn't care. All he knew was, she was home.

"Jasmine," he murmured. And, *fuck him*, if he didn't feel the sting of something caught in his eye. He blinked it clear.

"Hey!" his customer yelled. "Have your fucking touching reunion another time. I'm paying you to get this thing done today."

Jazz jerked within his arms at those irritated words.

"That's okay, *Kachina*, I got this," he murmured into her hair. Without letting her go, he twisted his head and pointed his gaze to the man sitting in his plastic-wrapped chair. "I'm closed. Get gone."

"But—"

"Didn't fuckin' stutter. Closed. Family emergency."

"But—" the man sputtered.

"Wipe it down, keep it covered, keep it clean. A&D Ointment. Come back in two weeks, I'll finish it on the house. Got me?"

"But—"

"Ain't no buts." Crow jerked his chin toward the door. "Out."

With a grumble and a scowl, the man climbed out of the chair and nabbed his nearby T-shirt. Crow tracked him as he passed by, keeping Jazz's face tucked against his chest.

"Two weeks," the man said before heading out of the front door.

Crow gave him a sharp nod. "Two weeks. No charge."

"Right."

"Right," Crow echoed him.

Once the door closed, Crow took a long, deep inhale and slowly let it out. Then he released her and held her out in front of him by her shoulders, so he could take a better look. "*Kachina*," he murmured. "Baby." While on the surface she looked okay, it didn't mean she was.

Her blonde hair was now dark. Actually pitch black, making her fair skin look even paler.

He hated it.

She wore thick black mascara, and too much caked-on shit covered the natural beauty of her face.

He hated that, too.

But it was her eyes. Something she couldn't change, couldn't hide, that twisted his insides. Those formerly vibrant green eyes seemed hollow. Empty. Dull.

Nothing like when she was twenty-two. The last time he saw her. When she was Hawk's house mouse. When she was a college student. Carefree.

Living the good life. Not a care in the world. Her whole future ahead of her.

That future had been kicked right in the fucking nuts.

Wrong place. Wrong time.

She had been collateral damage in a war that she had no business being a part of.

Yeah, she was DAMC because her grandfather was one of the oldest members who wasn't in prison, or underground. But she never asked for any of it.

Her mother wanted better for herself and her daughter, so Jazz's parents had moved hours away after she was born. Different town. Different state. Different life. Until they couldn't afford their daughter's college tuition.

So at eighteen, Jazz returned to Shadow Valley. Back to the club. Back to her grandparents so the club could cover the cost of her education.

What was supposed to help her turned out to hurt her instead.

And afterward, she returned home to New York. To heal. To hide. To forget.

He never thought she'd be back. No one ever thought she'd return.

She'd ignored everyone's calls, texts, and emails for the past six years.

Every fucking one of them.

He wondered, why now? And why him?

Maybe she'd stopped at church or The Iron Horse Roadhouse before heading over to his shop.

"You back to stay?"

She shook her head, not meeting his eyes. "No, I finished my degree online a while ago. There's no reason for me to stay. I only came to see you."

"Grizz an' Momma Bear are two good reasons. They miss you."

She nodded, staring at the floor. "Yeah, I'll visit them before I leave."

"Kiki... Hawk."

She tilted her head, peering up at him through that thick black mess of eye goop. She needed to wash that shit off her face. It wasn't her. It wasn't Jazz. "I... Kiki... It might be too hard. She'll understand."

"She feels it was her fault," he murmured. "We all tell her it wasn't. Might need to hear it from you."

"Crow..." she whispered.

"*Kachina*, Keeks needs to hear it from you. Thinkin' it'll be good for you both." He reached out for her arm, but she jerked it away and took a step back.

"I don't know if I can do that."

Crow studied her for a moment. She'd matured since he'd seen her that very last time, broken and battered in that hospital bed. Since then, her curves had slightly rounded, but not enough. Her breasts had become just slightly fuller. But her waist was too narrow, her face too thin. Her long legs like sticks in her torn jeans and tucked into heavy black combat boots. She was doing her best to stay unnaturally skinny, avoid the curves that may attract men. She wanted to remain unnoticed. Unapproachable.

No matter what, he could see her clearly. She was trying to hide who she should be, but she couldn't hide from him.

Whether she wanted to or not, she needed to stick around for at least the next six months so Mamma Bear could feed her well. Fill the hollows of her cheeks, put some flesh on her bones. Grow out that dyed hair and scrape that shit off her face.

Jazz was still there, hidden by someone else. She was wearing a mask. Wearing armor.

"Grizz an' Momma Bear know you're in town?"

"Not yet."

"But you're goin' to see 'em?"

"Yeah."

That didn't sound convincing. "Swear?"

To avoid him, her gaze bounced around the shop, landing on the now empty chair, the sketches taped to the walls, the uneven piles of ink magazines. His shop wasn't fancy, but it was efficient. It did the job, making him and the club decent money.

"So then... what're you doin' here, *Kachina*?"

"I need ink and I know you're the best. I'd be a fool to go elsewhere."

She had walked across the room and now stared at the flash tattoo designs that every tattoo shop in America had on their walls. But Crow hated doing the ordinary. He preferred custom art and always tried to convince his customers to go that route. He'd even teamed up with Jag to design some specialty pieces to tattoo on customers willing to pay some major scratch for an M. Jagger Jamison original.

"Got somethin' in mind?"

She shook her head, still staring at the boring tattoos that everyone and their brother had. Anchors. Hearts. Roses. Typical tribal bands worn by white boys thinking they were cool but would never understand those designs meant nothing.

"Gonna make somethin' special, just for you, then."

She nodded but still said nothing.

"C'mere, baby," he whispered.

Her head dropped, and her body went still.

"C'mere," he whispered again.

She slowly turned, her eyes shadowed, biting her bottom lip.

"Need to make sure you're real. You're really fuckin' here."

She nodded silently and slowly moved toward him. But he met her halfway and wrapped her tightly in his arms again. He couldn't get her close enough. He wished he could absorb her until he could take her past and all of her pain away, then help her move on and get back to the life she deserved.

"Missed you, *Kachina*," he murmured into her hair. "So fuckin' glad you came to me instead of some other random ink slinger."

She lifted her face and he pulled his head back to look down into her eyes. "I wouldn't go anywhere else."

He nodded, and his nostrils flared as he tamped down everything that was running through him.

After a moment, he let her go and moved back, giving her some space. "Where you want it?"

When her hand fluttered to her lower belly, he froze. He closed his eyes for a second. Hell, more like thirty seconds. Maybe even a minute. He'd never seen what they did to her. He'd only heard about it. He'd have to see it if he tattooed her there. He'd have to see where the Shadow Warriors left their permanent mark with a knife. Left their message to the Dirty Angels.

It wasn't enough to rape her. They destroyed her inside and out.

They left behind a clear message to all of them on just how vulnerable they were.

"Scar tissue's tough, baby. Gotta know that."

"The plastic surgeon did his best, but I can still see it. I see it every day, Crow. I don't want to see that ugliness anymore. I want to see something beautiful. I need you to do this for me."

He didn't want to see it. He didn't. He wanted to say no. Tell her it was impossible.

But she'd just go elsewhere. And that would be even worse for him. Knowing that she'd trust some stranger to make things better because he refused to. Or worse, she'd end up with some scratcher who would make it more of a mess, leaving behind a tattoo that looked like a kindergartener drew it.

His words caught in his throat, so he stopped, cleared it and tried again. "Jazz, gotta see it. Gonna have to show me so I know what I'm gonna be workin' with."

She stared at him for a moment, her eyes heartbreakingly empty. Then something switched inside her, almost as if she mentally shook herself, and she nodded. Her hands reached for the buttons on her jeans and he made a noise before he could bite it back.

She froze.

"Hang on," he muttered, walking quickly to the front door, locking it and flipping the "open" sign to "closed."

Then with measured steps, he took his time moving back to her as she stood in the center of his shop under the harsh fluorescent lights.

He could hardly get the words out. "'Kay, baby. Show me." He braced as her trembling hands unbuttoned her jeans. The zipper being lowered sounded way too harsh in the quiet shop.

He could hear someone's ragged breathing. Was it his?

Fuck no. It was hers. He was holding his breath. Waiting.

Fuck. He didn't want to see what those bastards did to her. It was better if he didn't.

Fuck.

Fuck.

Fuck.

She shoved her jeans down slightly and he caught a glimpse of black panties, then her hand fisted her shirt and she slowly tugged it up.

His heart thumped loudly in his ears, the lump in his throat went nowhere no matter how many times he tried to swallow it down.

Fuck.

Fuck.

Fuck.

"Jesus fuckin' Christ," slipped through his lips before he could stop it.

Her whole body jerked, and she quickly released her shirt and covered herself back up.

He needed a better look. He didn't get a clear enough view of it. He needed to see what he was working with.

Those fuckin' motherfuckers.

If he thought she was pale before, she was a ghost now. Her green eyes, rimmed with tears, appeared huge in her white face.

"I... I know... it's..."

Crow shook his head. "No, *Kachina*. Whatever you're thinkin'... Just no."

He approached her, and her wide eyes followed his every step. When he got toe to toe with her, he dropped to his knees at her feet. Moving slowly, he lifted her shirt carefully.

He stared at her reminder. The one she had to see every fucking day of her life.

"SWMC" had been carved with a blade into her lower belly. It had been cut deep into her tender, young skin.

So deep that the letters that bastard Black Jack had marked her with were still visible along with the suture marks, even after a plastic surgeon had most likely done his best. The lines were thin and ragged, but they were still there.

They'd never be gone. So he understood her need to cover it. But he wasn't sure if what he could do would be good enough.

"Doctor can't do nothin' more?" he asked softly. Because if he could, she needed to go that route first.

"No. I waited to see you until they did everything they could. They're done. But it's still there."

"Yeah," he murmured. "Gonna touch it, 'kay, baby?"

She didn't answer him, but when he glanced up at her, she was nodding.

"'Kay. Tell me to stop if you gotta. Need to see what I'm workin' with here. Yeah?"

"Yeah," she breathed.

With one hand holding her shirt up only to right above the top of the scar, he spread his fingers and gently touched her. He traced the tips over the marred skin, feeling the thickness, the toughness of the scar tissue. Wondering how the fuck he was going to do this for her.

She was relying on him to make things better and he wasn't sure what he could do would even be close to enough.

How was he going to fix her?

Fuck.

What should be smooth skin, a perfect canvas for his art, was anything but.

He kept talking slow and soothing. "Gonna be painful. Gonna have to trace it. Design it. Gonna take some time."

At least it was a good reason for her to stick around for a little while.

"Ain't gonna get it done in one sittin'. Gonna be crawlin' out of your skin from the pain, *Kachina*. Just want you to know that. Gotta do it in short sessions. Got me?"

"I would love to crawl out of my skin," she whispered.

He glanced up again. She was staring down at him, something haunted behind her eyes. "Not in this way, baby. Might be unbearable."

"I'm used to pain."

Crow winced at her soft words. "Wish I could take that from you but I fuckin' can't. Gonna do what I can, though. Promise you that."

She placed her hand over his, which was still splayed along the warm, but irregular, skin of her lower belly. "Just help me forget."

He wasn't sure he could do that, but he'd damn well try.

He nodded and pushed to his feet, tugging her hand and drawing her over to the tattoo chair. "Ain't gonna do nothin' tonight. Just gonna trace it. Start drawin' tomorrow, yeah?"

"I can't stay here too long, Crow," she said as she slid onto the reclined chair and laid back.

He grabbed a marker and a large sheet of tracing paper and headed back to the chair. He glanced down at her as she laid there, her jade green eyes staring up at him. Trusting.

With all that she went through, she trusted *him*.

He couldn't let her down.

"Gonna place this over the area an' trace it out, 'kay? So I know how big of a design I need to make."

She nodded and pulled her shirt higher with one hand, while shoving her open jeans down lower with the other.

He settled onto his stool and rolled closer. He carefully placed the tracing paper over her damaged skin and with the Sharpie made some marks. Where her protruding hip bones were. The top of her pubis bone. Her belly button. Mapping out his canvas.

When he was done, he lifted it and put it on the tray next to him. As she started to tug her clothes back into place, he stopped her. "Wait."

She jerked when he lowered his head and placed his cheek over that area, facing away from her.

I'm sorry, baby. So fuckin' sorry.

Her stomach rose and fell under his cheek with each breath she took, and he closed his eyes. He wasn't sure how long he stayed that way, but eventually her hand smoothed over his hair, down his long braid. Then he felt it, her fingers pulling off the band at the end, untwisting each plait.

Normally, he didn't want anyone touching his hair, but he didn't stop her.

He allowed her to do something he didn't allow anyone else. Slowly, methodically, she worked at it until his hair fell free. She smoothed it across her exposed skin and began to lightly comb her fingers through it.

"I love your hair. Always have. I've always wanted to do that," she said softly. "The color is beautiful."

He turned until his left cheek laid along her belly and he faced her. "The color belongs on me. Doesn't on you."

She nodded. "I needed a change."

"It's not you, *Kachina*."

"I don't know who I am."

Hearing that made it feel as if a knife stabbed him in the gut. A pain he wouldn't soon forget. "She's still in there. Maybe you can't see her clearly, but I can. I see you, baby. And everyone else will remember who you are, too. Nobody's forgotten. Gonna take a while for that tat. While you're here, everyone will wanna see you."

"Not sure if I'm ready for that."

"At least Grizz an' Momma. Yeah?"

"I promise I'll visit them before I go. But truth is..." Her words paused, but the movement of her fingers in his hair didn't. "I didn't come to see you just for ink. I was hoping..."

"Hopin' what?"

CHAPTER TWO

She came to town with a purpose. Not just for ink, but for something else entirely. Something she wasn't so sure, now that she was here in his shop and seeing Crow in person after all these years, that he'd be willing to give her.

However, it was time.

She didn't know who else would be better than him to help her move on.

Her past needed to stop controlling her future. She needed to do her best to fade those memories.

She couldn't do it at home in Buffalo. She needed to do it here. In Shadow Valley.

She needed to do it with the man who had his cheek pressed gently to her belly, his warm breath sweeping across her skin. The area she always did her best to hide. No more bikinis. No more baby doll shirts. Nothing that would expose her outer scars to the world which, in turn, could expose her inner ones.

She hid it so no one asked questions because she didn't want to think about the answers.

Now Crow was saying that the tattoo would take some time. That meant she'd have to stick around the Valley for a little bit.

And while she promised to visit her grandparents, she wasn't sure she wanted to stay with them. She didn't want to be coddled or babied. It may make coming back even harder.

But she also wasn't ready to stay with anyone else, either. Hawk and Kiki would probably insist she stay with them. But then, they had Ashton now from what she'd been told by her grandmother. And Hawk's house in town had only been a two bedroom.

Again, she wasn't sure if she wanted to see Kiki yet. Or Hawk. She had only known Kiki for a short time before *it* happened.

She tried to save Hawk's woman, but she couldn't. She failed.

Jazz wasn't sure if Hawk ever forgave her for that. She wouldn't blame him if he hadn't.

No matter what, she was glad Hawk and Kiki's relationship had endured everything his woman went through. From what Momma Bear said, they were perfect together.

Perfect.

Unlike her.

She was imperfect. Unsure if she'd ever find what those two had.

But one thing she was sure about, she never would if she didn't move past the barriers that were holding her back.

So, it was time. Coming to the Valley, coming to Crow for ink, was the perfect excuse to see the man who had always called her *Kachina*.

Spirit.

From the moment she spotted him in Hawk's house as she danced across the living room, her earbuds in her ears, her body moving to every heart-pounding beat of AC/DC's *Thunderstruck*.

She had been belting out the lyrics at the top of her lungs, most likely out of tune. Alternating playing air guitar and air drums as she rocked out with her eyes squeezed shut. The music moved through her, shutting out the rest of the world.

She'd barely been eighteen at the time. And when she opened

her eyes, noticed him watching her, she screamed in surprise, her heart almost leaping from her chest, then she lost her breath.

Not from fear, but from the beauty of the man who stood there, arms crossed over his chest.

Dark almost-black eyes, perfect golden skin, that long black braid that would make any woman envious. His narrow hips, the ropy muscles of his arms and neck. And not a tattoo in sight.

If Crow hadn't been wearing a DAMC cut, she would've had no idea who he was or why he was in the house.

She had foolishly left the front door unlocked. When she moved in not two weeks earlier, Hawk had insisted she always lock it. Especially when he wasn't home.

And he wasn't home.

No, she had been alone with the handsome stranger whose lips curled at the ends and the lines at the corners of his dark eyes crinkled as he watched her intently and with amusement.

She remembered how hard her heart thumped in her chest that day, even after her initial surprise. How her pulse pounded in her throat and a warmth ran through her, settling in parts untouched by anyone but herself.

She had never reacted to any boy—or man—like that before. At the time she chalked her irregular heartbeat up to being startled.

Later she knew that wasn't what it had been.

Not even close.

"If it's going to take some time, then I'll need somewhere to stay. Just temporarily. Just until... I know..." She shook her head. "You only have a room above church, so—"

When he lifted his head and sat back, she felt that loss. She took his offered hand, his warm fingers wrapping around hers as he helped her sit up.

His now loose hair fell like a black, silky waterfall around his shoulders, rippling as he shook his head. "No. Moved out. Got a house. Safe. Secure."

"You got a house? Where? In town?"

"Club built a place not far from church. For any of us with families."

Her stomach churned, and she worked hard to keep the disappointment from her words. "You have a family now?"

He shook his head again and Jazz wanted to touch his hair one more time. To resist, she curled her fingers into her palms since his hair was sacred to him and he never let anyone touch it. She was surprised he didn't stop her a few moments before. "No. But I'm forty now, *Kachina*. Was time to move the fuck outta church."

And that might be another issue he'd have. Their age difference.

The same problem he had all those years ago. When she was barely eighteen and he was well into his thirtieth year.

However... what she wanted from him... needed from him... wasn't long term. It was just something to get her moving in the right direction. Which was forward. Because she was tired of being stagnant.

Stuck.

Frozen.

She needed a gentle flame, not a roaring bonfire, to melt the ice crystals that had settled in her veins.

And now with her at twenty-eight and him at forty, the age shouldn't be such an issue. Unless he still saw it as such. If so, she hoped to convince him otherwise.

"How long will it all take?"

"How long you got?" he asked, his onyx eyes searching her face.

She lifted a shoulder. She had been hoping only to be in the Valley a day or two at the most. Now...

She was willing to stay as long as she had to in order to get what she needed. Ink or otherwise.

"Scar tissue's tough. Doesn't hold ink like..."

"Normal skin?" she finished for him.

"Not as porous. Gonna have to go over it several times. Let it heal, go over it again. Wanna make it right."

"That sounds like a long process."

"Could be. Won't know for sure 'til I start an' the first round heals. Then I'll have to do touchups."

"Sounds like months," she murmured.

"Yeah. Might be best to drive down here once a month, maybe. Do some, let it heal, come back, let me do the next round. You up for that?"

"It took me about four hours to get here." Four hours wasn't bad. It was doable once a month. But she wasn't sure she was willing to do it. It would delay both of her goals. And she'd waited long enough for both already.

"Or you could stay—"

"I don't want to be a burden on Grizz and Momma Bear." Or smothered.

"With me."

Her mouth gaped and her breathing shallowed.

Before she could answer, he continued, "Gotta bigger house than I need. Could use the help."

The help. The excitement of his initial invitation was dampened. "A house mouse," came out sounding flatter than she wanted it to.

"Yeah, but you probably got a fuckin' job. College grad an' all that shit."

The only job she had waiting for her was one at a guitar store that paid her minimum wage. She never did anything with her Business Management degree. It was just a piece of paper hanging on the wall in a cheap plastic frame in her parents' house.

She only finished school because of their insistence and the DAMC paying for her final year. She wasn't sure why. Maybe Z eventually wanted her help with the club businesses. But if he did, he never insisted on it once she graduated.

But a house mouse was worse than minimum wage. It was for

young women without a job. Someone going through school. Or whatever.

Not for a twenty-eight-year-old with her Bachelor's.

Being a house mouse paid nothing. You lived for free. You ate for free. You cooked. You cleaned. You grocery shopped. You ran the household. All for fucking free.

Your "payment" was having a roof over your head and food in your belly. You had protection. For the most part.

She loved every minute of it when she lived with Hawk. She could do what she wanted and got the house to herself most of the time.

And when Hawk was home, he was fun to be around. Not hard on the eyes, either. Especially when he walked around the house with just a towel hanging off his hips.

Hell, the few times she had her girlfriends over, she'd have to close their mouths for them since they'd be gaping at him, sometimes drool catching at the corner of their lips.

But as fucking hot as Hawk was, he wasn't for Jazz. Not that he would have made a move if he was.

No.

Nope.

That moment Crow caught her dancing and singing in the living room, after being totally oblivious to him watching her...

That moment she knew.

Though things didn't quite turn out the way she'd hoped.

"...Just a thought," he was saying.

What?

She missed something. "My job's just temporary," she murmured. Yeah, temporary for the past four years. "Just until I find something better." Not that she ever made an effort to look.

Though it paid shit, she loved working in the guitar store. She loved being surrounded by the instruments that took her away from reality.

With a guitar in her hands and lyrics on her lips, she was transported elsewhere. She lost herself when she played. She forgot about the past. She ignored the future. She lived for the now, as her fingers moved over the strings, playing the next note. Singing the next line in a song.

It filled her emptiness.

The store owner loved her. She'd sit in the corner and play, oblivious to the customers coming and going when she should be selling instead.

No, Jake never bitched because her playing drew people in. He'd prop the door open in nice weather. People visiting the strip mall and walking by would stop, enter and stay awhile.

Whenever she worked, he sold guitars and accessories, and booked more lessons than ever.

People would actually slip her tips, too. Jake saw it and said nothing. She was good for business.

But she'd never be able to live on her salary there.

So yeah, her job was just temporary.

"So nothin's keepin' you from leavin'," he stated, rolling his stool back and standing.

He offered his hand again and she took it. It was so much wider than hers and warm. His golden skin looked rich and beautiful next to her paleness. She used to worship the sun. Now she avoided it.

He helped her to her feet and she tugged her jeans back into place. Before she could fasten them, his long fingers were there, doing it for her.

She fought a shudder as the back of his fingers brushed along her skin.

He wasn't afraid to touch her, but she didn't find that surprising. She expected most men who knew what happened to her would be scared to be too close. To be hands-on. Even for a hug.

Not Crow. Never Crow. He was one who always had to touch. It was one way he communicated. Everyone who knew him was used to it. No one ever found it offensive because he was smooth about it. It just came natural. It was simply Crow's way.

A warmth spiraled through her and her nipples pebbled. As

he tugged her shirt back down into place, she closed her eyes and swallowed.

Holy shit, she felt alive. For once. He had no idea what he was doing to her. His simple, innocent touch.

The best thing was, she didn't recoil. She didn't feel a need to escape. Panic didn't rush in.

No, instead of wanting him to stop, she wanted to feel those fingers trail over the rest of her body.

"*Kachina*," he whispered. "You okay?"

Fuck yes, she was okay! She felt something she never thought she'd feel again.

Pure desire. A need for touch. The craving for intimacy.

To hold a man against her and let him touch her *everywhere*.

She opened her eyes and met his. His dark eyes were narrowed on her, filled with concern and worry. His hands now by his side. "Sorry I—"

"No. No, don't you dare apologize. Don't."

He lifted his palms. "I'll do better."

"No. That's you. It's who you are. Don't change who you are for me."

"I won't. I'll just be more careful."

"No. I'm not breakable. Don't be scared to... be you. I'm already broken so there's nothing left to break." Her voice had caught on the last word and she cleared her throat quickly.

"Jazz," he murmured, his brows dropping low.

"I accept your offer. I'll do it. For as long as it takes to get this piece done. I... I won't have any money, though, without a job. From experience, I know being a house mouse doesn't pay shit," she tried to joke, but his concerned expression didn't change. "If you want, I'll also keep things clean and organized here in the shop in exchange for the ink. Will that work?"

"Maybe—"

"No, too late. You're not backing out now. It's a deal, for however long it takes." She stuck out her hand for him to shake it. He only stared at it, so she dropped it back to her side. "I'm just going to ask one thing..."

He lifted his dark gaze from her hand, which was now pressed against her thigh, to her face.

"I just need you to keep it to yourself that I'm in town. Please. I'll visit with Grizz and Momma Bear. But everyone else. I need to do it on my own time."

"Ain't gonna be able to hide it for very long, *Kachina*. Livin' in a place that's full of DAMC. Gonna notice there's a female goin' in an' outta my house. Everybody's gonna be all over that. Got a cage?"

"Yeah. Out front."

He nodded. "Cage in my driveway's gonna be a red flag, too."

"I can leave it here. Be your back warmer."

The blood rushed through her as she imagined herself clinging tightly to him as they headed out to his place on his sled. But he might not want her there. That spot was usually reserved for someone special.

"Yeah," he finally said. "How much shit you got?"

"A small bag and..."

He arched a brow when her words drifted off. "An'?"

"My guitar."

He took it slow through town and Jazz wanted to press her cheek against his cut as she breathed in the warm air. The only bike she'd ever been on in the past was her grandfather Grizz's. And only after she'd begged him for a ride. Hawk would never take her out on his, no matter how many times she'd asked.

The brothers didn't like hauling women around unless they were getting something from them. Otherwise, they wanted the back of their sled empty.

With her overstuffed overnight bag wedged between them

and her guitar strapped across her back, she couldn't get close enough to Crow to fully enjoy the ride. It was only a way to get from point A to point B.

She was shocked when he didn't slow down as he entered a huge walled compound with a massive iron gate. The gate had the DAMC logo forged into the center. He never slowed down because somehow the gate opened automatically as they approached and then closed behind them.

She'd have to ask how. Maybe he had a remote of some sort.

Why did they need something like Fort Knox? Was it because of the Warriors?

"Grizz said that... that club... was almost extinct," she yelled into the warm night.

"Almost ain't good enough," he shot back over his shoulder.

Jazz nodded. She had a feeling that her grandparents kept any goings-on with the Warriors from her the few times she spoke to them over the years.

She didn't want to know. On the other hand, she also needed to know.

As soon as they pulled into a paved driveway in front of a house in a cul-de-sac, he remotely opened the garage and drove them inside. Shutting down his sled, he hit the button on a key fob again and the garage door shut behind them, effectively closing them in.

She didn't get a good look at the exterior of his house. She'd have to do so in the light of day.

She quickly dismounted, and he followed, taking her bag from her, and heading to the left where a door separated the garage and the house.

She followed him down a hallway, watching his back and shoulders move smoothly under his cut as he walked in front of her, instead of paying attention to the interior.

They ended up in a kitchen, surprisingly larger than she expected, and he dumped her bag on the center island. After swinging her guitar off her back, she propped it against the end of the island.

The kitchen was sparse, and she wondered if he'd only recently moved in.

Her thoughts went back to why Crow was living in what looked like a middle-class neighborhood in a typical two-story house where someone with a family would live. She braced herself when she asked, "What else did they... Who else did they... hurt?"

Crow dropped his gaze and turned away from her, heading to the fridge. He jerked it open, grabbed a bottle of Iron City beer and after ripping off the top, threw the cap onto the counter. It pinged as it bounced down the granite top and landed in a corner. A corner where, in most kitchens, small appliances were normally tucked. Crow had nothing but what looked like a top-of-the-line coffee maker and a shiny new toaster.

But then, it shouldn't be a surprise he didn't have a blender or mixer. He wasn't domestic. He was a tattoo artist and a biker. He didn't bake pies or cookies. But she would bet that he at least had a grill outside.

He tipped the beer to his lips and Jazz watched in fascination as his throat worked as he swallowed half the bottle in one shot.

Shit. Was what he was about to tell her that bad? Maybe she needed a beer, too.

"Got something stronger than that?" she asked, jerking her chin toward his beer.

He pulled the bottle from his lips and wiped his mouth with the back of his hand. Without a word, he opened a cabinet, grabbed a bottle of Jim Beam and placed it on the counter.

"Got any pop?"

He opened the fridge and pulled out a can of Pepsi before putting it on the counter next to the JB. Then he grabbed a glass from another cabinet and slapped that down with the rest. He waved a hand toward it and stepped back.

She guessed she had to make her own. Stepping past him as

he leaned back against the center island of the kitchen, she could feel the heat radiating from him. She wanted to pause, plant her palm on his chest and feel his heartbeat, too.

But she didn't. Instead, she went over and cracked open the pop, poured about an inch of cola into the glass, then glanced over her shoulder at him. "How much am I going to need for this?"

He lifted a shoulder, his face grim. "Not enough booze in the world to wipe away the sins of that fuckin' MC."

With a nod, she turned back, unscrewed the JB top and poured a good three fingers-worth into the glass, then topped it off with more cola. She jabbed her finger into the drink and swirled it around before pulling it out and sucking it clean. When she turned around with the drink in hand, Crow's eyes had darkened, and he was staring at her mouth.

Her lips parted, and a puff of breath escaped. Her nipples pebbled at how heated his look was.

Then it was like he shook himself free and he dropped his gaze to his beer before lifting it back to his lips.

Jazz took a sip of her drink and fought back the cough due to the strength of it. She wasn't a big drinker, so she wasn't used to the bite of whiskey, even mixed with the overly-sweet cola.

They stood for a while in companionable silence until Jazz had downed half her drink and he finished his first beer. Warmth now swirled through her belly. Though, she wasn't sure if it was the whiskey or Crow causing it.

Or a combination of both.

"Tell me everything they've done. After me and Kiki, that is." She already lived that nightmare once, she didn't need to live it again.

"Sure you wanna hear it?" His voice was low and sounded troubled.

"Yeah, I want to know why the club felt the need to build a," she lifted a hand, "place like this. A gated compound with high concrete walls and an electric gate."

"Just a precaution."

Jazz shook her head. "No. Don't bullshit me, Crow. You're not like that."

He nodded, went back to the fridge and pulled out another beer, gulping down a few mouthfuls before saying, "Don't even know where to begin..."

"That bad?"

"Ain't good. After you... left..." He dragged his fingers through his long, loose black hair, pushing it to the back and away from his face. "Took Jewel."

Her hand went to her mouth to stifle her gasp. "Was she..."

"No. Some fuckin' bumps, bruises, but... no, luckily. After that, Diesel got shot."

"By who?"

He hesitated, frowned, then watched her carefully when he said, "Black Jack."

Her eyes went wide. That *bastard*. He was the one... She inhaled deeply. "But he's okay." It wasn't a question because she knew Diesel was alive and well.

"Yeah, that fucker's too stubborn to die."

Jazz would've laughed if what he was saying wasn't so serious. And if Crow saying Black Jack's name hadn't twisted something inside her. Something ugly, just like that Warrior.

"Then they stole all the Toys for Tots donations. Both ours an' the SVPD's. If that wasn't enough, they shot up The Iron Horse during the club's Christmas party."

"Holy shit," she breathed. "Anyone hurt?"

"Nothin' serious. Did a lot of damage. Hawk ended up reinforcin' the whole front of the bar, replacin' the chain link fence that separates the front parkin' lot to The Iron Horse, an' the back of church to somethin' more solid. A little more secure. Then after that..."

Holy shit. There was more? Of course, there fucking was. The Warriors were the scourge of the MC world. They'd had a hard-on for the Angels for decades.

"Slade was taken an' beat to fuck. Thought we were gonna lose 'im."

Jazz's eyebrows knitted together. "Slade?"

"Showed up after you were already gone. Now Diamond's ol' man. Solid. Trustworthy. Good addition to the DAMC."

Jazz nodded. Diamond now had an ol' man. She kind of found that amusing, but Crow continued.

"Then..."

Jazz took another big swallow of her drink. "Fuck," she muttered after swallowing it.

"Yeah." He sighed loudly. "Then Dex an' Brooke."

"Who's Brooke?"

He tilted his head. "Pierce's daughter."

"What?"

"Yeah. Was a bit of a surprise. Not just to everyone, but Pierce, too."

"That asshole still around?"

"No."

"Chased him off? Or did he leave willingly?"

"No."

Jazz nodded. She wasn't sure if she wanted to hear those details. Not tonight, anyway. "So Dex and Brooke?"

"Brooke is Dex's ol' lady. A couple Warriors, including their prez, busted into her house in Harrisburg in an attempt to take 'em both out, an'..."

"And?"

Something moved across his face. Like he caught himself before saying too much. "An' that's it. They were lucky, until they weren't. Warriors came back an' burnt Brooke's house to the ground, along with her business."

"Holy shit," she murmured, tipping the glass and drinking the last of the JB and Pepsi.

"Yeah. Ain't done."

She wasn't sure she wanted to hear anymore. What he'd told her so far was more than enough reason for Zak to build this compound in an effort to keep everyone safe and protected.

"Jayde..." he whispered.

"No..." Jazz lifted her gaze from her glass. "Jayde isn't DAMC."

"Fuck yeah she is. You know it's in her blood. Like it's in yours. But she's also Linc's ol' lady."

For chrissakes, did she even want to ask? "What happened to Jayde?" She wanted to cry before she even heard the details.

"Wrong place, wrong time."

That sounded too familiar.

"Not taken by the Warriors, but by some other fucknuts. Ended up those assholes were related to a Warrior, though. The Warrior was gonna buy her from those fuckers but before that happened..."

"What?" she whispered, waiting, her head spinning at the anticipation of what Crow was about to say.

"Kicked the fuckin' shit outta her. She lost..." Her eyes dropped to his throat when he swallowed hard enough to notice. "She was pregnant."

Jazz closed her eyes and covered her face with her hands as she tried to process his words. He didn't have to say any more.

"Guess you weren't told any of this shit."

She and Jayde were almost the same age. She couldn't imagine that devastating loss.

"Probably for good fuckin' reason," he finished.

She dropped her hands, but not before rubbing the tears out of her eyes so they wouldn't fall. "What's Z doing about it other than hiding everyone behind high walls?"

"D's handlin' it all. Him an' his crew."

"His crew," she murmured. A flash of that crew, those men, skittered through her mind. Men she had never met before, leaning over her in that abandoned house. Men wearing savage expressions, talking in low furious tones, then getting orders barked at them from Diesel. She remembered only bits and pieces, and never saw them again. She wouldn't recognize them even if she tried.

She also hadn't seen Diesel since that day. She heard he slipped into her hospital room once when she was knocked out on Valium and pain killers. And she faintly remembered others coming in and out of her room. But no one stayed long except for Kiki.

She couldn't forget Hawk's woman sitting by her side, day after day, holding her hand, talking to her. But Jazz had been so stone cold and dead inside, she couldn't even answer her or react. Or even thank her for being there.

She didn't know what to say, so she said nothing.

Hawk always hovered by the door like a sentry, watching both Kiki and her carefully. She couldn't look at him. The eyes were the windows to the soul and Hawk's eyes...

What they held...

It had been too much for Jazz to bear.

She struggled with Kiki's sorrow. So Jazz was glad when she was well enough, her parents whisked her back to Buffalo.

She couldn't stand to see the pity, the sadness in everyone's eyes anymore. She needed to go somewhere where no one knew what happened to her.

She studied the man before her.

He knew.

She had no idea if Crow visited her while she was in that hospital bed. If he had, no one mentioned it.

She mentally shook herself back to the present. She picked up her glass and regretfully realized she had emptied it.

Crow pushed off the counter and took the glass from her fingers, placing it back on the counter behind her.

His arm brushed hers and she shivered. She automatically reached out and he grabbed her hand, pulled it to his chest and his other cupped her cheek, his thumb brushing lightly over her skin.

She shuddered, and he immediately let her go, stepping back.

He mistook her reaction. She needed to clear that up with him, but not yet. She needed to know a little more first.

"So, how big is this compound?"

"About a hundred acres. Plus, Keeks is in negotiation for the woods behind here. Another hundred."

"Damn."

"Yeah. Z wanted to make sure there was room to grow."

"There's only a couple houses in your cul-de-sac." That was one thing she had noticed. All the empty lots.

"For now. The other one is Slade an' Diamond's. There's still a bunch of open lots throughout the compound, but other streets off the main one are fillin' up."

"Biker suburbia," she murmured.

"Yeah, no shit. D an' Z both have houses toward the front of the neighborhood. D wants his Shadows to move in if they're interested. Keep the compound more secure."

"Will they?"

Crow shrugged. "Dunno. They try to stay out of club business for the most part. Keep that separation. D's tryin' his best to keep the club clean. An' it doesn't help Axel lives here also."

"He does?"

"Yeah, him an' Bella. They needed to settle somewhere permanently so they could adopt."

Wow, that was news she didn't remember hearing. It surprised her that a cop would live in a biker compound. "Did they?"

"Not yet."

"Who else lives here? Who should I be worried about running into?"

"Like I said, Z an' Sophie..."

"With their two kids. Zane and Zeke?"

"Yeah. D an' Jewel."

"And their two girls." Jazz shook her head at the thought of D having two baby girls. "What's their names?"

"Violet an' Indigo."

"I assume Jewel named them. I can't imagine D coming up with those names."

Crow's lips twitched. "Also, Dawg an' Emma. Dawg's got three girls now. Caitlin, Lily and their baby Emmalee."

"Damn. Three girls, and he runs a strip club."

Crow shook his head. "No. Moose now runs it. Dawg took over the gun shop."

"Because Pierce is gone."

"An' 'cause of his girls. Dex an' Brooke gotta place here. Jag an' Ivy with their 'lil spitfire Alexis. Lexi's a redhead just like her momma. With the same flamin' hot temper, too."

"Poor Jag."

Crow snorted. "Fuck. He loves it."

Ivy swore up and down, inside and out, she'd never be a biker's ol' lady. Jazz had believed her, too. "He chased her forever. I never thought she'd give in. I was surprised when she did."

"Everyone knew she'd give in. Jag was too fuckin' determined an' stubborn to give up."

"Then everyone knew but Ivy. So, does no one live above church anymore?"

"Hell yes... Moose, Coop, Jester, an' Rooster. Plus, a couple new prospects. Then you got the steadfast bachelors... Nash, Rig an' Crash."

"And you."

"Yeah, but like I said, had enough of that shit. Mostly the younger generation's livin' above church. When I'm crawlin' into bed at midnight after a long day of fuckin' slingin' ink, don't wanna hear Rooster crowin' as he's stickin' his dick into one of the sweet butts."

"He probably doesn't want to hear you do the same thing."

He stared at her for a moment, his eyes intense, then his gaze slid to the side. "Right."

Why did it bother her that he didn't deny he took advantage of the women who made themselves freely available to any of the brothers?

Why would he be different from anyone else?

Because he was Crow, that's why.

He dropped his hand and stepped back. "It's late. Let's get you upstairs an' settled."

"I can't believe you live in a house that has an upstairs."

He grinned. "Yeah, me neither." He grabbed her bag off the island and jerked his chin. "Let's go."

Jazz's heart thumped as she considered her options. She knew what she wanted. She knew what needed to happen, but she had to handle it carefully. Last thing she wanted was to make the approach and Crow not only shut her down but shut her out.

He paused at her guitar. "When d'you start playin'?" He picked it up and headed out of the kitchen.

"A few years ago," she murmured to his back as she followed him down another hallway toward the front of the house, then up the polished wood steps to the second floor. From what she could see in the dim lighting, the house was full of real hardwood floors and the walls painted in rich earthy colors. That was fitting for the man she followed up the steps, as she reminded herself to watch where she was stepping and not his ass.

At the top of the stairs, he hooked a left and went to the far end of the house.

"How many bedrooms do you have?"

"Three."

"So, plenty of room for guests," she murmured, figuring he was going to set her up in a guest room.

And was surprised when he walked into what looked like the master, instead.

Maybe he was going to make this easier than she expected.

He tucked the guitar into a corner and tossed her bag on the king-sized bed. She didn't know what to expect for decor since, though he was half Native American, he was also a badass biker.

His furniture was black and masculine, his bedspread a plain tan. He had a couple framed photos on the wall that looked like they were taken at a reservation somewhere with Native Americans in real headdresses and wearing authentic garb. She'd have to look at them closer later.

Besides that, he had a large dreamcatcher hanging on the wall over the headboard. It looked like it was authentic and not bought at some retail store. Real white and black feathers hung from it, colorful beads, real sinew and leather cording were weaved around a willow hoop. It was beautiful. Stunning, actually.

"*Kachina*," Crow murmured behind her.

She tugged her gaze away and turned to him. "This is your room," she said needlessly.

"Yeah, the other rooms are empty. Had no need to buy furniture or anythin'. This is the only bed."

"We're going to share a bed?" That thumping heart of hers went into overdrive.

His mouth opened, and she stared at his lips as one breath, then two escaped him. "You're gonna sleep in here. I'm gonna sleep downstairs on the couch 'til I can get another bed delivered."

"I can sleep on the couch."

"No, *Kachina*, you're gonna sleep in my bed."

Fuck. That's what she was hoping she'd hear, but she'd also hoped he'd be in that bed, too.

"Got another set of sheets 'round here somewhere."

"No, it's fine. If I'm going to be your house mouse, I can take care of that. But not tonight, since, like you said, it's late." Hell no, she wasn't changing his sheets. She wanted to sleep in them just the way they were. "But, Crow, I don't want to put you out."

"You ain't. Want you in my bed."

Her pounding heart seized and then kick-started again. Her whole body began to tremble. She needed to sit the hell down before she collapsed into a puddle of goo at his feet.

He grabbed her elbow. "You okay?"

"Yes," she squeaked.

His dark brows lowered. "You sure?"

She sucked in a ragged breath. "I'm fine. I—"

"Not gonna bother you up here. Promise. You're safe."

From who? She wanted to ask. From him?

"Never doubted that," she whispered.

He gave her a nod and released her elbow. "First thing when I get to the shop tomorrow, gonna start designin' your piece. Yeah?"

"Yeah," she breathed. "I'll make you breakfast in the morning and clean up around here tomorrow. The days you tattoo me, I'll head in with you and help in the shop. Will that work?"

"Yeah." He turned away from her. "See you in the mornin'."

As he walked toward the door, she said, "Crow, wait!"

He stopped halfway to there and glanced at her over his shoulder.

"Thanks," she said softly.

"Glad you're home, *Kachina*. You're where you belong."

Jazz forced herself to take her next breath. Then the next.

He had no idea what those words meant to her.

None.

CHAPTER THREE

Crow shoved the colorful handwoven blanket off his body and rolled off the couch. He adjusted his morning wood in his boxer briefs and ran a hand up over his bare chest, his bristly, unshaved jaw and then through his still loose hair. He never re-braided it last night before he tried to crash.

He normally slept naked but figured he'd better wear something since Jazz was in the house.

He brushed his fingers over his hard-on and pushed the thought of her in his bed out of his mind. That was the last thing she wanted or needed from him.

He shouldn't even be thinking of her in that way, anyway.

Snagging his jeans from the floor, he yanked them on and, as he was fastening them, headed into the kitchen where he heard someone moving around.

He knew who it was because it happened all too often. The culprit had not only the key to his house, but the code to his alarm.

Stepping bare-footed onto the cold tile floor, he murmured, "Baby doll," then cleared the morning roughness from his throat.

Diamond glanced over her shoulder, her blue eyes alert, her

long dark hair tucked into a loose, messy knot at the top of her head. She was wearing a snug black camisole and what looked like cotton pajama shorts that showed off her shapely legs. Without a bit of makeup on her face, it reminded him that Jazz needed to cut that heavy shit out.

"Fuck, sorry. Was I too loud?"

"No, wasn't sleepin' anyway." He hadn't got a fucking minute of rest. Not because he was trying to sleep on the couch, but because of who was sleeping in his bed upstairs.

"You look like shit. What's wrong?"

Crow glanced back toward the steps, hoping Jazz had slept better than him and remained in bed while Diamond was there. Especially since his house guest didn't want anyone knowing she was back in town.

Yet, anyway. He was going to do his best to convince her otherwise.

"Nothin's wrong. Things are gettin' right."

She tilted her head, her blue eyes studying him. "Meaning?"

He shook his head and went over to stare out of the glass sliders off his kitchen nook. His place was at the back of the neighborhood with his deck facing the woods. The hundred acres of woodlands Z and Kiki were now in negotiations to purchase. The early morning sun was beginning to peek over the tops of the trees.

Behind him he could hear Diamond digging through the fridge to make them breakfast.

"Where's Slade? Why aren't you makin' him grub 'stead of me?"

"For one reason, he had to get up at the ass crack of dawn to open the gym."

He frowned. "What happened to the prospect who does that?"

"Apparently, according to labor laws, we occasionally have to give him actual time off."

Crow snorted. "Yeah. An' the second reason?"

"Because you don't eat like you should. Ever since you moved out of church and no longer have access to Momma Bear's cooking, you've been looking a bit thin."

Right.

"He know you're here?"

Diamond didn't answer.

So, of course, he didn't.

"C'mere." He glanced over his shoulder to where she was fussing with some eggs. "Baby doll, c'mere," he repeated more firmly.

With a nod, she left what she was working on and moved over to him. He pulled her in front of him, wrapping his arms around her waist, and turned her to face the glass doors. He spread his fingers wide and placed them on the rise of her belly.

"How is he?"

"Fine."

"How 'bout you?"

"Still scared as fuck," she admitted.

"Gonna be fine. You guys went through a rough patch, but you're strong. Made for each other. This baby will bind you two closer together."

"I wasn't ready," she whispered.

"Know it," he answered just as softly.

"I don't think he was, either."

"Slade's gonna be a good father."

"He's afraid he won't. This kid will have no grandfathers. None. Our fathers weren't the best role models for either of us."

"Yeah. But your pop was loyal as fuck. That's why he's where he is. You're loyal as fuck, too, baby doll. You guys'll do fine."

Diamond leaned her head back against his shoulder and sighed. "He'd be questioning my loyalty right now if he saw you holding me. You know how many times he's told me you aren't supposed to touch me?"

Crow released a low chuckle but didn't move his hands from

Di's stomach. Life grew in there. Life Diamond and Slade made together. He couldn't help but be in awe of it.

The club was growing like crazy lately. The brothers settling down, making families of their own. Though he was a bit envious, he also liked the way his life was and wasn't ready for that to change anytime soon.

His only regret was he was getting older and he might not get the chance to have babies of his own. But he also wasn't sure he even wanted any.

"I should respect his fuckin' wishes," he finally said.

Diamond twisted her head enough so he could see her grin. "But you won't. Why's your hair down?" She reached up and swept a piece of it away from his cheek.

She was the only one, besides Bella, that he ever allowed to touch his hair. But usually only a touch. He didn't allow them to braid it or unbraid it.

Not like he had let Jazz last night. Once his uncle had taught him how to braid it properly, no one touched it. Not even a barber. Sometimes he'd trim the ends himself but not often. He could go for years without a pair of scissors ever touching it.

"It needed to breathe."

"I'd be the envy of the whole sisterhood if you let me wash it for you."

He grinned and pressed his lips into her hair, murmuring, "Know that's not gonna fuckin' happen."

"One day."

"Right."

A noise behind them had them both turning their heads in that direction.

"Jazz is home," he murmured into Diamond's ear, causing her to freeze in his arms.

Diamond released an audible breath as she stared at Jazz, who stood like a scared rabbit at the entrance to the kitchen, ready to run at the slightest movement.

Jazz's gaze dropped to where his hands were, and something crossed her face.

"Go," Crow murmured under his breath and released Diamond.

With a nod, she crossed the kitchen and grabbed Jazz, crushing the younger woman in her arms.

"Holy fuck," Diamond sobbed. "Holy fuck. I almost didn't recognize you with your hair."

Jazz's eyes met Crow's over Diamond's shoulder and he could see her nostrils flaring as she tried not to break down.

"Baby doll, don't smother her to death."

Diamond nodded again and stepped back. "Jesus, you're a sight for sore eyes. Why didn't we know you were coming?"

Crow stepped closer to the two of them. "She doesn't want anyone to know she's back yet. So, keep it to yourself for now."

"I'm not here long," Jazz said.

Diamond glanced from Jazz to Crow and back to Jazz. "Why here?"

He understood Diamond's question, so he answered it. "Needs some ink. What she wants gonna take some time, though, so..."

"I'm going to help out here and the shop while it's being done."

Diamond arched a brow at Crow. "A house mouse?"

He sighed and moved over to the coffee maker he paid a small fortune for. It even ground the fucking beans, but the damn thing was worth every fucking penny. And right now he needed caffeine.

J azz watched the muscles ripple along his back as he grabbed stuff to make coffee, then fiddled with the machine. Her eyes traced each line and curve of the club colors tattooed over his golden skin. The one just like the rest of the patched members had inked into their skin to show their loyalty and love of their "family."

When she turned her attention back to Diamond, the other woman was watching her closely with what looked like surprise in her blue eyes.

"I live next door. I didn't mean to intrude. Until you..." Di waved a hand around, "finish whatever you're here for, I'll leave you two be. When Slade's not around for breakfast, I come over and make it for Crow so he at least eats a decent meal once in a while."

"I eat," Crow grumbled, keeping his back to them.

"Whatever," Diamond said on a sigh. "Not worth arguing about."

Her gaze landed on Di's belly once again. "Congrats."

Diamond pursed her lips for a moment, then said, "Thanks. We weren't really trying. It kind of smacked us upside the head."

"It's the water at church," Crow grumbled again as he pressed a couple of buttons and then turned to lean back into the counter, his hands planted on the edge behind him.

"I purposely didn't drink the water at church," Diamond muttered. She turned her attention back to Jazz. "You're not going to stay a little while and then just up and leave, right? Everyone will want to see you."

Jazz didn't want to answer that, so instead she jerked her chin toward Diamond's pregnant belly. "Slade's, right?"

Crow made a choking sound.

"Yeah, he's my ol' man," Diamond stated with a grin. "Like I said, we live next door, so if you need anything, just let me know."

"Like I told you last night, *Kachina,* Slade rolled into town after... after you left. Diamond set her eyes on him an' he had no choice but to pay attention. He was fuckin' toast."

Diamond's grin widened. "It didn't quite happen like that."

Crow made a noise.

"I'm happy for you," Jazz told her. "Sounds like the club's expanding."

Di laughed. "You have no idea. I mean, Diesel has two little girls now! Imagine that. And those babies had him wrapped around their fingers the *second* they popped out of Jewel."

"Jewel's so petite compared to D," Jazz murmured, trying to imagine the DAMC sister bearing Diesel's kids. It had to be like a chihuahua giving birth to pups whose sire was a Mastiff. Jazz winced.

"And he hardly lets them out of his sight because he's so protective of them. He wants to make sure that the W—" Di shut up.

"I don't blame him for being protective," Jazz answered.

"Well, anyway, glad you're home. Hope you're here to stay. Kiki could use the help at the law firm. She and Jayde are as busy as all hell. And if she doesn't need you, then Slade and I do at the gym. Our membership is growing like crazy."

"Gym?"

"Yeah, Slade and I run a gym now. Shadow Valley Fitness in town. I teach kickboxing and he coaches boxers. We have all the rest of the normal gym equipment, too." She placed a hand on her belly. "Though, I'm done teaching for now."

"For good reason," Crow muttered.

"Yeah, yeah. So, do you want me to make breakfast or are you going to handle it?" she asked Jazz.

"I got it, especially since it's my first day on my new 'job.' I don't want my boss to think I'm slacking."

She heard another snort from Crow's direction. He was now digging in the fridge.

Diamond nodded. "Cool. I'll head home... but not before I grab a cup of coffee. I never turn down his coffee. It's the best. The guys at church went into a deep depression after he moved out and he no longer brewed it."

She moved past Crow, snagged a large travel mug that had

been sitting on the counter, and filled it with the fresh brew that smelled so good.

"Ain't supposed to be drinkin' coffee, baby doll."

Diamond snapped the lid onto the plastic mug. "The doctor said I could drink a cup a day." He gave her a look and Di raised her palm. "I checked with the doctor, Crow. It's fine." She approached him, cupped his check and leaned in.

At first Jazz thought she was going to kiss his cheek, but then realized she was saying something quietly into his ear. The same thing that tugged at her when she saw Diamond in his arms earlier with his hands on her belly, pulled at her again as she witnessed how close the two of them were.

She never realized they were like that. Diamond never was at any of the pig roasts at church that Jazz had attended. Not that she had gone to a lot of them. Neither Hawk or Grizz would let her drink while she was underage, so Jazz didn't bother to go, either. Instead, she hung out with the couple friends she'd made in college and she could get away with partying freely without the club's VP or even her grandparents stepping in.

When Diamond pulled back and patted his shoulder, Crow's eyes shifted to Jazz. They were darker than normal, and something in them made her want to shiver.

"Remember, I'm next door if you need anything... Cup of sugar... To talk. Whatever."

Jazz nodded silently as Diamond left the kitchen, looking like she was fighting a grin.

When she was gone, Jazz turned her attention back to Crow, who was still eyeballing her. Then it looked like he mentally shook himself free and went back to making breakfast.

That was her job. She unfroze herself as well, her blood rushing through her veins, and moved over to the counter where he was working. "Let me," she said, her voice huskier than she expected it to be as she pushed his hand off the bowl he was holding and plucked the egg he was about to crack from his fingers.

"Go. I'll do it. Do whatever you normally do at this time in the morning."

"Normally sleepin', baby. Work late. Sleep late."

He didn't move away, and his heat seared her, especially from his bare torso. She was wearing an old, worn, loose Harley tank top and a pair of cotton shorts that she normally slept in. She wanted him to hold her the same way he did Diamond. She wanted him wrapped around her back and holding her close, murmuring his honey-smooth voice into her ear.

Her nipples pebbled under her top at the imagery.

"I can do it this morning, *Kachina*." It was his turn to push her out of the way, but his arm brushed against her painfully peaked nipple. She sucked in a sharp breath and froze.

He quickly stepped back, his face pale. "Sorry!" He ripped a hand through his long hair. "Sorry! *Fuck!*"

"I... you... it didn't..." How did she tell him he didn't need to be sorry? She wanted more. But the fear of asking that from him kept her silent.

Why would he want to be with someone who had been violated like she had? Why would he want to be with someone who was so much younger than him? He had women drooling over him daily. He could have anyone in his bed. And probably did.

Why would he want someone in his bed who might not respond like she should? She worried about that.

She worried about how she would react the first time with a man...

"Sorry, baby," he murmured one more time, planting his hands on the edge of the counter and staring down at it. "Fuck," came out on a breath.

"It didn't bother me. It didn't cause any kind of reaction—" Oh fuck yes, it did. "Bad reaction," she corrected, then whispered, "Please don't be afraid to touch me."

"Thought maybe..."

She shook her head. "No. I'm broken but not completely

shattered." She turned to face him head-on. She sucked in a breath to bolster herself. "And I trust you." Something flared in his almost-black eyes, but before he could respond, she continued, "I don't want that day to define me anymore. I'm ready to move on. I can't be afraid of someone... Of that happening again. I can't live like that anymore. Because if I do, then those fuckers won. I want to eventually find someone to..." She drifted off. Still unsure on how to approach this with him.

How to ask for his help without him instantly shutting her down.

He began to pull eggs from the open carton, cracking them into the bowl. "Just gotta remember how it was for you before that time, *Kachina*."

Did he mean life in general or sex? Because if it was sex... "There's nothing to remember."

"None of 'em left an impression?"

Oh yeah, he was definitely talking about sex. "Crow... there was nobody to remember."

His hand stilled as he reached for another egg. He twisted his head to look at her, his dark brows pinned together. "And not since?"

She shook her head.

"Nobody before? Nobody after?"

She shook her head again.

"Those fuckers took..." A thunderous look crossed his face. "How is it possible they took your virginity? You were in fuckin' college."

She stepped back as she felt the blood leave her face. "You act like I was some patch whore."

He grabbed her wrist and pulled her closer. "No. Fuck no. Know better than that. Didn't think it was possible these days. Fuckin' kids startin' younger an' younger."

She closed her eyes and said softly, "I was holding out."

"For what?"

"For someone in particular," she admitted.

"Yeah? Who?"

Should she admit the truth to him now? She opened her eyes and met his gaze directly. "Someone who looked at me like I was a kid."

"You *were* a kid to all of us. We all thought that."

"I know. But I didn't want anyone else and I didn't want to give it up to just anyone, just to give it up. I wanted it to be... special."

"First time usually ain't that special." Crow's head jerked back and he groaned, rubbing a hand over his eyes. "*Fuck*. Sorry."

"Yeah, I can honestly say that was true for me. It wasn't special but it was certainly memorable."

"Don't think 'bout it."

"It's all I think about some days."

"So, while you're back, you gonna finally take a shot at the man who thought you were a kid?"

That was all she could think about all night long. "Yeah."

"Lucky fucker."

"Yeah, maybe. Not sure how it's all going to go."

"Why? He with someone else now?"

"I don't think so."

"Then what?"

"Not sure if I can... I'm not sure I can get over... what happened. Or he can, either."

"Man's gotta just be patient, gotta take his time. If he's worth it, he'll do that for you. Make you see how it should be."

"I hope so."

Crow tilted his head as he studied her. "If he's DAMC... not many single ones left."

No, it didn't sound like there was, but the one she was thinking of was standing right in front of her, still holding her wrist. His thumb was rubbing back and forth over her pulse point and she wondered if he even realized it. Goosebumps broke out all over her body, and peaked her nipples even harder.

He'd noticed. His eyes dropped for barely a second before he raised them again. "Can't come back to disrupt the relationship of someone who's taken, *Kachina*. Can't fuck up their happiness."

"Didn't plan on it."

He nodded. "Good." He released her wrist and went back to cracking the last egg. He pulled a fork out of the drawer at his hips and began to whip the eggs, adding a little milk to them.

Staring intently at the bowl, he asked, "So, who is it?"

Her heart began to thump in her chest once again. She didn't know if it was fear or anticipation. Or anxiety at the thought of revealing her secret.

She opened her mouth and he stopped what he was doing to stare at her parted lips. She nervously swept her tongue over her lower one and he watched that, too.

It was almost like a stand-off. Him waiting for her to spill the name and her waiting for him to figure it out on his own.

She didn't even realize she was holding her breath until her chest heaved as she sucked in the much-needed oxygen her lungs were screaming for.

Something in his face changed and he broke their locked gaze, turning his attention back to the scrambled eggs he was making. "Don't gotta tell me," he murmured, then moved away, grabbing a frying pan from a cabinet and placing it on the stove. After a click, the gas burner lit and he placed the pan on it to heat up.

Her gaze landed on a loaf of bread Diamond must have put on the counter, then on the one small appliance he had besides the coffee maker. The toaster. She could at least do that part while he cooked the eggs.

"Toast?" she asked.

"Fuck yeah," he muttered.

The way he said that made her wonder if he was answering the question she meant. Or something else.

Diamond set her eyes on him an' he had no choice but to pay attention. He was fuckin' toast.

Jazz stared at his bare back and his jeans hanging off his lean hips as he moved the rubber spatula around the pan, his long black hair loose over his shoulders, his head tipped down.

She grabbed the bread and made toast.

Jazz ground her teeth and panted hard. She was doing her best not to squirm. Not cry out. Not cry in general. She had been biting her bottom lip so hard, she'd tasted blood.

She didn't think her first time would be this bad. But it was worse than she expected.

He had warned her.

And every once in a while, Crow would look up, ask her if she was okay and then continue on with his torture.

She had ridden on the back of his sled when they had come to the shop earlier than his normal hours. His day was booked solid and he wanted to get started on the outline before his first customer rolled in.

But him even drawing a simple black outline was like a hot scalpel slicing through her skin. She knew now why he wanted to break the tattoo down into short sittings and why it would take so long to finish the whole piece.

She had a tennis ball gripped in one hand and was squeezing the shit out of it. She was afraid it would either pop or be fused to her fingers before he was finished with this first session.

Fuck, how many more of these sittings would she be able to take?

All of them. She needed to suck it up, put the unbearable agony out of her mind and let Crow do what he did best.

No doubt, he *was* the best. Probably in the whole state. He was a man who took pride in his work. He was meticulous and charged appropriately for his skills.

She had lost her breath this morning in amazement, and actually had to fight back tears, when he showed her what he'd spent hours designing the day before. After he made breakfast yesterday, he had gone into the shop early to begin to draw something up. She had stayed behind locked in his house, the alarm set as she plugged earbuds into her cell phone and cranked up an eclectic mix of music as she cleaned his house from top to bottom.

He wasn't a messy or unorganized person, but the house, much bigger than she first thought, was definitely due for a thorough cleaning. He didn't have a lot of furniture or decorations to dust, but what he did have consisted of a few Native American pieces or motorcycle type knickknacks.

She had spent some time studying the few photos he had hanging on his walls. Most of them were of his time growing up on a Lakota reservation in one of the Dakota states. She couldn't remember which one. She just remembered him talking about growing up in his tribe when she had "interviewed" him for one of her college papers.

That assignment for speech class had been a good excuse for her to spend hours with him. Those hours were boiled down to ten minutes talking about her favorite subject, Crow, in front of her classmates.

He was a simple man on the outside, but down deep, he was complex and fascinating with a wisdom beyond his years. She was pretty sure all the females in her class wanted to meet him when she was done speaking. She had actually stopped reading off her index cards and just began talking, letting the words simply flow from her naturally. When she finally realized she should stop, that her time was up, and she glanced over the class, all of the women's mouths were gaped open.

Including the professor, who was a gay man, and actually asked about Crow after class.

But right now, she couldn't appreciate the man bent over her, his brow furrowed as he worked. The front door to the shop was still locked, the "closed" sign still hanging in the window, since she had her shirt pulled up and tucked under her bra. The yoga pants she wore for comfort—since she'd be freshly tattooed—were yanked down to the widest part of her hips.

But the intense pain didn't let her appreciate his warm breath sweeping over her skin, or the fact that his face was so close to a place where she wanted it to be buried.

His silky black hair was back in its restrictive braid as he worked intently on inking the beautiful design into her skin.

He had to have spent hours and hours on it. The sketch he had done was nothing other than an artist's masterpiece.

She had heard Jag was a good artist and had seen his amazingly detailed drawings on the M. Jagger Jamison website that Ivy ran, but nothing... *nothing* could compare to what Crow created for her. She only hoped what remained of the scar tissue would hold the ink.

Even more, she hoped that the letters "SWMC" would be no longer visible when he was done.

It was time to move on. She needed to get past this last hurdle.

Two really. The permanent reminder on her lower belly and having Crow assist her in getting past her intimacy issues. She didn't know if there would even be issues since she hadn't tried with anyone else. She had no desire to explain to a man what had happened to her and why she may be reacting as she was.

She knew Crow would be gentle. Understanding. Careful. Quiet about it all. And very patient.

It also helped that she wanted no one else and hadn't since the day he walked into Hawk's house.

Today proved that he understood her, what she needed when it came to this tattoo. It wasn't just to cover up the evidence left behind of what happened to her and Kiki in that abandoned house that day.

No. He had drawn something, not only colorful and feminine, but a piece that represented change and new beginnings.

When finished, the center of the tattoo would include a stunning realistic Monarch butterfly with spread wings surrounded by rich purple tulips that he said meant rebirth. Peppered in would be some Jasmine blooms. Tucked in the midst of the flowers, which almost reminded her of a bouquet, would be flaming feathers made from different shades of red, orange and yellow.

The feathers of a Phoenix.

Jazz already knew what the Phoenix represented.

Somehow he made all the different elements blend seamlessly. What could have ended up a complete mess by another ink slinger, ended up being perfectly done by Crow.

However, like it or not, now she had to grin and bear the pain.

After she heard him come home late last night, she had considered heading downstairs and inviting him back up into his own bed. She sat on the edge of his mattress for over an hour trying to convince herself to take those steps.

Instead, she ended up curling up in his bed by herself, tucking her head on the pillow where his head normally laid, and burrowing into sheets that smelled of Crow.

As she laid there in the dark, staring at the shadows on the ceiling, she was torn. She didn't belong back in Shadow Valley, but again she did. She didn't deserve to be in Crow's bed with the intentions that she had, but it also made her feel like she'd come home.

If he knew her plans, he might have insisted that she stay with someone else.

"*Kachina*," his smooth, honey-like voice swept into the recesses of her mind, pulling her out of her pain-induced haze. She'd had her eyes squeezed shut during the last part and hadn't even realized it.

He had put his tattoo machine down on the tray and taped plastic over the fresh ink. She wasn't sure when he had finished, since she had been so caught up in her thoughts. It was one way of dealing with the pain... by shutting down.

It reminded her of another time she had to do something

similar. To block out what was happening. She had turned into herself, avoiding the harsh reality of what those two animals were doing to her.

She had to block out the sounds, the harsh laughter, the rough actions...

A shiver went through her.

"Baby," he murmured, brushing his now gloveless fingers down her cheek. "You okay?"

She shook herself mentally. "Sorry, yes. Are you done for today?"

"Got most of the outline done. Some spots didn't take ink. I'll try those areas again next time an' will work some of the lines again once they heal."

"How long does it take to heal?"

"Two weeks." He pulled her T-shirt from under her bra and slipped it over her exposed stomach, then carefully rolled her yoga pants up enough to cover the area so the top of her pubic area no longer showed. But he made sure not to roll it back over the plastic. "Keep it low on your hips. Got me?"

"Yeah."

"Gonna hurt. Can't do nothin' 'bout it. Wish there was. If I could take the pain instead of you, I would."

He probably would. He was the kind of man who wouldn't want anyone else to needlessly suffer who didn't deserve it. But someone who deserved it... Hell yes, he'd want them to suffer greatly.

This morning over breakfast, he had talked about Pierce, getting her up to speed on everything that had come to light after Brooke came to Shadow Valley looking for her father. His eyes, normally warm and intense, had become absolutely frigid. Scary even. She'd never seen him like that before.

His tone was stone cold when he told her about Kelsea, Brooke's mother, Diamond, Pierce's involvement with the Warriors, and the asshole setting up Z to go to prison.

Jazz had a hard time wrapping her head around everything

that bastard had done. She was relieved that the cancer that ate away at the club from the inside was finally excised.

But her relief was short lived when he got up from the table and walked out of the house, disappearing for a good hour.

She wasn't sure where he went. She didn't see him in the woods behind the house, but there could be a path that he walked regularly through the trees. More likely he'd gone next door. To Diamond.

It shouldn't bother her. She had no reason to be jealous. Diamond was a club sister and Slade's ol' lady. She was even carrying Slade's baby. But Crow going to Di did bother her.

He had no ol' lady, not even a permanent piece, when Jazz first met him and even during the almost four years she remained in Shadow Valley. And almost six years later, he had none now. He was well into his fortieth year and remained free and his own man.

She was sure he'd had plenty of women over the years, but no one who stuck.

Maybe he just liked being a free spirit. Living life as he wanted. That would make sense for a man like Crow.

"Gonna clean up before my first job walks in. Gonna be a long day. Diamond will pick you up later an' take you home, if you want. Plan on bein' here until midnight."

Home.

It probably meant nothing to him to say that. But to her...

It was best not to read into his words, so she could avoid disappointment later if he shot her down.

She decided to start with emptying the trash while he worked on rewrapping his tattoo chair in fresh plastic. Who would have thought that tattooing created so much garbage?

If she didn't keep herself busy, she'd just sit there and watch him like a stalker all day. And he might find that a little creepy.

With a groan of discomfort from the fresh ink, she snagged the overflowing can by his drawing table and he murmured something about a dumpster being behind the building. He also warned her to wedge the back door open, so she wouldn't lock herself out.

Carrying the can, she moved down the short hallway, peeking into the bathroom as she went. She wrinkled her nose since what she saw was absolutely gross. She headed back through an open space that held a copier and a bunch of supplies until she spotted the back door tucked between some overflowing shelves. She made a mental note to organize things better for him in the back right after she tackled the bathroom with rubber gloves, nose plugs, and a huge bottle of bleach.

She stuck a block of wood between the door and the jamb and headed out back into the sunny, but mild, spring weather. The light breeze caught a few of the balled-up sketches off the top of the pile and blew them into the alley. She quickly put the can down and grabbed the fallen crumpled balls of paper. When she picked them up, she noticed whatever he drew on the paper was colorful. Like her proposed tattoo.

As she walked back to the dumpster, she opened up the first one and saw it was a sketch of her tattoo. Similar, but not exact. She smoothed out the other ball and found another version. She tossed them into the dumpster and then began to pick the wads of sketch paper out of the can one by one, opening up each one and inspecting them all.

He *did* spend hours and hours.

All for *her*. All those hours he worked diligently on making her the perfect tattoo. Hours he would never get compensated for.

Just for *her*.

To make her feel beautiful and whole again. To give her a new beginning. A fresh start.

He had gone through so many different ideas before deciding on what he did. She appreciated how hard he had worked. How dedicated he'd been to make it just right.

Perfect for her.

And he hadn't said much about it. He just did it without

complaint or any expected kudos. No matter what, she had to find a way to thank him. To show him how much she appreciated everything he was doing for her. And *would* do for her, if he agreed.

She hated throwing all of his sketches out, so she saved a couple of them and brought them back inside, hiding them behind some reams of tracing and copy paper. Then she headed back into the shop with the now empty can.

She slid to a stop when she heard the voice first. Then saw the bulk next.

Diesel was hard to miss. He took up a lot of space and, even more than his size, his presence was commanding.

His shoulders pulled back and straightened as he turned his head slowly to look over, his brown eyes following the direction where Crow's had landed.

Which was on her.

Fuck.

Now the Angels' enforcer knew she was back. She closed her eyes and blew out a ragged breath.

She hadn't seen D since that single time he peeked into her hospital room. His face hard and scary as he had taken in her injuries and state of mind. But that day he had remained silent and so had she.

He had been the first on scene in that abandoned house. Doing the job of the club's Sergeant at Arms and doing it well.

She doubted that he was one of Crow's appointments today, since Crow knew she wanted to keep her arrival back in town on the D.L. and he would never purposely out her like that.

"Shit," she muttered under her breath as D stared at her, his face a blank slate.

Becoming a father had not made Diesel any less intimidating. If his fury happened to be directed at you, you would most likely shit your pants. His fists, which had the letters D-I-R-T-Y A-N-G-E-L tattooed on each finger could be considered deadly weapons.

While the man might look dumb, he was anything but. No, Diesel looked like a meathead, but was wicked smart.

Even so, she wasn't ready to run into him. He had seen her at her most vulnerable. Naked, bleeding, abused, and totally destroyed inside and out.

"What the fuck did you do to your hair!" he bellowed as he completely turned to face her. That's when she realized he had a baby in his arms. A baby that looked like a tiny, breakable doll in his thick, heavily muscled, heavily tattooed arms.

She wasn't sure if she should run and hide or face him head-on.

Her first instinct was to run and hide, but the second one was part of being an adult. And, anyway, it wasn't like he'd forget that he saw her anytime soon.

She blew out a breath and moved forward. "Is that your daughter?" she asked even though it obviously was. What mother would allow a beast like Diesel to hold their child besides Jewel?

Crow stepped between them, catching her gaze. His eyes said a lot more than his words. "That's Indigo. The latest."

"And last," D grunted.

Crow's lips twitched and the lines around his eyes crinkled.

"It's hard to believe two girls came from your loins," she said, trying to lighten the mood as she moved forward, her eyes on what looked like a baby only a few months old. She had thick dark hair like both of her parents. A little pink bow-shaped mouth curved as she blinked pretty blue eyes at Jazz. "Can I hold her?"

Crow snorted behind her and Jazz shot him a glance over her shoulder. With a hand on his hip, he had his head tipped down and was shaking it. She had no idea why he thought her request was funny.

D glanced down at his youngest daughter and tightened the grip on her, ignoring Jazz's request.

She assumed that was a big fat no.

Which also surprised Jazz. She figured D would leave the parenting of his girls to Jewel. However, it seemed he was a hands-on father.

But then his big body jerked, and his arms extended, offering his youngest daughter to Jazz.

She stepped forward and carefully took the baby from his arms, Indigo's blue eyes blinking up at her father first, almost as if in surprise, then her gaze fell on Jazz's face and she let out a soft grunt.

Like father, like daughter.

But at least she wasn't crying. Indigo's little hand fisted Jazz's hair and jerked. Then she smiled.

Jazz returned the smile warmly and whispered, "Hi, Indigo. You're absolutely precious."

Her gaze lifted from the cooing child in her arms to Diesel.

His jaw was like stone as he stared at his daughter for a moment before his intense dark eyes landed on Jazz, pinning her in place. "When d'you get back?"

"Yesterday."

"Grizz know?"

She gave a quick shake of her head and winced when the handful Indigo had a hold of pulled sharply at her scalp. "No. Not yet. Was trying to fly under the radar."

D jerked his head back as he stared at her. "Ain't gonna happen. Home now. Part of the club. Ain't gonna hide shit. Got me?"

"Why?" she asked softly.

His face got dark as he barked, "Fuckin' family, woman. Time you got back home where you belong."

Jazz quickly glanced down at D's daughter to make sure his bellow hadn't upset Indigo. But it hadn't. Instead her pretty blue eyes were turned to her father and she let out a little laugh. Figures. "My parents live in Buffalo, D. I was raised there."

"An' your fuckin' grandparents live here. You fuckin' belong here. No lip." He took a step forward, pointing a thick index finger in her direction. "That shit fucked Kiki up, fucked Hawk up. Fucked us all up. An' then you fuckin' just split. You weren't the only one that needed to heal."

Was he saying it was selfish that she left? "I wasn't planning on staying in Shadow Valley after I finished school, D. You know that. Hawk knew that. Hell, Grizz and Momma Bear knew that. Maybe no one made that clear to you."

"Fuckin' DAMC, woman. It's in your blood. How the fuck am I supposed to protect your ass when you're in another fuckin' state?"

Jazz's chest became tight and the blood rushed into her ears at his words. Her rage, a feeling she fought so hard to keep under control over the years, bubbled to the surface. Before she could rein it in, her heated words escaped, "You didn't protect me when I lived here!"

His head jerked back, his nostrils flared, and his face looked as though he saw a ghost.

"Fuck," she whispered, then groaned. "It wasn't your fault."

As his face twisted into something she didn't recognize, he turned and in three long strides he was looking out of the front picture window of the shop. He roared a raw, "*FUCK!*" and his head dropped low.

The tension in his body was easy to see from where Jazz stood. She glanced helplessly at Crow but he was turned away as well, his back to her, his hands on his hips.

Fuck!

She never should have come home. Never.

It was a stupid fucking idea!

She should've gotten the tattoo elsewhere, found another man to help her get past her sexual barriers. She should have left well enough alone.

She tried to swallow the lump in her throat, tried to blink away the hot tears that burned her eyes.

She began to bounce Indigo in her arms, more to soothe herself than the baby. The baby was fine. Jazz, not so much.

She should have let them continue to live their lives without bringing back the reminder of what happened. Something that affected the whole club, not just her.

Her returning only brought back the horrible memories and emphasized the weaknesses of the club when it came to the Warriors.

Diesel had a lot of responsibility on his broad shoulders. None of what happened to her was his fault. No, it was because of a decades long beef between the two clubs. Something that started way before any of them were born. Somehow they all got pulled into a cluster-fuck that should have died many years ago. But didn't.

However, she was sure Diesel bore the burden of what happened to her and his brother's woman. He might not admit it out loud, but she was pretty damn sure it ate at him deep down inside. And most likely, ate away at him for the last six years.

He had to live with what he believed was his failure every damn day. She shouldn't have thrown it in his face.

She had to live with the result of what the Warriors did to her... every damn day.

While maybe he didn't have physical damage like she did, emotionally he did.

Though it was hard to believe the man had any emotions at all, it was proven time and time again that he did. He'd deny it, but they all knew he cared way too fucking much. He didn't want that vulnerability to be known because he probably believed it would make him weak.

Seeing his little girl in his arms drove home the fact that D was, in fact, human. He could suffer greatly like the rest of them.

And he was probably scared to death what had happened to Jazz and Kiki could happen to his own innocent daughters.

Having an ol' lady and two children made him so much more vulnerable to personal attacks by that outlaw club. And until there wasn't a threat anymore from the Warriors, he probably thought about that every waking moment.

Because that's how D's mind worked.

He had taken the job of the club's enforcer all those years ago and taken it seriously. So seriously, he started his security business with hand-picked, well sought-after badass men, who had no problems handling the tasks he required of them.

D was in charge of protecting the club and its property. Even "property" like the women and children, because in the MC world that's what they were.

Claimed property.

Any ol' ladies and any children born into the club belonged to the brotherhood. It was an archaic idea, but one that wasn't changing any time soon.

But now she stood there in the center of the shop floor, holding D's daughter, staring at the cut on his back. Colors he wore with pride. A club he would protect to his dying day.

She was nothing but a reminder of his failure. Property he couldn't protect.

She should've stayed away.

Maybe she just needed to get gone.

CHAPTER FOUR

Crow sighed as he punched the code into the keypad, reactivating the alarm. He wandered down the dark hallway and into the kitchen, where he snagged the Jim Beam out of the cupboard. Not even bothering to grab a glass, he untwisted the cap and took a long swig until his insides warmed as they filled with the liquor.

He'd gotten through all his clients and, surprisingly, not one of them had cancelled. Which was rare. Because of that, he was getting home later than normal.

He was tired and spent. Totally fucking torn up.

Watching Jazz suffer through the outlining of her large tattoo had killed him. He had a difficult time watching her fight against the pain. And then the exchange between her and Diesel had twisted his gut into knots.

Not much affected the big man, but Crow knew that the club enforcer took any failure at protecting the club, or its property, personally. It was one of the many reasons D had started In the Shadows Security and built it from the ground up to be what it was now.

Today in his shop, though... When he handed Indie over to Jazz... Crow never expected that. In fact, it floored him. The man never let anyone hold his girls. He was just that intensely protective of them. In fact, a bit on the obsessive side. But when Jazz took Indie in her arms, she missed the expression on D's face. Crow didn't.

Crow had a feeling that letting Jazz hold the baby was a way D could ask for forgiveness without actually asking for it out loud. Though, Jazz might not have picked up on that. She probably had no idea of the impact of that action.

So, after she snapped at him, it had taken a long time for D to turn around, to get his shit together, to face Jazz again. To look at proof of his failure in the eyes. And when he finally did, he did what D did best. Barked orders. He made it clear that Jazz wasn't going to hide from everyone while she was in town. She *would* be on the club run Sunday. She *would* be at the pig roast afterward.

She was going to see, what he told her in no uncertain terms, what was her family and wasn't going to give him shit about it.

No lip.

Crow thought about stepping in, defusing the situation, but he agreed with D. To fully heal, Jazz needed to feel the love and support of her DAMC family. She had ignored them all for way too long. However, now she would be forced to deal with it whether she wanted to or not.

D also had a direct order for Crow. Since she was staying at his house, sleeping in his bed, her ass was going to be on the back of his fucking sled Sunday. No exceptions.

While D had good intentions, his delivery was a bit lacking. Luckily, Crow saw through his bluster since he'd known the man for what seemed like forever, and he quietly accepted what Diesel wanted.

If it had been up to him, though, Crow would have avoided the whole confrontation in his shop. He had no idea that D was stopping in because he normally didn't, but it just so happened he wanted to drop off the copy of Indie's newborn footprints. He wanted Crow to prepare them for his next tattoo. Since he had Vi's baby feet tattooed on his ribs along with her birthdate and her name, he wanted Indie's there, too.

So now that the cat was out of the bag about Jazz being in Shadow Valley and word would spread, Crow had called Grizz. Momma Bear picked her up and, after a tearful reunion which also knocked the shit out of Crow, took her back to their house so they could spend the day with her. Momma B fussed over making her a good meal since she needed "meat on her bones." Crow didn't argue that fact, either. He agreed, Jazz was way too skinny for her frame. Plus, he didn't want her to be alone since he knew he'd be running late and didn't want her being home alone too long after her emotional confrontation with Diesel.

While he hadn't argued with D's order for Jazz to be on the back of his sled during Sunday's run, he wasn't sure if it was a good idea. But he'd leave it up to her whether to follow D's order or not, since Crow normally didn't like anyone hanging onto his back when he rode. But who else would she ride with? The brother she wanted to hook up with? The one she hadn't named?

He wondered if it was Crash, Nash or Rig? She didn't know any of the newer patched members and everyone else was already snagged.

He lifted the bottle to his lips once more, letting the amber liquor slide down his throat and fill his gut. He needed to numb his brain, forget her face as it twisted in pure agony this morning, her fingers gripping the tennis ball so hard, her knuckles had turned solid white.

He almost stopped a thousand times. Almost, but didn't. He gritted his teeth and continued on, knowing in the end she was going to walk away with something beautiful. Like her.

She was so fucking young when those bastards extinguished her light, dragged her into the darkness against her will.

Fuck. She was still young. So fucking young. She had her

whole life ahead of her. She could do anything. Be anything. She just needed the desire to move forward.

She believed this tattoo would help her do that.

But he could understand why she came back. To him. She trusted him to do the tattoo that she needed. Not just the artwork, but she trusted him with her body. Her skin. His touch.

She might not be the same with someone else. A random ink slinger. A stranger pressing on her stomach, working closely, having hands and fingers manipulating her skin. Seeing her exposed. Both her body and her past.

Maybe she shouldn't trust him. Because all those years ago, when she was barely twenty-two... hell, even before that. At eighteen, at that moment he saw her in Hawk's house moving to music, he knew it was wrong. She needed someone her own age. She needed to live her life, experience it with people her own age. Her college friends. The younger sisters in the club, like Kelsea.

He wanted to claim her, take her, make her his before anyone else did.

But there was no fucking way he'd be that selfish. No way he'd take her youth from her.

He'd find someone else. Older. On his level. Someone with more life experience. A little more jaded and less innocent.

But he hadn't.

Fuck no. Pussy came and went. No one stuck. Some of them tried their damnedest to do just that, but he got good at breaking it to them easy. Sending them on their way.

If they lasted a week in his bed, that was too long. Because on that sixth night, he'd be sick of their shit and couldn't wait until the morning light came and he could show them the door.

Because, *fuck*, they did not belong in his bed. And they certainly didn't belong on the back of his sled.

But Sunday Jazz would be there, wrapped around his back like she belonged there.

She'd come *home*.

And fuck him for his own impure thoughts about a woman who was twelve years younger than him.

Who had gone through a bunch of shit and trauma.

Who could be scarred for life. Not physically, fuck no. He didn't give a shit about external scars. But the mental ones? The emotional ones?

Hell, the sexual ones?

He took another swig from the bottle, noticed how much he drank, and with a curse, screwed the top back on it before putting it away.

Last thing he needed was to get fucking wasted, climb those steps to his bed and demand to know who the man was that she was interested in seeing while she was home.

Whoever it was better be right for her.

That was for damn sure.

She fucking hated crying. It solved nothing. Nor did it do anything to relieve the tightness in her chest or the anxiety that ate at her. Or the panic she experienced as they had ridden into the back lot at church late Sunday morning.

She thought everyone would have heard by then. But they hadn't. Diesel kept his distance but kept a sharp eye on her as stunned familiar faces and curious new ones took her in as she dismounted from Crow's sled.

She wasn't quite sure if the surprise came from seeing her or seeing a female wrapped around Crow's back on his bike. Maybe it was a bit of both.

But what upset her the most was the way people treated her. With kid gloves. The brothers wanted to hug her, but she could see the hesitancy on their faces. And if they were waiting for her to tell them it was okay, they'd be waiting for a long time. She never invited anyone to touch her, but if they did, she would grin and bear it.

66 JEANNE ST. JAMES

All the ones she knew, she trusted, but she still wasn't sure
she was ready for them to squeeze her tight.

One who didn't ask, or hesitate, was Hawk. He had buried
his face in her hair like Crow did the first day, and he stayed that
way for a long time. She wasn't sure if the man shed a tear but if
he didn't, it came close. And that didn't help the churning of her
stomach and the sting of tears in her own eyes.

She did not want to have a breakdown in the middle of the
parking lot surrounded by so many bikers and their women.

Hawk never let her go as he talked and talked to her until
finally Jag had everyone mount up and start their sleds. As Road
Captain, he was getting impatient to get the ride started.

D and Jewel took tail, so he could keep an eye on everyone
and Crow took one of the spots in front of him, next to Slade
and Diamond.

Jazz was shocked when she saw not only Di wearing a "Property of" cut on her back, but so were Ivy and Jewel.

She never thought she'd see that day.

The only one who could surprise her more would be Bella
wearing one. And from what Diamond told her, Bella actually
did wear Axel's cut, but they weren't usually welcome on one of
the DAMC's runs. Instead, Bella and Axel, along with Mitch and
April, rode with the Blue Avengers MC, a motorcycle club for
law enforcement.

Shit had certainly changed in the time she'd been gone. And
the club had certainly grown. New brothers. New Prospects.
And plenty of the new generation.

Grizz and Ace had the backs of their bikes empty since
Momma Bear and Janice stayed behind at church and were
watching all the kids. Janice was the only person, besides Jewel,
that D allowed to babysit his girls. But then, if he couldn't trust
either the mother or grandmother of his daughters, who could
he trust?

He probably had their rooms in his house booby-trapped.

Jazz smiled at that thought and it helped push away the last of the tears. She needed to get out of her funk and appreciate everything that surrounded her. The Angels, her grandparents, and the perfect weather. The day was sunny and warm, but not too hot. The breeze made her ponytail tickle one cheek while the other was pressed to Crow's back. Her arms circled his waist tightly under his cut, so she could feel his muscles shift and ripple when he took corners.

Every bump in the road, every lean into a curve, was a good excuse for her to hold on even tighter. Between the vibrations of the bike and her crotch being smashed into his ass, she began to feel things she hadn't felt in ages. Urges and desires she had buried long ago.

Tipping her face toward the sun, she closed her eyes and breathed deep, letting the spring air fill her lungs as she pressed even closer to Crow.

Her grandmother had scolded her for being too thin. And being so close to Crow made her feel small. He wasn't one of the bigger brothers. He wasn't bulky, he was made up more of lean, ropey muscle. But she still felt so much smaller than him. He might not be the biggest brother in the club, but he wasn't weak. Not at all.

She uncurled her fingers from the front of his tee and spread them along his hard stomach. He was warm under her palms and only got warmer as she slid them down, planting one low, the other brushing over his bulky DAMC belt buckle. With her eyes closed, she continued her journey, exploring, until the Harley wobbled beneath them and his fingers snagged hers, raising them back up to his waist.

But not before she had felt his hot, hard length.

She opened her eyes and, with heat rising into her cheeks, saw Diamond, who was riding on the back of Slade's sled, grinning at her. Then she gave Jazz a thumbs up before turning her attention back to the road ahead of them.

The roar of the straight pipes soothed her soul as they weaved throughout the countryside for the next four hours. It was almost as good as listening to the music she loved so much.

What lifted her spirits even more was not only Crow's reaction to her touch, but her own reaction, as well. That little exploration made her want so much more...

CHAPTER FIVE

"Why she with you?" Hawk asked as he approached, double fisting two beers.

Crow was sitting on top of one of the picnic tables at the very back of the pavilion, in a dark corner. He had a half-empty beer bottle of his own hanging from two fingers between his thighs. Since he had to transport Jazz home later, he didn't want to be buzzing when he did it, so he'd been just nursing it most of the night.

Hawk lowered his bulk next to him with a groan. He handed a fresh beer to Crow and put the other one down beside him before scrubbing a hand over his short mohawk. Without needing to look, Crow sensed the man studying him.

"Know you ain't a big talker for the most part but need a fuckin' answer."

Crow lifted a shoulder, then let it drop heavily. He lifted the bottle of lukewarm beer to his lips and took another sip. "Needs ink."

"Where?" Hawk grunted.

"You know where."

Hawk sat silent for a few moments, then said, "Still don't get why she's with you, brother."

Crow knew what he was getting at but was going to ignore it as long as he could. With Hawk, he knew that wouldn't be very long at all. His patience wasn't quite as short as Diesel's, but it was still pretty damn short. "D gave the order for her to be on the back of my sled today."

"You know what the fuck I'm talkin' 'bout."

Yeah, he did. "Wanted to keep bein' home on the D.L. That got shot to shit as soon as D spotted her."

"Right. Could stay with Grizz."

"Yeah, well, she don't wanna stay with her grandparents."

"So, she's better off in your fuckin' house with you?"

Crow let his shoulder lift lazily again. "Yeah."

"Not thinkin' that's true," Hawk grumbled.

Crow turned his head to meet his VP's gaze directly. "Sayin' you don't trust me with her?"

Hawk lifted a brow, then said, "Trust you, brother. Think she's been through too much to land in your bed. Too young."

Too young in general? Or too young for him? It wasn't so long ago that Crow had to convince Axel and Z that Jayde wasn't too young to be with Linc. And she had been the same age then as Jazz was now.

"She's sleepin' alone in my bed. I've been on the fuckin' couch."

Hawk studied him for a long moment and Crow turned to let his gaze sweep the courtyard once more. The only glow was from the roaring bonfire in the middle. Then there were the colored stage lights where Nash and his band, Dirty Deeds, were playing.

Other than that, it was hard to keep an eye on Jazz. She had made her rounds, talking to the brothers, talking with her sisters. Every once in a while, her head would lift, and her eyes would search the grounds. He wondered who she was looking for.

So far, since the run earlier and after she ate a good amount of roasted pig and all the fixings that Mamma B had set up inside, he hadn't noticed her spending time with anyone in particular, brother-wise.

She'd also been avoiding Kiki. He got it. Hawk might get it. But Kiki needed to spend time with Jazz. So, he'd have a talk with her about that as soon as he got a chance.

And just like that, his thoughts were back on that day her life changed. Hawk and D had seen everything in full fucking technicolor. It had to be worse for them.

Crow could only piece the devastation together in his mind from what he'd been told, though he tried like fuck to avoid picturing any of that shit in his head.

Because if he thought about it too often, he'd want to slit a few throats. And D's Shadows were already on that war path. They all knew that Squirrel and Black Jack had been dispatched. Hopefully, not humanely.

"Was a virgin. Know that?"

"Fuckin' Christ," Hawk barked, then dropped his head and shook it. "Nope. Figured since she was in college, was gettin' it somewhere other than my place. Never brought a guy home once."

"Said she'd been holdin' out for someone... A brother. One who thought she was too young."

Hawk released a loud sigh. "Wasn't me."

"No, wasn't you," Crow murmured.

"Who?"

"Not sure. Gave her a rundown on everyone already snagged. Said it was none of them. Figurin' has to be Crash, Rig or Nash. Not sure who else it would be."

"Fuck," Hawk muttered. His gaze sliced through the courtyard. "Well, it ain't Rig." He jerked his chin to somewhere across the yard. "He's gettin' head from Tequila along the fence right now an' don't look like Jazzy could give a shit."

Crow found Jazz by following Hawk's gaze. No, she was ignoring Rig hanging onto the chain link fence like his life depended on it as Tequila was down on her knees in front of him. Her head bobbed in time to the rhythm of the fast-paced Judas Priest song blaring over the grounds.

He never touched that well-used sweet butt. *Thank fuck.*

He eyeballed the stage. Jazz's mystery man could be Nash. The brother was busy jamming out, so, of course, she wouldn't be hanging around him there. Crow studied the man as he sang. His long, light brown hair was loose, so it would fly as he screamed into the mic and strutted across stage, tossing his head. Occasionally, he'd pull on his long beard that had probably grown about six inches since Jazz left town.

It would make sense that Nash would be the one in her sights, especially since she loved music so much and now played guitar.

And Nash hadn't been nabbed yet.

Yeah, fucking made a lot of sense.

But Nash declared himself a permanent bachelor. His band went on tour to biker bars across the tri-state area whenever possible and he had zero responsibility. He loved living upstairs for free and getting no-strings-attached snatch. He didn't want any clingers holding him back from being a free bird.

Yeah, Nash wasn't looking to be tied down with a woman.

She stated she wasn't planning on staying in the Valley, so he doubted Jazz was eager to be tied down, either. Maybe she was looking for her first to be with someone she knew. Someone she had a crush on when she was younger.

"I was holding out."

"For what?"

"For someone in particular."

It wasn't a "what" but a fucking "who."

Kiki and Diamond slipped under the pavilion and Kiki moved to stand in front of her ol' man.

"Where's Ash?" Hawk asked.

Kiki tilted her head toward church. "Asleep in his playpen. It's late."

Hawk's eyes narrowed on his wife. "Who's watchin' him?"

Kiki frowned. "Your mother."

Hawk's jaw got tight when he asked, "You get to talk to her?"

Crow didn't think Hawk was talking about his mother, Janice.

Kiki shook her head. "She's avoiding me." She lifted a hand to stop Hawk before he could respond. "I get it, honey. I do. It's going to take some time. I'm a reminder. Not a little one, either. A big slap in the face."

"You went through shit, too," Hawk muttered.

"Not like her," Kiki whispered. She turned to Crow. "If it's okay with you, I'm going to invite her to dinner sometime this week while you're busy working."

Crow took another sip of his almost flat beer before answering. "She don't need my permission."

"No, she don't," Hawk agreed. "Ain't her ol' man."

Kiki pursed her lips which made it look like she was sucking on a lemon, then she shook her head. "Honey, it's called respect. She's living in his house."

"So fuckin' what? Just temporary."

"Oh, good Lord, Hawk," Kiki grumbled, snagging the beer out of his hand and downing half of it. "See? You make me drink sometimes."

Crow dropped his head to hide his smirk.

But Diamond didn't bother to smother her burst of laughter. "Don't they all? Stubborn fucks." Her hand dropped to her belly. "Knock us up. Make us fat. Drive us to drink."

Crow lifted his head and eyeballed Diamond. "You love your ol' man."

Diamond tilted her head, still smiling. "Right. But still... None of you make life easy for us."

"If you wanted easy, baby doll, wouldn't've waited for a brother."

Diamond only *hmm'd* since she knew he was right.

Crow jerked his head at her. "C'mere."

With a sigh, Diamond slipped between his thighs and leaned back into him as he placed his hands long her lower belly.

"How is he?"

"Good." She looked over her shoulder at him. "You know Slade's going to have a shit fit if he sees you."

"Yep."

Diamond shrugged. "Okay, just so you're aware."

"Feelin' 'im move?"

"Yeah."

"When am I gonna feel 'im move?" he asked her.

"Ain't gonna feel nothin' soon, brother. Slade at three fuckin' o'clock."

Crow turned to look in that direction and Hawk was right. Slade was heading towards them. Even in the dark, he could see the man's attention focused on where Crow's hands were.

"Told you," Diamond whispered and pulled away.

Diamond stepped into her ol' man's path, but he skirted around her, approaching Crow. "Brother, had this conversation. Not fuckin' once. Not fuckin' twice. Too many fuckin' times. You keep pushin' me with this shit."

Hawk rose from the picnic table and wedged himself between them. "Slade, calm the fuck down. It's harmless."

Right. What he did was harmless in Hawk's eyes, unless it had to do with Jazz.

"Don't fuckin' see him feelin' up your ol' lady, Hawk."

"He ain't feelin' Di up, an' there's plenty of times Kiki let him feel the baby move."

"He wants to feel a baby move, maybe he should have one of his fuckin' own," Slade muttered. He swung on Diamond, pointing at her. "An' you let 'im!"

Crow's body went tight, but Diamond was smart by keeping both her temper under control and her mouth shut.

Slade shook his head. "Knew it was trouble, him takin' the lot next to ours."

"Slade..." Diamond murmured.

Slade lifted a palm to stop her next words and dropped his head to stare at his boots. His chest heaved a couple times, then he looked at Crow. "Gonna tell you again..."

Suddenly Dirty Deeds got quiet on stage and Crow glanced that way thinking everyone was waiting to see if a fight was about to break out between him and Slade.

But that wasn't it at all.

No. Fucking Jazz was up on stage giving Nash a small smile as she whispered something into his ear.

Fuck. Crow's gut twisted. It *was* Nash.

Was she suggesting for them to go upstairs together? If so, Nash was nodding at whatever Jazz was saying in his ear.

Everyone in the courtyard had turned their attention to the quiet stage.

He plunked his empty beer bottle on the table and quickly pushed to his feet but remained where he was.

What the fuck was he going to do? Stop her? Discourage her from moving on? Prevent her from finding even a sliver of happiness?

If she wanted to go upstairs and do Nash up one side and down the other, there was nothing he could fucking do about it. Nothing he *should* do about it.

He needed to let her handle moving forward in her own way. It had been six years since that fateful day... She already waited long enough to find some happiness. Long enough to get herself back on track. Even if it was being with Nash for one night. Or however long Nash would tolerate it.

Nash stepped back from Jazz and circled a hand in the air. The stage lights dimmed.

Were they cutting this set short, so he could...?

Crow, once again, stopped himself from rushing to the stage to interfere.

He was glad he did, because the next thing everyone knew, the Dirty Deeds' guitarist handed Jazz an acoustic guitar before jumping off the stage. Nash gave her a nod and followed his guitarist as she stepped up to the mic.

Then she began...

Jazz stood, lit only by the amber glow of the bonfire, as she began to play her borrowed guitar. Leaning into the microphone, her eyes were closed, her expression pained. He thought he recognized the song, but he wasn't sure until she actually started singing. Even so, something was different about it...

It wasn't fast-paced like the song from the 80's movie. No. This was slow, raw... haunting... The meaning behind the lyrics sent a chill down Crow's spine. Like him, everyone remained quiet, frozen in place. Afraid of even the slightest movement.

Her melodic words swirled around him, sucked him in, swept through his veins as he began to pay attention to each word passing over her lips.

Crow couldn't rip his gaze from Jazz when Kiki whispered, "She's singing *Holding Out for a Hero*. Not the Bonnie Tyler version, but the version Ella Mae Bowen sings. Oh my Lord, that's just... beautiful. And so..." Her voice became strangled.

Crow felt the same tightening in his throat and chest. Every muscle remained frozen, every thought focused solely on Jazz, who stood there pouring out her hurt in a way that affected everyone who watched and listened to her.

She sang that she was searching for a hero and asked where all the good men have gone. The man she needed had to be strong, sure, and larger than life. A man who was her fantasy but just outside her grasp. Someone who would reach for her through her personal storm and sweep her off her feet.

Not one person could ignore her deep ache, even if they tried.

But when she finally opened her eyes and turned so that she faced the pavilion...

Somehow, even in the dim lighting, she found him.

Him.

She was staring directly at him as she sang the chorus, her fingers moving slowly over the guitar strings.

Fuckin' Christ.

He twisted his head to make sure Nash wasn't standing behind him somewhere. He wasn't.

No one was behind him.

His heart pounded so hard in his chest he was afraid he wouldn't be able to hear her voice over it.

Beside him, Diamond murmured, "She's singing to you, Crow."

He finally pulled his gaze from the stage to see Kiki clinging to Hawk's side, tears sliding down her face. The VP's arm hung over her shoulders, holding her close. Diamond had moved into Slade's arms. Her ol' man had her pulled against him, her head leaning back against his collarbone.

He returned his attention to the stage.

Was Diamond right? Was she singing to him? About him? For fuck's sake, was she expecting him to be her hero?

Was she still that naïve she could believe someone like him could fix everything that was wrong?

Him. Who never faced his own painful past. But she wanted him to help her?

Finally, when the last word drifted off and the last chord strummed, no one said a word, no one moved. Only the crackling of the bonfire rose up around them.

"Go to her," Diamond whispered. "Before she sings another song that will even have you guys bawling in your beer."

He forced his muscles to unfreeze and turned to Diamond, who gave him an approving nod. Then he glanced at Kiki who also gave him a little nod. At that, Hawk muttered a low, "Fuck."

Fuck was right.

Should he go up on stage and claim her? Is that what she wanted?

She was so fucking young...

She wasn't for him.

She wasn't.

She needed someone her own age or at least closer. She needed to pick up her life where it had left off all those years ago. She needed to finish living out her youth before she settled.

"Fuckin' go, dumbass," Slade muttered.

Crow's lips flattened out and he did just that. He went.

He had no idea what he was going to do. What he was going to say... He'd figure it out when he got there.

He got to the edge of the stage and hauled his ass up. She hadn't started a new song yet, instead she waited silently and had watched him approach, uncertainty in her eyes. When he got to her, he took the guitar from her fingers, propped it nearby and then snagged her hand.

"Goin' home, *Kachina*."

CHAPTER SIX

E xcept for the growl of the straight pipes, the trip home was quiet. Nothing was said as they dismounted from his sled and entered the house.

Nothing was said as he suddenly stopped, pressed her into the hallway wall with his chest and hips, quickly taking her mouth.

He expected her to push him away, but she didn't.

Fuck no.

She kissed him like she was drowning, and he was much-needed oxygen.

He wanted to pull away, take it slow, but she wasn't allowing that. She took his mouth, their tongues tentatively touching.

Then he took over by crushing his lips to hers, exploring every part of her mouth. When she made a sound at the back of her throat, he tried to pull away, but she dug her fingers into his braid and kept him right where he was.

He was torn in two different directions, wanting to toss her over his shoulder and take her immediately to bed or backing off like he told himself he should because he worried about her reaction.

Though she seemed fine with them kissing, that was all it was.

Kissing.

And he wanted to do so much more.

She might not be able to.

Her mind might not allow it.

When he had seen her in that hospital bed, staring at nothing, saying nothing, feeling nothing—just a shell of herself—he knew there had been a break. Her mind had separated and compartmentalized the shit that happened to her, so she could eventually deal with it. Eventually heal.

He broke the kiss but kept her pinned to the wall. "*Kachina*," he breathed.

"Don't say no."

"Think you expect somethin' from me I might not be able to give you."

She shook her head. "No. I don't expect anything from you but to be my first."

My first.

The lump in his throat grew. "That's a gift to give a man you love, *Kachina*."

She said nothing.

"Why that song, baby? Why that one? Who was that song for?"

She still didn't answer.

He pressed his forehead to hers and whispered, "If that song was for me..."

"They made me feel powerless," she whispered fiercely. "I never want to feel that way again."

Crow closed his eyes, simply breathing her in as she talked. Wishing he could inhale her past, absorb her nightmare. Make her whole again.

"They took so much from me. They left me empty. Like a husk of my former self. I no longer had anything left to give anyone. I still might not." Her trembling fingers brushed lightly over his jaw. "I'm afraid I have nothing to give you... But I want to try."

"*Kachina*..."

"No, Crow, I want to try... with you."

"Why?"

"Because I've always wanted you," she said on a shaky breath.

He opened his eyes and pulled back. But he didn't step away, only leaned back enough to study her face.

"You treated me like a kid."

"No—"

"Yes, you did."

"You were so fuckin' young. Still are..."

"I'm a woman, Crow. Far from perfect, but I am. I *need* to move on. I *need* my life back or they..."

Or they won, he finished in his head.

She was so right.

Those fucking bastards took so much from her and even though they no longer walked the earth, they still took from her to this day. She needed to shake them loose. Put them totally behind her. Forget about them. Prove that they lost that day, that she was stronger than what they did to her.

She was a survivor.

He needed her to be sure. "Don't you want someone your own age?"

Her warm fingertips traced over his lips, then down his neck. "I want you... Or I want to try with you."

He hated that her gaze dropped to their feet. Her self-esteem, the one thing she had an abundance of all those years ago... Now...

The badly dyed black hair. The unfeminine way she dressed. She was compensating. Hiding. Or both.

"I want to try..." She lifted her gaze again. And the plea in her jade-colored eyes got him in the gut. "Please help me try."

Fuck. "Don't want to hurt you, *Kachina*."

"You won't."

No, maybe not physically...

"Is it because I'm damaged?" she asked on a broken whisper.

Jesus fuck. She might as well have stabbed him in the heart.

"Have a hard time not picturin' you when you were eighteen. Twenty... Hell, twenty-two."

"Before I was damaged," she said.

"When you were—"

"Pure."

"Fuck, *Kachina*, never been with a woman who was 'pure.' Never cared if a woman was that way. That ain't it at all."

"So, you're turning me down." She nodded and turned her face to the side, to avoid his searching gaze once more.

He had to ask again, "Why me?"

"If it's not you, it'll be no one."

That was extreme, and he didn't like that pressure being put on him.

"I know you want me." She reached between them and found the proof. He did his best not to groan when she traced his hard length. "You're just afraid I'll freak out. I get it. I won't."

She couldn't guarantee that.

"I know you'll be slow and careful."

He didn't know if he could be that way with her. He was afraid that once he started, he'd take what he wanted. He'd never been with a woman who he'd had to handle delicately. So, fuck yeah, he was afraid.

He also worried about if he was inside her and she froze, said no, stopped him in the middle of what she asked for... he'd be devastated.

If she wanted him to make her his, then he wanted her completely his. Not partway.

But he was willing to take his time, be who she wanted him to be to get there.

Because if he was doing this, he was all in.

And she needed to know that.

"*Kachina*, gotta promise me somethin'."

She turned her head again until she met his gaze. "What?"

"Gotta promise to tell me what's goin' on in your head. Need to tell me to slow down, need to tell me to stop, make sure I hear you."

Her lips curled up softly at the corners. "I can do that."

"You like somethin', you tell me. Don't fuckin' retreat into your head, either way. I won't know what's goin' the fuck on if you do."

"I can do that, too." Her words were breathy, and her eyelids dropped low. A flush ran up her neck into her cheeks. It brought some color to the paleness of her skin.

"One more thing," he started.

"What?"

"Want you as Jazz. Not what you're showin' the rest of the world. Want your hair back to your natural color, none of that thick makeup, want you to dress like you should. No hidin'. Got a deal?"

She hesitated too long for his liking. "Deal."

"An' when your tat's done, we're done. Want you to find someone your own age." She needed to go back to living her life as if it had never paused.

The jerk of her body told him she wasn't expecting that last part. Her sensuous look turned to surprised.

"Plenty of good men out there that'll be good with you, got me? Someone you can marry, have kids with. Build a family. Want you in Shadow Valley, but want you to find happiness, even if that means somewhere else."

"Crow..."

He shook his head. "That's the deal. Want me to be your first, then you gotta agree. Doin' this for you, all for you. An' only want what's best for you, *Kachina*. Need to hear you agree to that."

"Crow," she repeated his name in a pained whisper.

"No, ain't doin' it if you don't agree."

She closed her eyes, turned away again and a few heartbeats later, he almost didn't hear her answer. "Okay."

Once again, he was torn. Deep down he didn't want her to agree with that last part but he'd backed her into a corner. It was one way to make sure she didn't regret the decision she was making by wanting him to be her first.

Fuck yeah, he was torn, because he knew once he had her, he wasn't going to agree with that.

Not at all.

"**K**achina, talk to me." His low, silky voice washed over her, his warm breath swept over her heated skin.

"I'm... good. You're... *good*."

Oh hell yes, he was good. Just like she thought, he took his time, talking to her, touching her lightly here and there. Experimenting with her, judging her reactions.

She wanted to simply close her eyes and let him do his thing. But no...

He wanted her to communicate everything she was feeling.

However, that was difficult. Because she wasn't sure sometimes. She'd never before experienced the pleasure he was creating.

And not by fucking her.

No.

They hadn't even gotten that far yet. An hour later, and he was still simply exploring her naked body. Every crevice, curve, and plane. With his fingers, his lips, his tongue. Kisses, licks and touches.

He moved so slowly sometimes, she wanted to scream.

It was one thing to be cautious, it was another to be as slow as a snail.

"More... faster..." she groaned.

He'd avoided the areas where she wanted him to touch the most. Her nipples were pebbled so hard that they hurt. The only thing that was going to take that pain away was his mouth or fingers... Or...

Another place she wanted him to touch... below her unfinished tattoo. An unfamiliar ache had settled at her core and she wanted him to relieve that, too.

But he didn't.

And she was about to scream "stop" but not for the reason he'd think.

He was torturing her. She wasn't sure she could take much more.

"Crow, youuuuu..."

"Tell me, *Kachina*."

"You..."

"Tell me," he murmured against the curve of her breast as his long, warm fingers trailed lightly over her belly, but avoided her fresh tattoo.

"You need to... touch me..." Goosebumps broke out all over her body.

"Where? Where do you want me to touch you?"

"Everywhere."

"No, wanna hear exactly where you want me to touch you."

"There."

"Where?"

As she blew out a breath, her head rolled back on the pillow and her eyes rolled in the same direction. "Down there."

"Show me." He was now kissing along her shoulders, over her collarbones, the hollow of her neck.

"I... I can't."

"You can, baby. Show me what you want."

She blindly reached out for him, finding his braid, shoulder, then elbow, before sliding her hand down to his, interlacing their fingers and guiding him to the exact spot she wanted him to touch. Where she ached so deeply for him. With her hand controlling his, she tucked his middle finger into her cleft where she found herself slick and hot.

Was she going to have to do *everything* for him?

"Please," she moaned. She didn't know what to tell him. He was the experienced one, not her.

She tried to disengage her fingers from his, but he kept her there. Kept her with him, she was touching herself as he did. He slipped their fingers between her folds and stroked her lightly, gently touching her clit with his thumb. He pressed, circled, and teased.

Her lips parted on a groan and she began to pant. She tilted her hips trying to encourage him to take it further. He was being *too* careful.

"Crow," she groaned.

"Wanna taste you, *Kachina*."

"Yesss," she hissed.

She expected him to go lower, but he didn't, instead he alternated flicking the tip of her puckered nipples with his tongue, making her pulse race and her nipples bead even more. Then a gasp escaped her as his warm, wet mouth drew one nipple between his lips.

Lightning shot from her breast all the way down into her core as it clenched and throbbed. He needed to fill that emptiness inside her.

She wanted to feel his full weight on her. He had done his best not to do that, not to pin her down on her back. And she knew why...

Their fingers on her pussy continued to move, explore, but he avoided going inside. He stayed on the surface and when he moved to suck on her other nipple, her body tensed and did something so surprising...

The pulses radiated from her center as she came and cried out. She hadn't had an orgasm in years. Since before...

Even then, they were all self-induced.

Her pulse raced when he didn't back off, but continued

sucking and stroking, making her thrust against his hand, her body squirm against the bed, her breath become even more ragged.

She needed his hair loose. She needed to feel that black silk all over her skin. Without asking, she found the end, rolled off the elastic band and began to undo the braid. He hesitated for a split second, then began to suck her nipples even more intently.

When she had it undone, she spread his hair out over her, smoothing it against her heated skin.

Then he lifted his head, surged up and took her mouth again. It wasn't gentle. No. His tongue swept between her lips and hers tangled with his for a few moments, before he broke the kiss, his breathing as ragged as hers.

He was hard and hot against her hip, and she needed to touch him, but every time her hands got near, he'd move them away.

"*Kachina*," he whispered again, then moved down her body, kissing her flesh as he went. He was...

Yes, he was going there. *Finally*.

He gently cocked her legs, spread her thighs and took her clit in his mouth. She whimpered and grabbed long strands of his hair, rubbing the silky length between her fingers as he did amazing things with his lips. With every stroke of his tongue, every flick to her clit, her hips jumped off the bed uncontrollably.

She forced herself to lift her head and stared down her body to see his dark head moving between her too pale thighs. She lost her breath when he tilted his head just enough to catch her eyes.

Then she slammed her head back into the pillow as another orgasm ripped through her, much more intense than the first one.

The Warriors stole this from her. Years of pleasure. Years of intimacy. Years of being with someone she loved.

She squeezed her eyes shut and shoved that as hard and as fast out of her head as she could.

No. This was her time. With Crow. Without them. She wouldn't let them win.

"Talk to me, *Kachina*." He kissed along her inner thighs, scraped her skin lightly with his teeth.

"That was... everything I expected from you and more."

He rose up with a smile, kissed the top of her pubis and then one of her protruding hip bones. "Are you ready for more?"

Her pussy clenched, at not only his words, not only the smooth satin of his voice, but at the imagery of the two of them being connected so intimately.

She wanted that. Oh, did she want that.

She nodded and whispered a "yes."

He studied her for a moment, his eyes darker than normal, his cock hot and heavy against her thigh, the tip of it sticky against her skin. He lifted himself even more, leaning to the right, reaching out for his nightstand drawer. She knew what he was digging for so she didn't need to watch, instead she studied the long, lean line of his body. Perfect golden skin that she wanted to explore in the same way he had done to her.

She heard the wrapper tear and his body shifting against her. Then he moved back between her thighs, keeping his weight off her by planting his palms into the mattress.

"Talk to me, *Kachina*," he whispered.

She glanced down between them, seeing his cock, now wrapped, hanging heavy between them.

She wanted this. She wanted this.

She wanted this.

Oh, how she wanted this.

It was not fair to Crow to make him be the one to get her over this hurdle. She never should've asked him. She should have come to him already unbroken. It wasn't his responsibility to fix her.

While he'd been patient with her, like she expected, it wasn't fair to him.

"Talk to me," he urged softly.

"I want this... I do..."

"You're not ready."

He began to move away, but she stopped him by digging her fingers into his hair on both sides of his head and holding him right where he was.

"I want this," she said more firmly.

"Need you to be sure, baby."

"I'm sure."

He dropped his head and took her mouth again, kissing her long, deep, until she forgot everything that was about to happen. And then he moved, lowering himself just slightly. Another shift, and he was pressing the broad head of his cock against her slick entrance, sliding it up and down in between her folds.

He broke the kiss, pressed his forehead to hers and pushed forward, oh-so-slowly.

As she felt the pressure, the stretching, every muscle in her body froze as she waited for the pain. The tearing. The stabbing motion. Her breath caught, her eyes closed and she bit her bottom lip so hard she could taste blood.

She was not in that room in that abandoned house. She was not. She was in Crow's bed. She was in his house. His house had windows, not like that other one. His house had furniture, not like that other one. This one was a home, not like that other one...

He was being gentle, not rough. Slow, not fast. He wasn't slamming her. He wasn't holding her down against her will. He wasn't laughing, biting, grunting, digging his fingers painfully into her flesh, and taking his aggression, his anger, his revenge out on her.

He wasn't them.

He wasn't them.

He wasn't Black Jack. He wasn't Squirrel.

He cared about her. They didn't.

He didn't want to hurt her. They did.

He didn't want her to regret this.

She wasn't going to regret it.

She wanted Crow.

She needed Crow.

She loved Crow.

Then his weight just disappeared. He was gone. She forced herself to open her eyes as he slid to her side, ripped the condom off and tossed it to the floor.

He gathered her in his arms, rolled her to her side, and pulled her tightly against him, her back to his chest. His erection remained hard against her ass as he spooned her tightly.

"Crow." Her voice caught, because her throat got tight, tears burned her eyes. "I need—"

His arm tightened around her waist, not allowing her to turn to face him. "No. Not yet," he murmured in her ear.

"Crow..."

"No, *Kachina*, you'll know when you're ready."

"I'm ready, I swear."

"I ain't..." He blew out a breath and it ruffled the hair by her ear. "I can't... Not like that."

"Like what?" Even though she asked the question, she already knew the answer.

"You... Not like that."

"But you didn't..."

"Don't matter."

"It does. I need to take care of you. Like you did me."

"Not yet, *Kachina*. When you're ready it'll come easily. When it's time, you'll know it's me inside you, no one else. You'll have no thoughts of anyone else. Thought I got you there. I didn't. Fucked up an' rushed it."

He hardly rushed anything.

She bit back the sob that so wanted to escape.

She thought she was ready.

Maybe he was right. She wasn't ready. Maybe she'd never be ready.

Maybe she was so broken, she was beyond repair.

C row inhaled a shaky breath. His dick was throbbing and his nuts desperately needing a release. It didn't help that he was holding Jazz against him. Inhaling the fruity smell of the shampoo in her hair. Feeling her smooth, warm skin against his.

She was too skinny, yes. She could put on at least twenty pounds if not more, but even at her current weight, he wanted her. Even with that awful fucking black hair, he wanted her.

The most difficult thing he ever did was pull out before he was even completely inside of her. He wanted to push forward, to take her, to make her his. But he couldn't. Not yet.

If he had done so, she still wouldn't be his. Not when she had other thoughts running through her mind.

Black Jack and Squirrel still had a hold on her. Those fucking bastards. If he could dig those fuckers up and kill them again, he would. One death wasn't good enough.

When every muscle of her body locked. When her nails dug sharply into his flesh. When she whimpered, not because she was out of her mind with wanting him, but with fear. It was like a bucket of ice water had been thrown on him.

Forcing her to push through her fear, her memories, and continuing on with what he was doing, wouldn't have made things better for her. It might have made things worse.

And he couldn't risk that.

He couldn't.

He never wanted to be the one who might damage her even more. Push her to break once again.

No, they were just getting Jazz back. He needed to make sure it was Jazz who stayed. Not that other person she tried to be.

When they started this earlier, when he had led her upstairs to his bedroom, with excruciating slowness removed her clothes, placed her in the center of his king-sized bed where she watched him strip off his own clothes, he wasn't sure how far they'd get.

He knew it would take time, that's why he forced himself to take it so slowly that he thought he was going to lose his own mind.

He had to keep his patience, his control, while his brain screamed at him to take her.

His brain played tricks on him, telling him to go faster, make her his quickly before anyone else got that chance.

He'd be her true first. But not her last.

He knew that it wasn't smart to think he would be.

He was willing to help her get over her fear. To show her how good sex could be with someone who cared. But he wasn't willing to hold her back once she did.

She wanted him to be her hero.

But the hero didn't always stick around. The hero helped someone and then moved on.

She wanted him to help her heal.

But that's where he faltered. How could he do just that when he himself never faced his past? He'd avoided knowing all of the details, the complete truth, about his parents' murders.

If he wouldn't, couldn't, deal with that, how could he help her?

He couldn't.

Until his own past was dealt with, he'd be a hypocrite to think he could.

He needed to finally hear the truth. What currently was nothing but a gap in time. A black hole in his memory.

He needed that crevice filled. He needed to hear the details.

He needed to know.

He needed to go visit Rocky at SCI Greene.

CHAPTER SEVEN

A buzz sounded as the heavy metal door in the small room on the other side of the thick glass opened. A heavily tattooed man in an orange jumpsuit, with his hands shackled to his waist, stepped inside. The same door slammed shut with a loud metallic clank and Rocky shuffled up to the window with shackled ankles.

He stared at Crow for a long minute, then took a seat, his bound hands in his lap.

"What the fuck you do now?" Crow asked him.

Rocky shrugged then grinned. "What I had to."

Crow sighed and sat back in his chair, crossing his arms over his chest. "You get the hole?"

"Yeah, for a couple nights. Was a nice fuckin' break." Rocky's salt and pepper head tilted and his gray-blue eyes narrowed on him. "Been a while, boy."

Crow grunted a "yeah."

"Have you seen my baby doll?"

"Yeah, I've seen her." Crow didn't tell him Diamond now lived next door to him. He wasn't sure Rocky would care and their time was limited. He needed to stay on point.

"Ain't knocked up yet?"

Shit. Rocky didn't know. Diamond hadn't told her father that she was pregnant. It wasn't his info to tell. "Don't think it's for a lack of tryin'."

Rocky sat back in his chair, his cuffed hands resting on his gut, as his eyes got a distant look. "Practice does make perfect. Sure miss pussy in here."

"Ruby must miss you, too," Crow said dryly.

Rocky's jaw became tight. "What I fuckin' meant—"

Crow cut him off. "Right."

Rocky's narrowed eyes were now focused on him. "Why you here?"

"Ready."

"For what?"

"Closure."

"Why now?"

"'Cause I need to learn to let shit go. That toxic shit that rots my gut deep down inside. Need to help someone else do the same. So, need to be able to do it for myself first."

"Who you helpin'? Isabella?"

"Bella's got Axel."

"Yeah, right. That nephew of mine would never step into this place to visit his murderer uncle. Don't want to get his fuckin' hands soiled." Rocky paused with a tilt of his head. "'Kay, who then?"

"You never met her."

"Club property?"

Fuck. Was she? She was DAMC, so in Rocky's eyes... "Yeah."

"Who?" Rocky asked again like the stubborn cuss he was.

"Was involved in the shit that went down with Black Jack."

Rocky shot to his feet and slammed both palms into the thick glass separating the two of them so hard that the loud bang made Crow's head jerk back in surprise.

Fury masked the older man's face. "Was itchin' for that fucker to come here."

Fuckin' Rocky. "He was handled," Crow murmured.

"Just like Izzy's ol' man."

May Rebel's fuckin' rotten soul never rest.

"It was handled," Crow repeated.

"By who? You?"

The man looked doubtful that Crow could take out another human being. He could. He had. He just wasn't proud of that fact. He also didn't boast about it. "No."

"Too fuckin' soft for the club, boy. Ain't willin' to spill blood. Now your pop... Coyote... He was a true badass."

"'Til he wasn't," Crow muttered but Rocky must not have heard him. The speaker system between them wasn't the best.

"Too much like your little squaw ma. Soft. You ain't no hard warrior."

Crow's fingers dug into the arms of his chair as he struggled to let that roll off his back.

"Right, well, baby doll's ol' man... The Marine. What's the fucker's name?"

Crow had to loosen his jaw to answer. "Slade."

"Yeah. Slade's pop was a ruthless fucker. What he did to your ma and pop... Right in front of you, too... Least he left you breathin'... but you were crawlin' around in puddles of blood when you were found. Almost like you had bathed in that shit."

"Slade's pop..." Crow repeated softly, wondering if he heard Rocky right through the shitty speaker.

"Yeah... Buzz... That Warrior. That's what you came to hear 'bout, right?"

He came to hear the truth about what happened, but he didn't expect Slade's name to come up. "Right."

"So you're finally ready to hear all the down an' dirty details? All those times you came to visit me over the years, sat there hardly sayin' a fuckin' word, wouldn't let me tell you, but now, 'cause of some snatch, you're ready for me to give you the low down? Must be helluva sweet slit."

For fuck's sake, Rocky was lucky there was a wall and thick

glass between him, otherwise, the man would be finding out just how "soft" Crow was.

And the man had no idea he was insulting Grizz's grand-daughter.

He loosened his fingers from the arms of the chair when they began to cramp. "Just fuckin' tell me. Don't leave anythin' out. Want every fuckin' detail. Got me?"

Rocky settled back in his bolted-down chair with a nod and began to talk. His words washed over and through Crow. Chilling him one minute. Burning him the next. Rocky spared no details. It was graphic. Heartbreaking. Soul crushing.

Crow heard every detail Buzz and another Warrior were forced to spill before Rocky and Doc finished them off. He heard every detail of the bloodshed that law enforcement pieced together during their investigations. He heard every detail of what the brothers put together while doing their own.

During it all, Rocky kept calling Crow's mother a "little squaw." He knew the man didn't mean anything bad by it, it was just the way Rocky was, but it still pissed him the fuck off.

He talked about Coyote getting his throat sliced but not before watching his "little squaw" get raped and slaughtered. Every one of his mother's orifices had been assaulted with a knife. All while she still breathed, even if barely.

His mother, the woman he hardly remembered, was tortured by a fucking monster.

Rocky was wrong. Coyote wasn't a badass. That mother-fucker watched everything that happened. A badass protected his fucking family. A badass would die before allowing anything like that to happen to the woman he loved.

But Crow's father didn't die until after his mother did. And he died because his throat was sliced, not because he was fighting off the other Warrior to try to save his ol' lady.

Fuck no.

Crow would have taken his last breath, let the last drop of his blood fall before sitting back and watching that.

He would've done whatever he could to make sure those fuckers died first.

Coyote was no badass. He was a coward.

Rocky's words brought him back to the room. "Me an' Doc took care of 'im, though. Eye for an eye. Or more like a good guttin'. Hung 'im up like a buck an' sliced that fucker open from his dick to his throat. Shoulda seen the look on his face while we did it. Did the same for that other fucker, too. What was 'is fuckin' name... A tool of some kind... Hammer. Yeah, that's it." He grinned. "So, what kinda closure you expectin' to get from hearin' all that shit?"

Just the complete truth. Not sugar-coated bullshit like his mother's side of his family gave him. He needed it raw and knew if anyone would give it to him, Rocky would.

Grizz and Ace would have glossed over it, too. After what he just heard, he wouldn't blame them one fucking bit.

But one thing he wasn't sure about was if Grizz and Ace knew—and maybe they did and kept it a secret—that this Buzz was Slade's own blood.

Slade's father raped, tortured and murdered Crow's mother, Soaring Dove. Buzz's club brother, Hammer, sliced Crow's father's throat. Though, from what Rocky said, it turned out Hammer had a round with his mother first before Buzz finished her off.

"Slade know his pop did what he did?" Were Diamond and Slade keeping that from him?

"Yeah, he knows. Baby doll an' 'im visited me a while back. Slade's pop killed your ma, I killed Slade's pop, an' here I fuckin' sit. Doc killed Hammer an' he sits on death row. Ain't quite even, but close."

Ain't quite even, but close.

Just like that. Simple.

And close was where the son of his parents' murderer lived. Right fucking next door. With Diamond.

Slade lived and breathed among the Angels. The son of a

Warrior. The son of a murderer. Another child would be born. The fourth generation of the DAMC would include a grandchild of a Warrior. A grandchild of someone who was a mortal enemy.

How fucked was that?

But, even so, that child would be wanted. Loved. Raised and protected by the club. Unlike Crow, who ended up being raised elsewhere.

"No one wanted me."

Rocky pursed his lips and studied Crow for a moment before answering, "Everybody wanted you, boy. Your ma's family came an' got you against our wishes. Thought it was best for you to be raised Indian an' not biker. Don't blame 'em. The shit goin' down at the time was bad. Too dangerous for you kids. That was one of the reasons my brother wanted nothin' to do with the club. Kept Z an' Axel from that shit. Tried to protect them. Z wasn't havin' any of that, though. That boy made me proud. Buckin' his father, doing what was in his fuckin' blood. Bein' a pig wasn't in his blood. Fuck no. Bein' DAMC was."

Being DAMC landed him in prison for ten years, too. Rocky sure didn't mention that part. Being DAMC caused a huge fucking rift between him and his blood family for way too long.

That wound was healing, but not without leaving a scar.

"Why do you think I fuckin' did what I did? Not just revenge. To protect Diamond, Jag and Jewel. To protect Ruby."

No, what he and Doc did landed their asses in prison for life, leaving the club down two brothers to protect their families. They didn't take the Warriors out smart. They did it with big egos, wanting the Warriors to know.

They did it as a warning, but that warning was never heeded by those nomads. Instead, it drew that fucking line deeper in the sand.

It turned it into a never-ending war in which no one ended up the winner.

The tables were finally, but slowly, turning, not due to Doc and Rocky, but Diesel.

Z strived to keep the club above board as best as he could, which forced D's hand to get a band of men together that could be used as a weapon. A precise weapon.

D's Shadows could move in, take Warriors out and no one was the wiser. And it kept the DAMC clean. At least on the surface.

They cut off the head of the snake when they took out Sandman, the rival club's president. But that didn't mean another head wouldn't grow back.

And that was one reason why Z worked so hard on building the compound. Encouraging his brothers to move in. Stay close. Circle the wagons, almost.

The third generation had children and ol' ladies to protect now.

"Gotta convince Jewelee to bring my grandkids in here to visit me. Can you do that? Keep askin' Ruby, but she tells me Jewel says she will, but then doesn't. Want to see my grandbabies. Tell Diesel to drag my fuckin' daughter in here, got me?"

Crow wasn't getting involved with that shit. No fucking way. He'll mention it to D, but he wasn't pressuring the man or his ol' lady to drag two baby girls into a max-security prison.

"Jag, too. Fuckin' family's growin' an' everybody forgot their old man. Did all that shit for 'em an' they don't appreciate it."

"Right. I'll say somethin' but that's all I can do."

Rocky nodded. "Better than nothin'." His shackles rattled when he shifted in his chair. "The day the Warriors quit existin' is gonna be the best fuckin' day ever."

"That day's comin'."

"Yeah, so Ruby says. But ain't soon enough." Rocky tilted his head as he peered through the thick glass. "So now that you know the fuckin' details, how's that gonna help you?"

Crow had no idea. Maybe it never would. But not knowing the truth, the details had eaten away at him for a long time. Now he knew, he wasn't sure things would change. He was in that room when his parents were killed. As Rocky had talked, he had

expected bits and pieces to come back to him. Things he'd
tucked away into the corners of his mind, just like Jazz probably
had during her ordeal. They'd both lived through violence and
tragedy. He hoped hearing just how bad it was would help him
deal with her past.

Hearing what he was lucky to live through, reminded him no
matter how bad things had been in the past, things could get
better. It reminded him that the mind was a complex organ.

Maybe today wouldn't help him deal with Jazz but he at least
needed to try. Only now it unsurfaced something he never
expected.

The son of the enemy living next door in their secure
compound. The compound that was supposed to protect them.
Slade was now deeply ingrained in the club. Not only being a
brother, but being Diamonds ol' man, by being the father of her
unborn child.

He had no reason not to trust Slade, but it sure made him
fucking think twice about how easily the enemy could plant
someone amongst them. When Slade was new, their guard was
up. Now that he'd been around for a while, no one was watching
him.

"Hammer got family?"

"Don't know, boy. He did a lotta jabberin' when we had 'im
strung up, but don't remember 'im beggin' for his life because of
any kids... Now, Buzz...."

"Mentioned Slade?"

Rocky shook his head. "Fuck no. But he mentioned another
son. Said his kid's momma was gone an' the kid would be left an
orphan. Figured after baby doll was here, that kid was Slade.
Maybe not. Maybe he had another one. Wonderin' if he even
knew 'bout Slade."

That kid had to be Slade. It only made sense.

"Why you wanna know? You gonna take Diamond's ol' man
an' possibly this other son out in revenge for your ma an' pop?"

Before Crow could answer, a loud buzzing sounded again and the door behind Rocky swung open.

"Times up, Rock," the guard yelled. "Let's go."

"Fuck," Rocky muttered. As he pushed to his feet, he said. "Get my grandbabies here, Crow. Do it as payment for what I just told you, yeah?"

Crow didn't have to answer, because now two guards were there, grabbing Rocky's elbows and pushing him out of the room.

"Yeah?" Rocky yelled over his shoulder. "Got me, boy?"

Instead of answering, Crow stood and watched the door close behind Jag, Jewel, and Diamond's father.

He'd do what the man asked and tell them what their pop requested, but that was all he would do. It would be up to them to decide what was best for them and their kids.

CHAPTER EIGHT

Where the hell was Crow? She'd woken up this morning to an empty bed, though she had no idea when she finally fell asleep. In fact, she didn't think Crow got much sleep, either. But she somehow gave him the chance to slip out undetected.

After he had held her for a little while last night, he had gotten up, pulled on a shirt and a pair of boxer briefs, tossed her one of his T-shirts and told her to put it on and then climbed back in bed to pull her against him once more. Besides the order to cover herself, he didn't say much else.

Being wrapped in his arms last night made her feel safe and wanted, even though she knew she was damaged goods. But Crow wanted it to be perfect for her. And he didn't think last night it would be.

He didn't think she was ready.

This morning she expected to head back to the shop, possibly spend the day with him. Instead, she found him gone. Maybe he just needed some separation. For his sanity. He had to be suffering after he abruptly stopped as he was...

As he was...

A warmth swirled through her and settled in her core. Yes, she had been about to have her first sexual experience with a man of her choosing and that had gone sideways.

She closed her eyes and tried to imagine what it would have felt like if he had continued to press forward, to finish what he started before she froze up like a fucking idiot.

She bounced her fist off her forehead in frustration. They had been so close.

She headed into the bathroom and flipped on the light to study herself in the mirror.

For the most part, she didn't think much of how she dressed and what her hair looked like anymore. She never tried to look "cute" or "sexy" or even pretty. The cheap over-the-counter hair dye was horrible, she knew that. The flat black color made her look goth. Hell, with her thin face and the dark circles under her eyes, maybe even like a meth head.

But in truth, she wasn't trying to look like anything. Just blend in. Not be noticed.

Only exist.

The heavy makeup she normally wore was more like a shield she hid behind.

This morning she wasn't putting any of that on. She was throwing it out. She also needed to find a ride to a hairdresser to see what could be done with her hair. Crow wanted it back to its natural color. That was the deal. She wasn't sure that was even possible until the black grew out.

But she could get it bleached and dyed back to a color as close to her own blonde as possible. Hopefully that would be good enough for now.

Unfortunately, she didn't have a way around town on her own. Her car was still parked behind In the Shadows Ink. Maybe she could call one of the sisters to help her out. Or if she could find Crow, he could drop her off at her vehicle, since there was no reason to hide that she was back in town anymore.

Nope. That cat was out of the bag.

She sighed. No matter how she got there, she needed to shower first since she smelled like sex, even though they never finished what they started.

Maybe tonight they could try again. If he was willing.

After her hair looked better. Maybe that would make her more attractive to him.

She should call Momma B and have her grandmother give her some cooking lessons, so she could feed Crow better. While he said she was thin, he wasn't much better.

Hawk had always eaten at the bar before coming home, so she rarely had to cook for anyone but herself. Grocery shop so he had crap to snack on, yeah. But meals? No. And her being in college at the time, microwavable shit had been good enough for her.

But maybe if she learned to make Crow a real dinner, he'd appreciate and realize she was now a grown woman.

She wanted to look good for Crow. Remind him of what she used to look like before...

She released a slow breath.

Before.

She felt the need to impress him. Show him he was making the right choice if he decided to be with her. Maybe not forever since he said they were "done" once her tattoo was finished.

While she hadn't planned on sticking around the Valley, she also had expected Crow would shoot her down right from the get-go. He hadn't. So the only reason now that he wanted whatever they had, or might have, to be temporary was because he believed she was still too young for him.

So yeah, learning to cook. Helping him out in the shop. Looking like the old Jazz. Getting past those sexual barriers. They might help Crow see her for who she was deep down, past the fractures at the surface.

She wanted to be better and she wanted to be better with Crow.

She ran a hand over her flat black hair. She needed to show him she could be everything he wanted.

And desired.

Age was just a fucking number.

J azz watched Momma Bear's car turn the corner as she exited the back alley where Jazz's car had been moved that first night. Crow hadn't wanted to leave it on the street. While Shadow Valley was safe for the most part, he was worried about someone clipping it if it remained parked at the curb. Plus, it took up valuable parking real estate in front of the tattoo shop that he needed for customers.

After calling Momma B for a ride, her grandmother had insisted on taking her to her own hairdresser, a lady who lived right outside of town and worked out of her own home. And though Jazz was skeptical at first, it ended up that the woman was excellent at what she did.

After her hair was bleached, colored, highlighted, washed and trimmed, even styled, Jazz looked in the mirror afterward surprised at who looked back at her.

The sex that Crow and her *sort of* had last night had brought some color back to her face and life back into her eyes. Going easy on the makeup after her shower earlier hadn't hurt, either.

She forgot who that woman was who had wide green eyes and stared back at her in the reflection. She had forgotten her because she hadn't wanted to deal with her for so long.

But Crow insisted he wanted Jazz. The before. Not the after.

She would also need to go shopping and grab some new clothes, since she had only brought an overnight bag with her from Buffalo. Momma B had jammed a wad of cash into Jazz's purse before pushing her out of the car with a knowing smile. She gave the order to go shopping with Jayde, since the woman had a decent sense of style without looking like a patch whore or a stuck-up bitch.

Yes, that's exactly what Momma Bear said word for word.

Jazz rolled her lips inward in amusement and dug in her purse to find her key fob.

She had tried to text Crow earlier to find out where he disappeared to, but she got no answer. Most likely because he didn't answer to any woman, especially her. Or was somewhere without coverage... Possibly. But more likely the first than the second.

She'd also had her grandmother drive past the front of the shop to see if he was inside before taking her around back to her vehicle. She was disappointed to find out he wasn't working, either. The storefront was dark, the sign on the door turned to "closed."

Was he with Diamond?

Jazz pushed that thought away. Diamond seemed happy with this Slade, the newer patched member Jazz met yesterday at the club run and during the pig roast after. And she needed to remind herself that it was Slade's child the older club sister carried, not Crow's.

But still... did Crow have feelings for Di? More than brotherly love?

Finally finding the remote at the bottom of her bag, she pulled it out and unlocked her old Hyundai.

She lifted her head when she heard another vehicle enter the ally. Frowning, she noticed it was a blacked-out some sort of SUV on steroids which looked like it could be driven by some drug kingpin. The exhaust rumbled, and the engine growled powerfully. Unfortunately, she couldn't see who was driving.

Her heart began to race when the vehicle accelerated as she yanked open her door. Her fingers began to shake as she tried to keep one eye on the vehicle that was quickly approaching. Before she could throw her purse inside, she dropped her keys.

"Fuck!" She needed to get into her car, lock the door and get the fuck out of there. The only problem was, the oversized SUV was now blocking her exit. And she didn't have enough room to turn around.

None of that might matter since she might not have time to start her car before whoever driving was upon her, anyway.

She reached for the dropped fob, snagging it and jumping in, tried to shove the key in the ignition with trembling fingers. The damn key kept missing the slot. Using one hand to hold the other, she did her best to steady her hand. Finally, it slid home.

Fuck. Her driver's door was still hanging wide open.

She was reaching for it when suddenly a tall, very large man was standing in the open door, blocking her from closing it.

Losing her breath, she told herself to keep calm. Not to scream. Not to freak the fuck out. She needed to think clearly and not freeze up.

She reached to turn the key, because she could at least reverse out of the alley if she had to. She couldn't care less if she mowed down the man who continued to tower over the car and say nothing.

"Jazz," the deep voice said. Not in a threatening manner. Not in an angry manner. But surprisingly chill.

She didn't recognize the voice. And because he was standing in the doorway, she couldn't see above his waist.

She ignored him, turned the key and... she only heard a click.

Fucking piece of shit car! She should have known it wouldn't start and asked her grandmother to wait until she tried. Her car never started after sitting for a few days. The battery needed to be replaced and she didn't have the money to do that.

Her heart leapt into her throat when the man squatted down next to the car just inches from her. She jerked back when she saw his face.

He had a thick scar running diagonally from the top of his hairline and down across his nose. The end of it stopped at the corner of his mouth and it pulled his lip up slightly.

"Jasmine," he murmured again.

How did he know her name?

She had no idea who he was. Never saw him before. Was he a Warrior coming back to finish what they started?

No, couldn't be. If he was, he would have dragged her out of her car by now, even dragged her by her hair back to his vehicle. He also wasn't wearing colors. He was wearing a black T-shirt that clung tightly to his well-built torso and bulging arms. And that was not the body of a typical biker.

"I—I have no idea who you are," she whispered, the tremble in her voice too revealing.

"Don't remember me?"

She let her gaze roam over his face again. Maybe she met him before the scar? "Should I?"

His expressionless, piercing gray eyes narrowed. "Maybe not."

"How do you know me?" While she was talking to him, she was reaching slowly behind her, trying to hide the motion by blocking it with her body. Her cell phone was still tucked into her purse. If she could only get it... Press three numbers...

But his eyes caught her movement and his jaw tightened. "You're safe with me."

Oh sure. Just him announcing that made it believable.

"I'm Mercy."

Mercy.

Suddenly, her thoughts began to spin, and she couldn't catch her breath.

Mercy.

"You saw... You saw..." *Everything. Me naked, bleeding, bruised, broken.* "What they did to me."

She turned away from him and grabbed the steering wheel, pressing her forehead to it and trying her best to suck in oxygen. "You were there," she whispered.

"Yes."

She squeezed her eyes shut as a flash of a memory hit her. A sliver of remembrance. Diesel. Hawk. Kiki... Other men. She didn't know what they looked like, just heard them while they were in the room for a very short time. She heard Diesel bark orders at them. And then they were gone.

But everything was just bits and pieces. Some of those splintered memories of that day. The memories that haunted her.

Changed her forever.

That feeling of helplessness.

That loss of hope.

The fight to survive slowly leaving her body like the blood they drew.

Giving up.

No longer holding on.

Just…

Letting go. Letting the darkness take her. Enshroud her. Make it all end.

"Jazz."

Her fingers ached from how hard she was gripping the steering wheel. But she couldn't let go.

She jerked when fingers brushed hair away from her face. She opened her eyes and turned to him. "What are you doing here?"

"Want to show you something."

Jesus. Was that how her eyes looked? Like his? Devoid of emotion?

When he didn't continue, she asked, "What?"

He shook his head. "Not here."

"Where? What is it?"

"Will you come with me?"

Should she trust this guy? Yes, he was one of Diesel's guys. His crew. One of his Shadows. But still…

"My car won't start, so I can't follow you." A lame excuse not to go with him. But true.

"You can ride with me."

Her eyes flicked to the black SUV wide enough to block the ally. "I don't know."

"Just need to show you something."

"Why?"

"You need to see it."

She studied his face closer. She looked beyond the scar. She could see what he looked like before, how handsome he'd once been. He was in no way ugly now, but the scar was distracting. It caught your attention first and you really had to concentrate to see the rest of him.

Kind of like her. She existed somewhere beyond her "scars." But you had to get past them first. "What does it have to do with me?"

"You'll see."

Her eyes flicked to her purse, then back to him.

"Bring your phone, but I swear you're safe with me. Won't keep you long."

Won't keep you long.

Keep: To retain possession of.

Retain possession.

She mentally shook herself. Where the fuck did that come from? She couldn't be scared of every male that crossed her path. Worried that they were going to take her, possess her against her will.

She jerked when he reached into the car, cupped her cheek and brushed his thumb lightly across her skin. "Do I scare you?"

Yes. Because you're big and strong and there's no way I could fight you off.

"Sorry, baby, I promise you're safe with me. Wanna prove that to you." He stood and reached his large hand into the car.

She stared at it for a second, chewing on her bottom lip. Then, fighting the instinct to flee, she took it. He assisted her out of the car, yanked her keys out of the ignition and slammed the door behind her.

Her heart thumped in her chest as she followed him back to his vehicle.

She hoped she wasn't making a dangerous mistake.

CHAPTER NINE

Mercy pulled up to a detached garage behind a two-story, Cape Cod-style home. A house out in the middle of nowhere with a mini-van parked out front and a swing set in the backyard.

"You live here?" Because if he did, she was surprised. No, more like shocked.

He didn't answer her, instead he parked directly in front of the garage, shut the vehicle off and got out.

He wanted to show her he had kids? A normal life? What?

The passenger door swung open and he once again offered his what-seemed-like-enormous hand.

Like he ignored her question, she ignored his hand and got out on her own, climbing down carefully from the beast of a vehicle. "Is this thing bullet-proof?"

He only grunted, then turned his back on her to head around to the side of the garage. She followed a few steps behind.

"Trusting you not to tell anyone about this place. Expecting you to trust me, also need to trust you. Deal?" he shot over his shoulder.

"Shouldn't you have asked me that before you brought me here?"

He grunted again, then stopped at a windowless metal door that had a keypad on it. He pressed a five-digit code and Jazz heard the lock release.

When Mercy opened the door, Jazz peered around his bulk into the dark interior. Her heart skipped a beat when his big hand pushed her inside. She froze as she stood just inside the door since she couldn't see shit. At least until an overhead light suddenly blinded her. She blinked and looked around. The section of the garage they stood in had a solid wall separating it from the front portion where vehicles would be parked.

He moved past her and approached another door to what only could be another room inside of the room where they stood. It had a hasp with a padlock on it. Did he just unlock it using his thumbprint?

"Haven't stopped thinking about you since that day..." he said as he unlatched the door.

Well, that was a bit creepy. She wasn't sure how to take that news.

He pushed the second door open and reached in to turn on the light. Then he stepped back. He lifted his hand, indicating she should move forward and into the room.

Was this where she was going to be hacked apart into a million pieces? Were there plastic sheets lining the walls, like on the series *Dexter*?

A shiver ran down her spine. What the hell was going on?

Before she let him shove her into the second room, she stepped inside on her own power. At first, she didn't understand what she was looking at. Her brain wasn't letting her process just what it was that hung on the walls in this smaller room.

If she thought his words had been creepy, this... this...

The blood drained from her face and she became a little lightheaded. What was all this?

Why did he have a room full of cuts that bore the insignia and rockers of the Shadow Warriors?

She wobbled. She put her hand out for balance but only hit air. She needed to sit, but there was nowhere to plunk her ass down. Besides the floor. Which she very well may hit when she passed out.

Mercy came behind her and, with his hands on her shoulders, steadied her. "Needed to show you this. Not going to stop until the cut of every fucking Shadow Warrior is hanging on these walls. Every fucking single one."

These cuts were trophies he took. Like a fucking serial killer. Was she right about the *Dexter* part, only she wasn't his target? Was he a serial killer? Who would do such a thing? What type of person would keep this kind of evidence of what they had done?

He didn't do this just for her, right? There had to be another reason besides what happened to her all those years ago in that abandoned house. Because why else would someone go to that extreme unless the Warriors had done something to him personally?

She eyeballed him. He was watching her, an empty expression on his scarred face.

"Did they do that to your face?"

He barked out a sharp laugh, but it wasn't warm. No, it was frigid and made her shiver once again. "No."

"Why... Why are you so intent on taking all of them down? I'm assuming that's what all this is? The owners of these cuts... they're..." Dead. Gone. Maybe even had been tortured?

She knew Diesel's guys were former Special Ops who had done things most humans would never do, things most humans could never bear doing. While doing their patriotic duty, they were most likely asked to do things above and beyond the norm. But still...

"Because of you, baby."

His "baby" and Crow's "baby" affected her totally different.

Crow's sounded warm and meaningful when he called her that. Mercy's was...

She didn't know how to describe it.

"Because of what I saw. What I'll never forget. I do this for you. But also for Kiki. For Jewel. For all you women that the Warriors ever... *touched*, ever hurt."

"So, not just me."

"No, not just you."

She let her gaze sweep around the room again, looking closer this time. "Are their cuts..."

Was Black Jack and Squirrel's cut among them?

"Yeah."

She closed her eyes for a moment, feeling relieved that neither of those two would ever hurt anyone again. She didn't feel bad for them, she felt a strange satisfaction.

She wondered if she'd ever rid herself of the hatred for the men who took her and changed her life forever.

When she opened her eyes, her gaze landed on an oddball cut. One that was not like the rest.

Holy shit.

Holy shit.

Holy motherfucking shit.

It was not a Warrior's cut, and it was held in place to the wall with a huge knife stabbed directly into the center of the very familiar patch.

She pulled out of his grasp and went over to it. Even though it was halfway up the wall, she could still reach it. Carefully flipping the right side over, she read the identifying patches. The spot where the president patch used to be was not only bare, but the leather was darker there, and only a few stray threads remained. But the patch below that empty spot remained.

Pierce.

She couldn't breathe, she couldn't swallow. They didn't just strip the former DAMC president of his colors.

Hell no, they didn't.

They stripped him of his life. She released the cold, stiff leather from her trembling fingers and blindly took two steps back. She collided with a warm, solid body.

She pulled away quickly and turned to face him.

"That one was for Diamond. For Brooke's mother. For Zak. And everyone else who's life he touched and not in a good fuckin' way."

"Diamond? What did he do to Diamond?" Her question was whispered, her mind racing on all the possibilities. Crow had mentioned he touched Diamond when she was fifteen, but had the former DAMC president done more than just touch?

But Mercy ignored that question, too. "Once I get the last Warrior, I'm going to burn them all. They'll all cease to exist."

"How many are left?" Did she want to know?

"Hard to get a good head count. But that one right there," he pointed toward one that had dark, dried blood stains on it, "was their prez. Being nomads, they were never organized well, but now? A complete cluster fuck. Club's been pretty much disbanded, thank fuck. Just a couple stragglers left behind hanging onto history from what we can tell."

"I don't know whether to thank you or be horrified," she told him truthfully.

"Just wanted you to see how we've been working our asses off. Making Shadow Valley safe. Hoping you'll realize you don't have to worry now you're home."

"I'm not sure I'm staying," she answered. "In fact, my plan was never to stay."

Suddenly, he was there. Toe to toe with her, grabbing her chin and lifting her face to his. "Was hoping..."

Oh shit. "What?" She studied the lift the scar created at the corner of his mouth. It made him look more sinister than as if he was smiling. Because he certainly wasn't smiling right now. And she wondered if he ever did.

"You and I are a lot alike. Both been through some fuckin' shit. Some unspeakable shit but we both came out on the other side. May never be the same again, but we endured. You're a fuckin' survivor, Jazz. That takes a strong fuckin' woman."

No, he was wrong. She shook her head, but that didn't shake his grip loose. "No. I'm not strong. I... I hid. I ran away from here as soon as I was released from the hospital. I didn't want to deal with anything I left behind. I hid behind clothes, dyed hair and heavy makeup." At first, unconsciously. Then, on purpose. "I became someone else, so I didn't have to deal with who that person was. So, no, I'm not strong."

"Here now."

She broke his gaze, letting hers slide to the side for a moment. Because they were too close. And he was right, too alike. The only difference being she could only imagine doing what he did to the Warriors, while he actually followed through. "I'm only here to get one more scar covered. The one that's visible. That's the only reason I came back."

"Don't believe that."

"Well, it's true. But even when that's finished, I'll still be scarred on the inside. I wish I could move past it. I *hope* to move past it. But I don't know if I ever can."

"They took a lot from you," he murmured, his gray eyes intense as he swept his thumb back and forth over her cheek.

In a shaky whisper, she agreed. "They took everything."

Mercy shook his head with a frown. "No. Not everything. You're living, breathing—"

"Barely."

"Bullshit," he barked sharply. "You got more than most people. Family who loves you. Family who wants you in their life. Family who'll support you with whatever choices you make. That shit's everything. You got everything, Jazz. Don't let those fuckers," he swept the hand not holding her chin around the room, "define you. Decide how *you* live. How *you* love."

Jesus. She expected a speech like that to come from Crow, not from a guy like Mercy. Was there more to him than met the eye?

"By keeping those cuts, aren't you letting them define you? By keeping their memory alive?" she asked him.

His gaze slowly roamed the room before meeting hers again. She fought the urge to shiver at how icy his eyes became. "No. Got a mission. Gonna carry it through. Once the mission's over, it's over and all this will disappear. But I do need that reminder of what goal I'm working toward. By taking you, Kiki, Jewel, they cemented their future. The moment I saw you... saw Kiki. Then D's face. Hawk's. Don't feel much fuckin' pain anymore, but I felt theirs to my fuckin' bones. That shit devastated them. Fuckin' rocked them to the core."

Diesel's reaction the other day at Crow's shop proved how much it affected everyone. And rightly so. To see D almost break down...

"This was all by D's order, right? He wants them all gone."

"He wants them gone, but we don't do this on the clock. Me, Walker, Steel, Ryder, Hunter, and Brick... All of us. We want to do this."

"Do they know you've kept those cuts? Does D?"

Mercy shook his head slightly. "No. Just you. That's why I'm trusting you to keep this shit to yourself. I've kept them to show you. Needed to show you. Wanted to let you know you're not alone in this shit. Not dealing with this by yourself. We got your six."

We got your six.

What did that mean? She should feel honored, right? Thankful?

Her gaze skipped around the room once more. What she saw turned her stomach. It didn't make her feel any better at all. She doubted any one of the owners of those cuts were innocent, but did they *all* deserve the sentence they were given?

"Again, hoping you'd stay in town and—" His phone went off and he grabbed it from his hip.

He scowled as he read the text. He closed his eyes for a

second. "Fuck." When he opened them again, they were pinned on her.

Did that text have to do with her? "What?"

"They think you're snagged. Just put out an alert."

"What? Who?" Of course, those questions went ignored, too.

He turned his back on her and put the phone to his ear. "She's good. She's with me." His shoulders jerked and he quickly pulled the phone away from his ear. Even though he didn't have the speaker on, Jazz could hear a loud roaring coming through the cell phone.

Uh oh. Sounded a lot like Diesel.

Once the booming stopped he put the phone back to his ear. "Need to get everyone to stand down. She's safe, boss. She's with me." Mercy shook his head and planted a hand on his hip. "Yeah. Right. Got you." Then he pulled the phone from his ear. His head dropped forward, and he muttered, "Fuck." He turned to face her, his eyes as hard as steel. "Gotta get you back. Apparently, leaving your car behind was a big mistake."

"My car's been sitting there for the last few days."

"Yeah, well, seems as though Momma Bear called fuckin' Crow to see how he likes your hair. Said she dropped you off at the shop."

"And now they think I'm missing..."

"Yeah. *Fuck me.*" Mercy scrubbed a hand over his head. As he herded her out of the room and locked up, he asked, "Why would Crow care about your fuckin' hair?"

He was beyond pissed. Crow let the fury eat at him.

And it didn't lessen as he saw Mercy's big black Terradyne pull in front of his shop. Fuck no, it didn't.

He'd been standing out front waiting on Mercy and Jazz for almost a half hour. Every minute that ticked by made him want to smash that fucker's face in even more.

He was normally not one for violence—unless it was warranted—but right now that was all he could think about.

Getting that call from Momma B, then finding Jazz's car still out back in the ally with no Jazz...

Fuck.

He had lost it. His first call was to D, who also lost it, but even worse in his typical raging bull style.

The thought that fucknut MC might have taken Jazz again was beyond thinkable. He'd never been so fucking scared in his life.

She would never survive a second assault from those mother-fuckers. They would make sure she mentally snapped in two. Most likely never to be fixable again.

And if that happened...

Fuck.

His jaw felt welded together as the RPV came to a rolling stop in front of him. He ripped the passenger-side door open and ignored the surprised woman in the passenger seat to stare past her at the driver.

Fucking Mercy. What the fuck had he been thinking?

Mercy studied Crow's expression and his gray eyes narrowed. His gaze then flicked to Jazz and back to Crow.

Then the one side of his mouth, the side without the scar, curled up slightly.

Fucking son-of-a-bitch. He'd been making a play.

"Got everyone freaked the fuck out!" Crow shouted, then reached in, unlatched her seatbelt and yanked her the fuck out of the vehicle. "Get in the shop," he ordered, his gaze once again locked with Mercy's.

She yanked her arm from his grasp. "But—"

"Get in the fuckin' shop. Need a word with Mercy, here."

"He—"

"Jasmine, get inside. Now."

"I'm not a fucking child."

He twisted his head to glare at her. He took in her now

blonde hair, her practically make-up free face, her slim body tucked into jeans and a royal blue loose tank top that had the logo of a Buffalo-based guitar store on the front.

He sucked air through his nostrils in an attempt to calm down. "No, you're not." She certainly wasn't that. Apparently, he wasn't the only one who noticed. "*Kachina*, go inside." This time he made the order softer, more of an ask than a demand, though he certainly wasn't giving her a choice.

Her green eyes bounced from him, to Mercy at the wheel of the RPV and back to Crow. She opened her mouth, paused, then closed it. Spinning on her heels, she went inside his shop with a huff.

Crow watched her through the picture window as she walked a little deeper into the shop, turned, crossed her arms over her chest, then stared at them through the glass.

Fuck.

He would try to keep it civil.

Try.

"What the fuck do you think you're doin'?"

"She belong to you? You claim her?"

Crow set his jaw. He wasn't going to answer that because Mercy already knew the answer.

"Right," Mercy continued. "Didn't think so."

"She don't need the likes of you."

"Says who? You?"

"She needs a soft hand. Patience."

"Got lots of fuckin' patience."

"Got nothin' in that chest of yours. Your fuckin' heart's ice cold. She don't need frostbite."

Mercy's hard-as-steel eyes got even harder. "You an expert on what she needs?"

"Known her for a long fuckin' time."

"And she's been gone a long fuckin' time, brother. She's not the same as when you knew her before."

Wasn't that the truth. "No one knows that better than me."

"I disagree."

"Get you're tryin' to make a move, but put that shit out of your head."

Mercy snorted. "Again, she belong to you?"

"She doesn't belong to anybody."

Mercy gave him a smile that didn't reach his eyes. Not even close. "Yet."

"When she does, it won't be you," he growled, his hands curling into fists.

"We'll see." Mercy's words were ice cold. He shoved the shifter into first gear and stomped on the accelerator. As Crow quickly stepped back, the passenger door slammed shut on its own.

Crow watched the oversized military-style vehicle speed away, its tires squealing as it took the corner at the end of the block.

If that fucking guy thought he was getting his hands on Jazz...

He shook his head.

Over Crow's dead body.

He closed his eyes and willed his blood pressure to go down before he went inside to deal with her.

Because what she pulled by going somewhere, wherever the fuck they went, without telling anybody was just plain bullshit.

When he turned, she was gone from the large picture window. With a curse, he went inside, his gaze landing on her sitting in the office chair behind his counter where his cash register was kept.

Her bottom lip was tucked between her teeth and her eyes tracked him as he strode toward her.

"He touch you?"

"No."

"He wanna touch you?"

She pursed her lips for a second before saying, "He's a bit intense."

He studied her face when he growled, "Didn't answer the question." When she avoided his gaze, he ground his back molars.

"Because I don't know that answer. He wanted to show me something."

"Sure he did." Mercy wanted to show her his dick, no doubt. "What he show you?"

The color that had been in her cheeks fled. She was thinking way too hard to come up with an answer. He decided to put her out of her misery of making up something that would very well be a lie. "You want 'im?"

Her green eyes went wide. "No."

Hell, he almost believed that. "Sure you don't want 'im to be the one to help you?"

"Help me..." she drifted off.

"What you're askin' from me," he clarified. "Want 'im to be the one instead?"

The color flooded back into her pale cheeks. "No!"

"Sure?"

"Yes."

"Just gotta tell me now, *Kachina*. Gotta be upfront with me." *Before I get to a point where I can't return. Where you ending up in someone else's bed does something to me that...*

Fuck.

She slowly got up from his office chair and came around the short counter to stand inches from him. So close he could feel her heat. Smell her scent. See the different flecks of green in her eyes. There was life behind them today. Unlike the other night when she first walked into his shop. Did he put that spark there or did Mercy?

She tucked her hand under his cut and placed her warm palm over his beating heart. "No, I need it to be you."

Fuck, if those softly spoken words didn't land right in, not only his heart, but his dick.

He reached for her hand, pulled it off his chest and lifted it to his mouth. He kissed her open palm before dropping it and stepping back from her, giving himself some breathing room. "We're goin' home, *Kachina*."

"Why? Don't you have clients today?"

"Cancelled all of 'em thinkin' you were snatched. Thinkin' our asses were gonna have to go out an' find you. Shoulda let someone know where you were."

She curled her fingers into the palm that he'd kissed and held it against her chest, like she was afraid to let that kiss go. "Are you more pissed because you thought I fell into the hands of the Warriors or because I was with Mercy?"

He wasn't going to answer that because right now, it was pretty fucking even. Right now, he was taking Jazz home.

And also right now, he could only think about one thing...

Taking her to bed.

Nobody else was going to claim her first.

No fucking way.

Especially Mercy.

CHAPTER TEN

"Sorry," Jazz whispered as she dismounted from the back of his sled after pulling into the garage. "I should've known. I should've called or texted. But I did text you earlier and got no answer."

Right. Because he couldn't have his phone while visiting Rocky in Greene. "Shoulda at least checked in with D first. Mercy's his man. Mercy answers to D. You know that."

"Maybe it's best if I head home to Buffalo and just come back once a month for my tat. I don't want people worrying about me." With that, she turned and headed toward the door that led into the house.

He swung off his bike quickly and snagged her wrist, stopping her forward motion. "Hold up."

She turned to look at him over her shoulder, but didn't say anything.

"It scared the fuckin' shit outta me, *Kachina*. To get a call sayin' you were dropped off at your car, then when I check out back, I find your car sittin' there an' you nowhere around? What the fuck am I supposed to think?"

"Him showing up was unexpected."

No shit.

"It brought back some deeply rooted shit." She took a deep inhale. "I didn't remember him. I didn't recognize him."

That shouldn't bother her, but it did. He could read it all over her face. There was probably a lot from that day she didn't remember. Maybe it was better that way. "But you got in a fuckin' vehicle with 'im. *Alone*. Not smart, baby. Not fuckin' smart at all."

She turned to face the door again and his chest tightened as her head dropped. "I know."

"He ain't gonna hurt you." While that was true, that didn't mean Crow trusted him. And that was certainly true if Mercy had a hard-on over Jazz. Them being "the same" and all that bullshit. Had some "connection." As fucked up as that may be.

That man was not right for her. No matter what Mercy thought in his fucked-up head.

It took everything in his power to ask, "Need to know, *Kachina*, if you still want me to be your first?"

She jerked within his grasp and he pulled her back to him, turning her to face him.

"Wanna know if what we did last night... you wanna finish."

She lifted her face to him and he could see the sheen in her eyes.

Fuck. She was going to rip his fucking heart right out of his chest.

Her lower lip trembled as she whispered, "Yes. Today didn't change that. I told you back at the shop, it needs to be you."

"Needs an' wants are different," he reminded her. He *needed* her to *want* him, not just use him because she considered him the best man for the job.

"What if it's one and the same for me?"

"Is it?"

"Yes."

Thank fuck. Because he had plans.

Last night he had backed off, but maybe he shouldn't have.

Maybe he just needed to push past those walls. Break down those barriers.

Yeah, she needed a soft hand. Yeah, she needed patience. And, fuck yeah, she needed someone who genuinely cared for her.

That wasn't Mercy.

No, that was fucking him.

Him.

No one else.

He had told her to stop wearing that shitty makeup. Her face was almost make-up free. He told her he wanted her hair to be her natural color. It was very damn close. And he could certainly live with what she was wearing today.

Who did she do that for? Not fucking Mercy.

No, she did that for him.

"*Kachina*."

She lifted her green eyes to his.

"Thank you," he whispered.

"For what?"

"For bringin' her back."

She blinked a couple of times and her bottom lip trembled. "Just on the surface."

He shook his head slowly. "No. I'm seein' her for the first time since you've been home. She's in there."

"You going to help her break free?"

He hoped to fuck that he was. "Gonna do my best."

She gave him a small smile. "Then I should be thanking you."

Crow wasn't sure this was the best idea. In fact, he almost wanted to say this was the worst fucking idea in his life. But at least it was an idea. Last night hadn't gone as it should have, so he was hoping this would work out better.

Let her go at her own pace.

But the problem was, he was going to die.

Just fucking die.

Normally, he'd love this kind of shit. The kind of shit where he was spread eagle on a bed naked as a woman straddled him and did whatever she wanted to him.

But this wasn't "normally."

No, he couldn't move. Not because he was tied down. Because he certainly wasn't restrained. But, *fuck him*, he had promised her he wouldn't move. So he needed to keep his shit together and keep his promise.

And worse, he couldn't touch her. Again, another fucking promise he wished he hadn't made. And, *fuck him twice over*, he was never making that one again. Because with what she was doing to him—he blew out a frustrated breath—he wouldn't be surprised if he just came all over himself. Simply blew his load like a knocked over fire hydrant.

Because this was fucking *torture*.

Now he knew how she felt last night when he had spent over an hour just worshipping her body, taking his time, letting her appreciate everything he was doing to her.

For fuck's sake, that table was now turned. He had the bright idea to let her control everything that was about to happen. Or *hopefully* happen. It would be up to her how everything proceeded and how everything ended.

He only knew his fucking balls were cursing him out and his dick was throbbing to the point where he might snap and break his promise.

A few times—*fuck*, more than a few—he had to close his eyes and clench his jaw and fingers to keep from grabbing her, throwing her on the bed and just taking her like he wanted to.

Consequences be damned.

But his genius-self volunteered for this, so he wouldn't go back on his word. He was also not a quitter.

He bit back a snort. His damn brain was turning into a steaming pile of dog shit.

Like he did to her last night, she was exploring every inch of his body. He swore there wasn't one spot she missed. Once she took the whole tour with her fingers and her soft exploratory touch, she started all over again with her lips. And now her tongue was flicking at his fucking nipples.

And, *oh, fuck him...* His hips jerked, and his chest caved in as she moved down his body and the tip of her hot little tongue licked off the bead of cum at the very tip of his dick.

But he kept his eyes closed because, otherwise, he wouldn't be so patient. If he saw her blonde head down there as she...

Fuuuuuuck. Now she nipped at his inner thighs.

He tried to swallow, but found it impossible.

"*Kachina.*" He hardly recognized his own voice as it escaped him. He groaned as she wrapped her lips around his sac and sucked his balls gently.

Holy fuck. This woman had zero experience. Zero that he was aware of.

If she was this skilled as what he considered a "virgin" ...

When her mouth wrapped around the head of his painfully hard dick... His back bowed and he gripped the sheets so hard he thought he heard them tear.

"*Kachina...* not a good idea," he panted.

"You said I could do whatever I wanted." Her husky voice, thick with what he could only hope was need, swept over him and then swirled around in his muddled brain.

Did he? Did he say that? That was fucking stupid of him. Maybe because he expected her to be more timid about touching him, exploring. Not taking the bulls—or his balls—by the horn —or her hand—and...

He threw his head back as she sucked him deep within her mouth, almost to the back of her throat. He fought to keep from thrusting up, but *shiiiiit...*

"*Kachina.*" Did he say that out loud or was he just screaming in his head? Her mouth was small but hot, wet, and she sucked him *hard*. He tried to gather his breath so he could tell her to stop. Beg her to stop before he...

Then she was gone.

Thank fuck.

His pulse not only pounded in his dick, but also in his temples. Hell, his whole body throbbed.

He forced his eyes open to see what she had planned next.

She was straddling his thighs and pulling off her tank top, reaching behind her back to unclip her bra. Then her tits were bare, her nipples hard peaks. She didn't have a lot there, but what she did have fit her frame perfectly. He expected once she put weight on, they'd fill out even more. Even so, his mouth watered at seeing those pink puckered tips begging to be sucked.

When she stretched out on top of him, those nipples pressed into his chest.

What the fuck was she doing? All he could see was a cloud of blonde hair in his face as her body wiggled back and forth. What kind of fucked-up torture was this?

He realized she was wiggling out of her jeans. But instead of getting up and off him to finish getting undressed, she was doing it on top of him.

Fuck me.

A man could only take so much. "*Kachina*, need to touch you."

The wiggling paused. "You said—"

Know what I fuckin' said! Did he scream *that* out loud? Was he totally losing his shit?

"That I could do what I wanted and you were just going to lay there and allow it."

Fuck. Did he really say that? Yes, he did. He did.

Jesus, he was going to let her finish what she started. And do his best not to whimper. Beg. Or shoot his load between them.

The wiggling resumed and a groan came from deep within his chest.

He stared sightlessly at the ceiling as she jerked a couple of times and he could only imagine she was yanking her jeans off the rest of the way, then slipping out of her panties.

He wondered how damp they were.

Shit. Fuck. Goddamn. She was crawling up his body.

Now what?

He couldn't look.

He couldn't.

But then he didn't have a choice. She was straddling his head and perching above his fucking face.

What the fuck.

"Do what you did last night. Make me come that way."

"*Kachina*, need to touch you," he repeated as he stared up her body. So slim. So young. So inexperienced. But still...

He wanted her.

She shook her head. "No touching. Except with your tongue and mouth."

She probably had no idea how torturous this whole thing was.

"*Kachina*..." He wasn't beyond begging.

"Stop talking, start eating."

What the fuck?

He stared up at her and she stared back down at him, her now blonde hair framing her face, her eyes unfocused. He wanted to kiss her, flip her over and actually make love to her.

He'd never done that before. Never had that urge before. Not with anyone. No. His whole life he simply fucked. He got what he needed. He gave the woman what she needed. And then he got gone. He never made love. He never stuck. But staring up at Jazz, shit was just different. He had no idea why. Seeing her naked and staring down at him with those jade green eyes of hers, her lips parted... He wanted to take her slow and gentle, show her just how good this could be. How right.

How satisfying.

Show her that sex wasn't for punishment or revenge. No, it

was for connection and closeness. He'd never had that before. All the women in the past were now... women in his past.

The woman above him was his future.

She was so fucking young, though... Even naked and aroused she still looked too innocent for him. He was hardly that.

"Crow."

"Yeah, baby?"

"I'm going to sit on your face now."

His lips twitched. "Yeah, baby, I'm good with that."

She shifted forward and then her plump, shiny folds were right there... in his face and he did what she wanted.

He loved every fucking second of it. Even when she ground down on his face and he was almost smothered to death.

Jazz's thighs trembled as she circled her hips slowly. The man was good with his tongue. No doubt about it. She had her fingers dug into his hair at both sides of his head—she should have undone his braid before they started, *damn it*—as everything he did to her made her arch her back and want to pull him closer.

Alternating between flicking her sensitive, swollen clit and sucking hard on it, she threw her head back and moaned. She wanted to experience what she did last night when he did the same thing, but that time she'd been on her back. And he'd had all the control. Tonight, hell, *today*—it was only midday—he had given *her* all the control.

At first, she was unsure of what to do. Then she let herself relax, tried to clear her mind and did what came naturally. The man was beautiful inside and out. His smooth, golden skin, his black silky hair, his onyx eyes, his soul-searching gaze.

And what surprised her last night was that he was tattoo-free except for the club colors on his back. She needed to ask him why. She assumed most tattoo artists had loads of ink. Why not him?

But that was a question for another time, because right now... Right now, even with him not "touching" her, she felt the heat sweep through her and her pulse race. This man knew what he was doing. She was sure he'd done it plenty of times with plenty of women.

Unlike her. When she had taken him into her mouth, she had worried she was doing it wrong. But his reactions proved she was doing something so right. The noises and the way his body arched and tensed, the tight grip of his fingers in the sheets. It didn't seem as though he hated it. Not at all.

That gave her some hope. She shouldn't have waited for the right man all those years ago. But she was waiting for a man like Hawk or Zak before she gave up her virginity. Not those immature high school classmates of hers. She had wanted someone who knew what they were doing. She listened to girls her age brag about banging so-and-so to all their friends, then turn around in private and complain how much it sucked.

She didn't want to be disappointed, she wanted it to be worth it. So she waited. Then she came to the Valley for college. And she spotted Crow and knew he was the one. So again, she waited for the right time. The time when he stopped seeing her as too young.

Unfortunately, things went sideways before any of that could happen.

So she had a lot of catching up to do. A lot of things to experience. And she only hoped her mind wouldn't cock block her. She only hoped her body would remain open and willing to Crow so he could show her things she missed out on. The intimacy, the pleasure, the connection of two people.

That's what today was going to be. Breaking past that barrier. And it was all in her hands. No pressure, right?

Well, except for the pressure of Crow's tongue and lips on her clit. She ground her pussy down into his face. She was getting slicker by the second and wasn't sure if it was from him or from her. Either way, it felt like heaven. Pure ecstasy.

When his tongue slid through her folds, he made a noise. When it dipped inside her, he groaned.

Her breathing became ragged as he continued to turn her into jelly. Her legs weren't the only things trembling now, her whole body quivered from what he was doing.

While his tongue slipped in and out of her, she imagined it was his cock. Long, hard, smooth... skilled. She imagined him pumping his hips slowly, making sure she enjoyed every second of him being inside her. Completing her. Gluing her pieces back together, making her whole.

Maybe she was expecting too much from him. For the most part he was a simple man. Unlike her, who was far from simple. She was messy.

Her thoughts. Her body. Her life.

But if she tried hard enough, maybe, just maybe, she could overcome all of that. For him.

For Crow.

Be the woman he needed.

The woman he wanted.

The woman he claimed.

Would he ever think of her like that?

Those thoughts exploded like a cloud of dust, disintegrating into nothingness as something built deep inside her. A tension. A swirl of heat that rippled through her, landing in her core, where he continued to relentlessly lick, suck and fuck her with his tongue.

The man gave good tongue.

Yes, he did. And she needed to concentrate on that and not the rest of the bullshit that wanted to distract her. The garbage sitting at the edge of her consciousness wanting to pull her from this moment. She wouldn't allow it. No.

This moment was for him and her.

The man she wanted for so long, she had him right at that moment, so she needed to remain here in the room with him.

And like last night, the tension that built slowly within her suddenly exploded like her thoughts had. She cried out as she came, her pussy pulsating, her muscles spasming uncontrollably.

It was an indescribable high. The rush of blood, the rapid beat of her heart, the loss of her breath. After she reached the peak, the float back downward was just as satisfying.

Her mind calmed. Her body relaxed. Her thoughts now only of Crow.

"Fuckin' taste so good, *Kachina*. You have no idea."

No, she didn't. But she would. She quickly slid back along his chest until his cock was wedged between her ass cheeks and she took his mouth greedily, finding not only her own scent, but the taste of her own arousal.

Now she knew what she tasted like.

He allowed her to take control of the kiss, permitted her tongue to explore him with no complaint.

Still, he didn't touch her. His control was unreal. She pulled back until only their lips were touching and they were softly kissing. He was breathing her in, then giving her breath back. Back and forth. She gave, he took. He gave, she took.

She pulled away just enough to say his name. She loved his name and she couldn't say it enough. "Crow."

His name fit him perfectly. When she had done her college paper about him she had learned the large black bird symbolized intelligence, flexibility and destiny.

His mother couldn't have picked anything more appropriate.

"Yeah, *Kachina?*"

"That was awesome."

"Yeah, 'specially when you exploded all over my face."

She jerked her head back. "I did?"

"Yeah, baby, you did."

"Is that good?"

Those skillful lips of his curled at the ends. "The fuckin' best."

"We'll have to do that again, then."

His warm, low chuckle sent a shiver sliding down her spine. "Whatever you need, *Kachina*."

She knew what she needed. He had gotten her primed and prepped and she was so ready to take it further. She only hoped her mind wouldn't fuck with her.

There was nothing more she wanted at that moment than to give herself to Crow.

Her gaze slid to his nightstand and when it did, his cock flexed against her ass.

He was ready.

She needed to be ready, too. She didn't want to leave him hanging like last night. She didn't want to disappoint him.

Hell, she didn't want to disappoint herself.

"Ain't gonna move, baby. It's all you. Take your time. Make sure it's right. I'll be here. When you're ready, you'll know it."

She glanced at the nightstand again. "I'm ready," she whispered, more for herself than for him.

"Wanna touch you so fuckin' bad, *Kachina*, that it's killin' me. But it's all on you. So take it as far as you want to. I'm here for you."

He was always good with his words. Wise. Knew just what to say for the most part. And she recognized what he was doing, trying to bolster her confidence. Make her comfortable.

For that, she was grateful.

"Wraps are in the drawer."

She worried her bottom lip as she looked at the drawer for the third time and gave herself a little pep talk. She wanted this. She could do this. She needed this.

Then she took that next step, leaning over and reaching for the drawer, yanked it open, felt around for the box. Her fingers found it open. Found it half empty.

Of course, the condom he'd used last night wasn't the first one from the box. Of course, he'd had sex with other women.

Of course, he'd had sex with other women in this very bed.

She'd be a fool to think otherwise.

She had saved herself for him.

He didn't do the same. It was stupid to even let that thought bother her.

He was forty years old. He wasn't a love-sick teenager. He wasn't celibate. He was a sexually active adult male who could have almost any woman he wanted.

He was only doing this to help her like she asked. He was doing her a favor.

She probably wasn't his choice in who he'd like to have naked in his bed.

He'd want someone curvier. More experienced. Sultry and sexy.

She was none of those things.

She was thin and bony and... and... scarred.

"*Kachina.*"

But even so, she needed to do this. He was the right one to help her get over this hurdle. She knew it. He knew it.

"*Kachina.*"

She nodded and plucked a condom out of the box and held it between her fingers as she leaned back and finally let herself look at him once more.

His eyes were darker than normal. His gaze flicked from the wrapped condom in her hand to her face, where it searched.

He was expecting her to back out. To call this whole thing off. To tense up and shut down.

But she couldn't do that. Not this time.

She needed to push all thoughts away that might paralyze her.

She needed to remind herself who was beneath her.

She lifted her weight off him and shifted until his cock no longer was wedged between her ass cheeks, until it was in front of her.

She tore the wrapper open, slid out the condom, threw the wrapper over the side of the bed, and then when she grabbed his cock, he hissed out a breath. Ignoring that, she concentrated on rolling the latex down his length slowly, making sure it was on properly. At least she knew how to do that. Something she learned in high school thanks to a good Sex Ed program.

Not releasing it, she held it steady as she lifted herself up again and shifted forward once more.

"*Kachina.*" This time his name for her came out a bit choked.

Was he going to stop her?

He couldn't. Not now. She needed to do this before he bailed.

"*Jazz.*"

She couldn't look at him. Not yet. She lined herself up and once he was right where she needed him, she slid down on him with a whispered, "I'm sorry."

Instead of a look of pleasure, he appeared confused. "For what?"

"For not being who you want me to be. For asking this of you."

She closed her eyes as she lowered herself even further, concentrating on the way he felt inside her. Stretching her. Filling her.

She dropped lower.

Lower.

Finally, when all her weight rested on his lap, she took a slow, deep inhale, opened her eyes and met his.

She was shocked with what she saw.

He was fucking pissed.

Suddenly his hips bucked up, throwing her off balance. With an *oof*, she landed on her back on his mattress with him on top of her.

Somehow he remained inside her but she expected him to pull out and roll away.

He didn't.

No, he stayed deeply seated and he dug his fingers into her hair and held her head so that she couldn't look away.

"Fuckin' listen to me, Jazz, an' listen good. Only sayin' it once... You ain't askin' anythin' of me that I don't wanna give you. Got me? I'm right where I wanna be. Inside of you. *You*, Jazz. No one else. Wouldn't do this for anyone but you. I hated your hair black. I hated that shit on your face. I hated those clothes you showed up in. That's fuckin' true. But you ain't wearin' any of that shit right now. You're fucking one-hundred-percent Jasmine right now. I asked for her back. You gave her to me. I thank you for that gift. You didn't have to do it. You did. Know you did it for me an' not yourself. You have no fuckin' idea how much I appreciate that. You were willin' to come back for me. An' ain't talkin' about comin' back to Shadow Valley, baby." He put all his weight on one arm and slapped his bare chest with his other palm. "You came back for me. That means more to me than what you realize. Know it wasn't easy. Know what we're doin' right now ain't easy, either. Will cherish this fuckin' gift from you forever. Got me?"

She could hardly see him through the tears that had gathered in her eyes. She wasn't crying because of what they were doing. She was touched by his words, no matter that they were angry ones.

His next words were softer, gentler. "Now... you okay with my weight on you?"

She sniffled and nodded, unable to see the beautiful features of his face through a blur of tears.

"Sure?"

She nodded again. "Yes."

He melted against her and put his mouth to her ear. "Good. Gonna show you what you mean to me an' how much I care 'bout you. An' show you how much I appreciate everythin' 'bout you. So hang on tight, baby. Yeah?"

"Yeah," she breathed.

Then he began to move.

CHAPTER ELEVEN

The tight heat that surrounded him pushed all the anger aside. He should've kept his cool, but he couldn't. Not when it pissed him the fuck off that her self-esteem was in the shitter.

He understood why. But he hated it.

It was one more thing those motherfuckers stole from her. He was going to do everything in his power to make sure it returned.

But right now, the last thing he wanted to think about were those asshole nomads. Not when he was deep inside Jasmine.

He was her first, so he needed to make sure she enjoyed the journey he was about to take her on. This wasn't about him. This wasn't about him getting off. Fuck no. This was all about her.

Because if he could get her through this without stopping him, he was going to prove to her how special it could be.

Yeah, sometimes sex sucked with the wrong person. Or if someone was a selfish fuck. But that wasn't him.

He was the perfect person.

For Jazz.

She was the right person.

For him.

So even though he got angry when she worried about disappointing him, the truth was, he was more worried about disappointing her.

He couldn't let her down.

He was moving in and out of her slowly but completely, her mouth near his ear. His mouth near her ear. He could hear her breathing change, her little gasps and shuddered breath with each unhurried, deep thrust.

This was no "slam it home" fuck until he busted a nut. This was a distinct dance he was teaching her. Or an intimate song she was learning the lyrics to.

The surprise in her voice when she said his name made him smile and whisper, "That's it, *Kachina*, say my name. Tell me, show me how good that feels. You feel so fuckin' good to me."

"Crow."

"Yeah, baby, I'm right here." He had his arm curled beneath her shoulders, holding her close as he let his hips move in a rhythm similar to the song she sang the other day on stage. Unrushed and with a whole lot of meaning behind it.

"You always remember your first, baby. Always," he murmured low into her ear. "Want you to remember how perfect this is."

"Yes," she answered on a hitched breath.

"Like what I'm doin' to you?"

"Yes."

"Love what I'm doin' with you?"

"Yes."

"Want more?"

"Yessss."

"Feel you squeezin' me tight, *Kachina*. Feel you ripplin' 'round me. You can't imagine how good that feels."

She whimpered and tilted her hips, letting them rise and fall with each painstakingly slow thrust.

"Want you to remember this moment, baby. Just me an' you, makin' that music you love so much."

Her arms tightened around his waist, her nails digging into his skin. But he didn't care. She could shred him if she needed to. He wasn't going to stop until all the thoughts of her past were swept away and all the possibilities of her future took their place.

He buried his face in her slender neck, licking along her pounding pulse, sucking her delicate skin, the moans and groans that moved up her throat vibrating against his cheek.

Those noises drove him wild, made him want to pound her hard, take her fast, but he forced himself to take it slow. Stretch out their pleasure. Push away her pain. But, even so, those whimpers, sighs and his name on her lips...

He did that to her. He did that for her.

He kissed along her collarbone, over to the hollow of her throat. Then removing the arm he had wrapped tightly around her, he pushed up with his upper body and drove deep with the lower.

He stayed that way. Both of them fitting together so fucking perfectly as he curled over her, snagging one of her nipples into his mouth. His teeth scraped against her heated skin ever so lightly. Enough for her to feel it, not enough for her to panic.

He flicked the pointed nipple with the tip of his tongue, then with a groan, sucked it deep within his mouth.

Her body bowed off the bed, encouraging him on. Encouraging him to suck harder. His palm swept over her other pebbled nipple and once again she cried out his name.

Would he ever get fucking tired of hearing it come from her?

As he sucked one, he gently twisted the other between his thumb and forefinger. Once again, enough for her to experience this new pleasure, but not enough to cause pain.

The pad of his thumb brushed over the tight tip. His fingers then swept along the outer curve before sliding along the bottom and around, exploring, kneading, squeezing just enough to bring about his name on her lips once more.

He moved to the other one, sucking it, his fingers now finding the wet, swollen nipple his mouth had left behind.

And though he remained still, remained deep inside her, he could feel her reaction around his dick. That left no doubt how much she liked what he was doing.

Her fingers found his hair, traveling down his braid and back up. Then her fingers were digging into his scalp.

"Gonna start movin' again, baby. This time gonna stay at the same pace 'til you tell me to change it. Tell me to go harder, go easier. Go deeper or not. How ever you want it, I'm here for you. What ever you say, gonna listen. Yeah?"

"Yeah," she sighed.

"Want me to stop, tell me to stop." *But for fuck's sake, don't ever tell me to stop. This feels way too fuckin' good an' I wanna feel you come around my dick.*

"I don't want you to stop."

Thank fuck.

It killed him to reassure her, "If I gotta, just say it. 'Kay, baby?"

"Okay."

He began to move again, rolling his hips, digging his knees into the mattress, sliding one arm underneath her again, this time to lift her hips just slightly. Her head tipped back, and her eyes closed, her lips parted, little puffs of warm breath beat against his cheek.

It was going to kill him, but he was going to keep the same pace until she told him otherwise.

Yep, he fucking was.

He wanted to grab her thighs and wrap her legs around his hips, but he didn't want to trigger any memories of being manhandled.

"Good, baby?"

"Yes."

Please tell me to fuck you harder an' faster. Even a little...

Her hands smoothed down his back and she grabbed his ass, digging her fingers in deep. He took one of her swollen nipples into his mouth again and while sucking it, circled his tongue around the tip.

Her fingers flexed and dug deeper into his ass muscles.

Whatever she needed...

"Crow..." she breathed.

He didn't stop what he was doing, he continued to tease her tight nipple and draw it fully into his mouth.

"Crow..."

Yeah, Kachina, cry out my name... Just like that.

"Crow... faster."

He picked up his pace, not much faster than he was previously moving, but enough so she could tell.

"Faster."

He quickened his pace a little more, still taking long, deep strokes.

"*Crooooow*," she moaned. "Fuck me."

He lifted his head. "Tell me how you want it, baby. Gotta hear it."

"Harder. Faster. I... I want to come."

So do I. But waitin' on you.

He began to do what she asked: thrust harder and faster. Not as hard and as fast as he could, but more than he was previously. He watched her face for any other kind of reaction other than bliss. But there wasn't one. Everything he was seeing, every reaction he witnessed, showed him that she was enjoying what he was doing, but her eyes remained closed and he worried about what was running through her head.

The mind could play tricks. One minute things could be good, things could be moving along as planned, then the next...

She could tense up and order him to stop. The slightest sliver of that past nightmare could come back to haunt her.

He needed to keep her attention on him. On them there in this room, his bed.

"*Kachina*," he murmured. "Open your eyes. Look at me."

She ignored him at first, and he leaned in to brush his lips over hers. To remind her who was above her, who was inside her. Where she was at that very moment. Where she was going.

"*Kachina*," he whispered. "Need to look at me."

Her eyelids fluttered open and he noticed that her pupils were wide, narrowing that beautiful sea green.

"Tell me you're good."

She nodded slightly. "Yes... Yes. I... This is good."

He couldn't fight the smile that curled his lips. "Just good?"

"No... it's... amazing."

That was more like it.

He took her mouth, savoring the taste of his *Kachina* for a moment, then lifted his head once more.

"Eyes on me," he reminded her. "Tell me to slow down if you need to."

She gave him a silent nod and he began to do what he was dying to do, what he was waiting for.

He claimed her thoroughly, inside and out. Their gazes remained locked and he watched her face change. Not from panic, but from pleasure. Maybe even a little surprise.

He increased his pace once more, tilted her hips even higher and he drove deep over and over.

Her eyes were heavy and hooded, but she kept them pinned on him, obviously fighting the urge to close them. And he did the same.

He wanted nothing more than to rip the wrap off, throw his head back, pound her hard and come deep inside her. Mark her as his.

All of that would be fucking stupid, so it helped to keep their gazes locked to remind him who was beneath him, as well. To remind him how important it was to be careful with her.

For now.

Later when...

Later...

Fuck.

Later when her tattoo was done and she learned how great sex could be with the right person, they'd go their separate ways. She'd head back to Buffalo or wherever and he'd go back to living by himself.

In this house that was way too big for him.

Way too empty.

In a house that didn't make sense if he was going to remain a bachelor.

"Crow."

It was then that he realized it was he who closed his eyes. He had got caught up in his own thoughts, something he was trying to help Jazz avoid.

He opened his eyes. "Yeah, baby?"

"I'm... I'm going to..." Her back arched. "Come. Keep... doing what you're doing."

Jesus. It wasn't like he was going to stop. Fuck no. "*Kachina,* let go."

Her mouth gaped open and her head tipped back as she let out what seemed like a silent scream. Nothing but hissing breath escaped as her body convulsed beneath him, tensing, jerking.

Then he felt it. The muscles squeezing him, rippling around him, the heat, the slickness. Her hips lifted again and again as she rode out the orgasm.

He dropped his forehead to hers and he stayed right there with her, struggling to hold back until she was done.

And the second she was, he let himself go, too.

He met her on the other side of something he never experienced before with any other woman.

And that fucking scared the shit out of him.

Crow stared at the digital clock. 5:45 PM. They'd been lying in bed for hours now and he'd soon need to make sure she got something to eat.

He hated to move because Jazz was asleep in his arms, though he hadn't slept for a second.

Instead he had burrowed his nose into her blonde hair and inhaled her scent which was becoming way too familiar. He'd lightly stroked his fingers over her warm, soft, smooth skin as she slept soundly, her breathing steady.

They didn't talk afterward. He'd gotten up, rid himself of the wrap and slipped back into bed with her, covering the two of them with the sheet.

It was weird being in bed during the day, especially when he should be at his shop working. But he wasn't. Because right now being in his bed with Jazz in his arms after he just became her first, was more important than anything.

He should feel satisfied and at peace with the way she reacted. It was a big step for her.

Instead, he was feeling restless. And the reason was, after Jazz fell asleep, everything he found out this morning at SCI Greene, everything Rocky told him, began to invade his thoughts.

He wasn't sure what to do with that information.

He wanted to hear the truth, the details of the violence he'd witnessed when he was just a toddler, to see if he was repressing any of the memories. To see if he could deal with a past that changed his path. A violent event which ripped him from his parents, from the DAMC and sent him "home" to his mother's reservation.

Would he be different now if he'd grown up with his parents in the club? If he never experienced everything he did with his ancestors and his real blood?

Maybe Rocky was right. Maybe he was too soft. Maybe being raised among his mother's tribe instead of his father's MC made him incapable of being emotionless like Diesel when he needed to be.

He had listened to Rocky's words carefully, trying to pull up any memory of being in that room, but he had none. Maybe that was for the best. Remembering his mother raped and murdered in front of him may have filled him with a lingering hatred. And he didn't want to live his life like that.

But like every one of his brothers, the thought of a man turning sex into a weapon, an act of violence, control and revenge, burned in his gut. It stirred that hatred he wanted to avoid.

The thought of what Jazz endured at the hands of their enemy chilled his blood.

But Diamond... What she suffered as a teenager at the hand of their trusted brother. Someone who was supposed to be family. Someone who led them as president. Someone who had access to vulnerable females. Females each and every one of them were tasked to protect.

They should have known. Someone should have known how downright fucked in the head Pierce was.

That was on all of them. They allowed a monster to remain amongst their midst.

His nostrils flared, and his chest got tight. When Pierce confessed what he did to Diamond...

He *hated*.

He *despised*.

He had lost all softness that Rocky said he had.

Crow normally didn't condone violence, but on this occasion, he required it to cleanse his soul.

He knew D's crew was going to make Pierce disappear. Not run him out of town, not just strip him of his colors. But ghost him.

That fucker was going somewhere he'd never touch anyone ever again. Never touch anyone else's life with his downright evilness.

While Mercy and the rest of the Shadows took pleasure out of avenging women who'd been hurt at the hands of a man, Crow wanted it even more than them.

He could taste that shit. It permeated every cell in his body. It tainted every thought.

After a quick word with Slade after Hawk and D escorted Pierce out of church, he'd run upstairs to his room, dug out the knife that was given to him by his uncle on his sixteenth birthday. A wide blade that was hand forged and the handle made out of a carved elk antler.

And because that knife had meaning to him, it was only appropriate it would be the tool used to remove Pierce from the earth.

Crow had caught up to Walker and Mercy out in the parking lot before they drove away. While they weren't happy about it, they reluctantly allowed him to follow. And no one else who was outside, Diesel, Hawk or Zak, tried to stop him.

He'd got on his sled and trailed the large SUV through the countryside, not knowing where they were headed. Only knowing what thoughts spun in his own mind.

He couldn't push out the image of Pierce forcing himself on a fifteen-year-old Diamond and then her remaining quiet about it.

Diamond was tough. Diamond was a fighter. It ate at him that she remained silent about what that bastard had done all those years prior. It was so unlike her. If she had come forward...

But that wasn't for any of them to judge.

None of them.

Though, it made him wonder that if no one knew or witnessed what happened to Jazz, would she have kept silent about it, too. Would she have suffered alone, trying to go through life without revealing what chewed her up inside?

He closed his eyes and remembered the day those devastating secrets were revealed... The sun had set by the time they reached their destination, which was an edge of rocky cliff at an abandoned quarry filled with water.

As Mercy dropped Pierce to his knees and Walker held him there, Crow's first instinct was to simply filet the colors from the traitor's back.

Between church and the quarry, Pierce's cut had been taken from him and he only remained with his long-sleeved T-shirt on, facing the quarry from the top of the cliff. It wouldn't take much to slice that tee free and do what he intended.

Both Mercy and Walker waited patiently as Crow studied Pierce's back. And surprisingly, at first, Pierce said nothing.

The man knew his fate. He should have known it the second he touched Diamond over fifteen years earlier.

Crow had expected vile words to spew from his mouth, to get in his last-minute digs. But again, he remained silent. His head hung forward, so maybe he was losing consciousness. Or trying to block out what was about to happen.

Probably like what Diamond had to do all those years ago.

Crow actually wanted the man to say shit, because that would stir up Crow's anger, make it easier for him to dole out the justice Pierce so rightly deserved.

But the more he pictured Diamond suffering at the hands of the man currently on his knees, the easier it became.

Stepping up to Pierce, he used the knife to slice open the worn cotton tee to reveal the black and gray ink that covered the man's back. The symbol of family and loyalty. History and future.

Pierce had pissed on all of that.

The man's head had jerked up, but he continued to face the water. "You never belonged in this club, half-breed. Shoulda stayed on your reservation where you belonged." Then he spat a hocker on the ground before sneering, "Soaring Dove's name shoulda been Whoring Dove. She loved that fuckin' white dick."

Crow stared at the back of Pierce's salt-and-pepper hair for a long minute and he let those words absorb into every fiber of his being.

This was Pierce. This was who he was. Cancer in the club. Cancer on the earth. A cancer that needed to be eradicated.

It would be Crow's pleasure to do it.

With deliberate slowness, Crow carved off the colors that he himself had inked into Pierce's back a couple decades ago. And when he was done, he whispered some words in Lakota. A request to the gods that Pierce never rest in peace. That what he'd done to others would be done to him for eternity.

He asked the gods to give Pierce no mercy.

Then with slick, bloody hands, he ripped Pierce's drooping head back by his hair, tempted to scalp him, but he didn't. Instead, he drew the blade across the man's throat, as Mercy and Walker continued to hold him upright. When it was finished, he dropped the now tainted knife, drew two bloody fingers of each hand diagonally across his own face, leaving twin streaks of warmth across both cheeks.

After giving Walker and Mercy a chin lift each, which they both returned, he turned and walked away.

As he headed back to his sled, he heard the splash. It sounded heavier than a body. Whatever weighed Pierce down would make sure he never surfaced again. His grave would be hundreds of feet deep.

Crow wondered who else was at the bottom of that watery grave.

Not that he gave a fuck.

He mounted up and began the long trip home. And once he returned to his room at church, he stood under the scalding hot water in his shower until it turned cold.

He waited to feel something. Guilt. Doubt. Anything. But he didn't.

He had no regrets.

Fucking none at all.

And now he wondered if he was no better than Buzz or Hammer, the Warriors who'd killed a mother and a father right in front of their child and didn't give one fuck that they did so.

Jazz's knee slid up his thigh and she adjusted her cheek on his chest. He was on his back with her pinned to his side. "What time is it?" she asked with a yawn.

"Almost time for dinner."

She groaned and shifted, tucking her face deeper into his neck. He tightened his arm around her, not ready to get out of bed even to make sure she ate.

No, he was liking right where she was at. He was liking right where he was at, too.

She trailed her fingers over his chest. "You have no tattoos."

He combed his fingers through her hair, gently untangling some of the knots it got during sex. "Got my colors."

"Other than that you have no tats. Why? Not only are you a tattoo artist, you're a biker. That's not typical."

Maybe it wasn't. Just because everybody else was doing it, didn't mean he had to follow the crowd. He never was one to do that. He did things on his own timeline, for his own reasons. Having his colors done on his back was a given, though. He didn't even think twice about it once he found the right slinger to do them.

"See too many people make the wrong decision when it comes to ink. Only gonna get ink I'll never regret. Like my colors. When I get a tat, want it to mean something. Refuse to tat myself an' there ain't too many ink slingers I'd trust."

Her fingers continued on their journey, lazily drawing circles over his stomach. "Who did your back?"

"A guy at Sturgis. He did a lot of club colors an' I saw some of his work. Trusted 'im enough to let 'im do it."

"Would you go back to him if you wanted anything else done?"

Crow thought about it. "Probably. But like I said, whatever it is gotta mean somethin' to me. An' I haven't been to Sturgis in years."

Yep, any tattoos he got had to have meaning. Unlike all the prison ink that Rocky now sported. That got his thoughts back on his meeting with the man that morning. Jazz had mentioned she couldn't get a hold of him and Crow didn't want her to think that he would ignore her on purpose. "Was a reason you couldn't reach me this morning, *Kachina*."

"Why was that?"

"Had business to take care of."

"For the shop?"

"Past business. Went to Greene."

She didn't say anything for the longest moment. "The prison? Why?" She began to lift her head, but he wrapped his hand around the back of it and held her there. Her warm breath washed over his skin.

He wasn't sure if he should tell her all the details, in fact, he knew he shouldn't. Not the brutal ones.

"To see Rocky. You comin' home made me realize a few things. Made me realize I've been avoidin' somethin' my whole life. Hidin' from it. Saw you doin' the same, figured I needed to face that shit head-on. Hear it, deal with it, move the fuck on."

This time he didn't fight it when she lifted her head. She shifted again, sliding over him until she laid across his chest, staring up at him. While he liked her face tucked against his neck, he liked her weight on him, too. Plus, he could explore the smooth skin of her back easier that way.

"What did you find out?"

"Found out my father was a coward."

She blinked wide eyes at him. "I don't understand. You went to the prison to find out if your father was a coward?"

"Went to hear what happened to my parents. The truth. All of it."

"I know they were murdered."

Of course she knew that, like everyone else did. But he had also told her that all those years ago when she "interviewed" him for one of her college courses. At that time, he simply said they were killed by Warriors and left it at that.

She continued, "But how does that make him a coward? Wasn't he one of the victims?

"Yeah, baby, he was a victim. But that's not the point."

Her brows lowered. "I'm still not understanding how a victim could be a coward. Wouldn't that make me a coward?"

Shit. He didn't need her to think that. Not at all.

He grabbed her chin and lifted her face to his. "No, *Kachina*, you were not a fuckin' coward, you were brave. You were a survivor. *Are* a survivor. Coyote was a fuckin' coward because he didn't fight to save my mother."

Her eyes widened again and she whispered, "How do you know he didn't fight?"

"Because, baby, if he did, he woulda either saved his woman or died first."

"But—"

There was no argument about it. What he said was one hundred percent true. "No fuckin' way could I sit there an' watch my woman go through what my mother did. She suffered, *Kachina*, she suffered bad. I'd die doin' whatever I could to save her. That's why Coyote was a coward. You die protectin' the people you love."

"Sacrifice," she whispered, snuggling back against him.

"Always."

"Loyalty," she murmured, suddenly sounding half-asleep.

"Always."

"Family."

Family.

As he heard her breathing slow, his thoughts went to the house next door.

His father wasn't the only spineless one that day. So was Slade's. Because what kind of fucking man did that to a helpless woman?

So, he and Slade had something in common.

Since Jazz was snoring softly once more, there wasn't a better time to slip out of bed and go have a conversation with Diamond's ol' man.

The porch light lit up, blinding Crow for a second before the door swung open.

Slade stared at him from in the doorway, his jaw set, his eyes hard. "Diamond ain't here."

"Ain't lookin' for Diamond."

"Well, that's a fuckin' first. Love to paw my ol' lady. Must get off on feelin' her up."

Crow set his own jaw. Slade was sporting for a fight and Crow wasn't going to give it to him. "Whether you fuckin' believe it or not, I'm happy for her. Fuckin' happy she found someone who's right for her. It wasn't me. Never was, never wanted it to be. Gotta admit we're close, yeah. Been close for a long fuckin' time. Longer than you've been existin' in this club, in her life. So get the fuck over it." Crow shrugged. "Or don't. Don't give a shit."

Slade shook his head then pinned his narrowed eyes on him. "Why? Why her?"

If he was in Slade's shoes, he'd probably have a problem with another man touching his woman. Even innocently enough. So Crow figured Slade needed an explanation on why he was so drawn to Diamond. "Truth? Knew somethin' ate at her. Never knew what. Just knew she didn't wanna hang at the club or be a part of the pig roasts. Didn't know why. Especially when she loved being DAMC. But being part of the club means being part of the shit that goes along with it. Like the parties. Bella, I understood why. Diamond, I didn't. She was a part of the family but stayed distant. Maybe she didn't know she was doin' it. Maybe she did it on purpose. Either way, don't blame her one bit. What fuckin' Pierce did—"

"Don't!" Slade barked as he lifted his palm up to stop what Crow was going to say next.

He respected that. He didn't want to bring that shit up, either. "Know you guys went through some hard shit 'cause of that. It sucks, but you both came through it. Shows just how strong the two of you are. Now you're bringin' new life into this club, into your relationship. It's gonna be good."

"Don't need you to tell me that, *oh wise one*." With a scowl, Slade crossed his arms over his chest.

A chest that had been built and honed even more since opening the gym he and Diamond ran. Crow didn't need to get into a fight with him. He'd fucking lose for sure.

So instead, Crow flattened his lips, took a calming breath through his nose and continued, "Let me fuckin' get somethin' straight. I see how fuckin' good you are for Diamond. Fuckin' see it. Ain't ever gonna fuck that up for the two of you, no matter what you think. Want her to be happy; want her to love her life. She got there 'cause of you. I see that. Everybody else sees it, too. She wasn't happy for a long fuckin' time. Now we all know why. Can't change history but can change the future."

Slade didn't say anything. His tight, closed-off body said it all.

"An' I'm here to talk to you 'cause of both history an' the future. Need to get some shit out on the table."

Slade watched him cautiously. "What shit?"

"You know what shit. Shit you an' she's been keepin' from me. Shit you both know."

Slade's eyebrows dropped low. "You didn't know?"

"Didn't wanna know. Like Diamond, kept shit buried, didn't wanna bring it to the surface."

"Why now?"

"Got a good woman in my house. Got a woman who needs to bury the past, too. Look to the future. If I wasn't willin' to do it, how the hell am I supposed to help her?"

"Jazz," he murmured, dropping his defensive stance.

Crow let himself relax, too. "Yeah."

Slade nodded. "You serious 'bout her?"

"Wanna help her. After that?" Crow shrugged. "Don't know. She's young. I'm fuckin' old an' set in my ways. Wanna help her move forward but don't wanna hold 'er back."

Slade snorted. "You think you'll hold her back 'cause you're forty an' she ain't? That sounds like a fuckin' bullshit excuse, brother."

Whether it was or wasn't, it was still true. "Maybe."

"No fuckin' maybes 'bout it. Look at Diamond an' me. Our fathers were enemies. Her father killed mine. Mine..." Slade drifted off, pursed his lips and tilted his head. "Yeah, got you. Wasn't sure if you knew." He shook his head, then jerked his chin, indicating Crow should come inside before turning to walk deeper into the house. Crow followed him down the hallway toward the kitchen while Slade murmured, "Sins of the father..."

In the kitchen, Slade stopped in front of the refrigerator, opened it, grabbed two beers and offered one to Crow.

He didn't really want a beer, he wanted to get back to the woman waiting in his bed. He wanted to make sure she ate a good meal. But he also didn't want to pass up this opportunity to smooth shit out with Slade. They were brothers, neighbors and he was Diamond's ol' man. Crow didn't want tension between them, so he accepted the beer and twisted off the cap.

"His shit ain't your shit, Slade. Just like your ol' lady ain't Rocky, you ain't Buzz. Wasn't you who was in that room. It wasn't you who—"

Slade's grunt cut him off. "Yeah." He took a swallow of his beer, then turned to face Crow. "Yeah. But that fucker's blood runs through my veins."

And Coyote's runs through mine. "Don't matter. Ain't you."

"What he did to your ma. Your pop." Slade dropped his head, shook it again and planted his hand on his hip.

"Yeah," Crow murmured as he raised the beer to his lips.

"Glad I never knew 'im."

"Yeah," Crow repeated because he wasn't sure what to say to that. It had to be difficult to know your father did some violent, foul shit to people who didn't deserve it.

It was also tough to learn that your own father didn't do everything in his power to save your mother. He should have died trying.

"Keeps me up sometimes, worried I'll turn into him."

"That won't happen."

Slade's eyes slid to the side and he blew out a breath. "Did some awful shit in the service."

Slade never once mentioned his stint in the Marines. He always avoided it, even with Diamond, so Crow was surprised he was bringing it up.

"Look back at some of that shit an' see the possibilities of it bein' genetic. That fuckin' evilness. That cold-hearted..."

Killer, Crow finished in his head. He was sure Slade did some ugly shit while serving overseas. Shit he wasn't proud of. Things he had a hard time living with.

But that was in the past. He now had a good future. He was finally settled where he belonged.

"Need to push that shit outta your head, brother. Got a good woman who loves you. Live your life for her. For your son. Do your best for them. Future, remember? Not the past. Fuckin' can't control the past. Don't let that shit stop you from bein' the best fuckin' father you can be. Best ol' man you can be. You saved Diamond. You fuckin' saved her an' I'm grateful for that. I tried, but it was you."

Slade nodded then lifted his beer to his lips, draining the rest of it in one swallow.

"Got a successful business. You're an asset to the club. Got a great house. An' fuckin' best of all, you got a great motherfuckin' neighbor."

With a grin, Slade tossed his empty bottle into the trash can. "Yeah, had me worried when you moved next door. Was figurin' I was gonna come home to find you bangin' my ol' lady in my own fuckin' bed. An' that's the truth."

"Never touched her. Wouldn't disrespect one of my brothers like that, either."

"You touch 'er," Slade muttered.

"Not in that way."

"Right."

"Ain't gonna promise not to touch her, especially when she's carryin' the future. The second she tells me no, I'll respect that."

"I've told you no."

"Right. Diamond's her own woman an' makes her own decisions. But you want me to stop, I'll stop, brother." It would be a great loss for him not feeling that life growing inside of her, but he'd do it. If only to keep the peace.

Slade didn't say anything for a while, only stared out of the window over the sink. "Right an' when she asks why shit with you has changed, she's gonna make my life hell."

Crow chuckled. "Know it. So pick your fuckin' poison. Happy wife, happy life."

"Ain't my wife."

"Same shit."

Slade glanced over his shoulder at Crow. "Need to make her my wife. Got a kid on the way. It'd be smart."

Crow shrugged. "She knows you love 'er. Knows you're loyal. A ring ain't gonna make a difference."

"Yeah," he grunted, then turned to lean back against the sink, crossing his arms over his bulging chest once more. "So you came over here to settle shit. But not 'bout Diamond, 'bout my sperm donor."

"Yeah, been thinkin' 'bout it since I visited with Rocky this mornin'. Jesus, hard not to think 'bout it. Didn't want you to think I'd hold it against you. Like I said, you ain't your pop. Will never be your pop. You're family, brother. An' that's the truth. Just wanted to lay it out there. Gonna talk to Diamond, too. Gonna reassure her since your pop's gonna be her son's granddaddy by blood. Just wanna make sure there ain't no misunderstandin'."

"'Preciate you comin' over to talk 'bout it. Sorry it happened. Sorry it affected all of us."

"Gotta only look forward," Crow reminded him.

"Yeah, the future. My son... Your godson."

Crow suddenly couldn't breathe as he stood in the middle of

the kitchen and stared at Slade. Did he hear that right? It took everything he had to say, "Ain't blood, brother." A reminder that if they were looking for someone to fill those shoes, it shouldn't be him.

"Don't matter. Still family."

"Diamond okay with that? She got real blood to step in." He couldn't imagine that Jag, Jewel or even Ruby would be okay with naming Crow as Diamond's unborn son's guardian.

"She's the one who mentioned it. Didn't agree with her at first. Now I do. She's right."

Jesus fuck. "Brother..."

Slade shook his head. "No, she's right. She loves her family, loves this club, but she loves you more. That shit fuckin' bugged me for the longest time. That day I came down the steps at church an' saw her in your fuckin' arms..." He shook his head again. "It fuckin' killed me. Ripped me wide open."

"You kicked her from your bed."

"Yeah, I did. My mistake."

"Wasn't doin' nothin' but soothin' the sting," Crow reassured him.

"Know that now, too."

"Worked out."

"Yeah, it worked out. Know she loves her family an' the club, an' though she still loves you, know I fuckin' knocked you outta that top spot. That's my baby in her belly, not yours. That's my bed she climbs into every night, not yours. And it's my dick she sits on."

Crow pinned his lips together to keep his smile contained. "Glad you finally see that shit clearly."

"Didn't until just right now. So gotta thank you, brother." Slade pushed off the counter and approached Crow.

When the man held his hand out, they clasped palms and bumped shoulders. And the tension Crow hadn't realized he was carrying around for a while disappeared.

Slade stepped back. "So, you gonna do it?"

"Be the godfather? I'll think 'bout it."

"No, you know Diamond won't take a no on that issue. I'm talkin' 'bout helpin' Jazz out. Showin' her her future, help get her over her past."

"Gonna try my fuckin' best."

"She in your bed?"

What happened in his bedroom, in his bed, stayed there. He never shared. He never discussed pussy with his brothers. Never saw a need for it. But Jazz wasn't pussy.

"Don't even gotta answer that, brother, can see it in your face." Slade chuckled, went into the fridge again, pulled out another couple of beers and offered him one.

Crow shook his head. He needed to get back before Jazz woke up.

Slade slapped him on the back with a laugh. "Brother, if you could see what I'm seein' right now, you'd know you're fucked."

That's what Crow was afraid of.

"Welcome to the club."

Fuck.

CHAPTER TWELVE

J azz sat in the middle of Crow's bed as naked as the day she was born. She felt no need to hide herself. At least from the man whose bed she was in.

However, she was *sort of* covered. By her guitar. Sitting cross-legged, she strummed the strings letting the music not only swirl around her, but fill her. Though that hollow spot she normally filled with music wasn't so empty anymore.

Hell no.

The other night, she had woken up to a dark bedroom and an empty bed. And when Crow returned, she watched him carefully.

"Where'd you go?" she asked softly, really not expecting him to respond because he didn't answer to her. In truth, he didn't answer to anybody. But the house had been dead quiet, so she knew he'd left. She also guessed he went next door.

Her assumption was confirmed when he stated, "Next door."

Jazz had nodded and wasn't going to ask anything else, but before she could stop it, the jealousy that clawed at her made her say, "To Diamond." She didn't ask, she stated it.

She had thought back on the conversation when he said he'd

do whatever he'd have to to protect his woman. Whether she was his ol' lady or not, he'd probably kill for Diamond.

Crow had moved farther into the room, his almost-black eyes taking her in as she curled up in his bed under his sheets.

"No. Had to talk to her ol' man."

She wanted to ask about what. But it wasn't her business, especially if it was club business. She knew *that* drill.

However, he kept talking. "Had to straighten some shit out with Slade."

"And did you?"

As he slowly approached the bed, his eyes not leaving her, he stripped off his cut and his clothes. "Yeah."

Jazz gave him a half smile. "Good."

"Gotta get you fed soon, *Kachina*. But..."

She was finding it hard to catch her breath because he was now naked, his golden skin gleaming in the soft glow of the lamp on his nightstand. "But?"

His cock was hard and jutting out from his body. He wasn't thinking about food. Or Diamond.

Well, now neither was she.

"Wanna be inside you again. Gonna be okay with that?"

"Yes." Because it was true. The sex she'd had with Crow, was not only everything she imagined, but even better. And she truly couldn't wait to do it again to make sure it wasn't a fluke.

"Sure?"

She gave him a small smile and pulled back the top sheet in invitation. "Yes."

It ended up that the second time wasn't as long as the first. Or nearly as excruciatingly slow.

Jazz realized the sex with Crow—how good it had been—wasn't a fluke at all.

And now, two weeks later, she was feeling much more comfortable in her own skin. Even naked. Tomorrow, she'd go back to the shop and he'd work some more on her tattoo. She looked forward to it but also dreaded it.

While she couldn't wait until the piece was done, she also wasn't ready to endure that pain again. And she knew the sooner he got the tattoo done, the sooner she'd be out of both his house and his life. She'd have to restart her own life for real. No more hiding.

Once again this morning, she had woken up and the bed was empty beside her. She had no idea where he went. The familiar smell of coffee brewing was curiously absent. And while it was her job as house mouse to go down and make him breakfast, she didn't want to see where he'd gone.

Most likely it was next door. Again.

While Diamond had kept her word and stayed away, giving them space, that didn't mean Crow didn't go over and spend time with the woman in her own house.

Because he probably did.

So instead of heading downstairs and letting that thought eat at her, she had grabbed her guitar and climbed back into bed to play a little while she waited. To let the music she loved so much soothe her soul.

She played a few different riffs and kept humming along until she found the right song that fit her mood. The perfect song that expressed what was going through her.

Bound to You.

Because that's what she was. Bound to Crow.

She found a man she could trust. And because of him, she was breaking down the walls she had built around herself all those years ago.

Her worry was, when Crow finally walked away, she would suffer all over again. Maybe even rebuild those walls, because she didn't want to think about being with anyone else.

She couldn't imagine letting anyone else in. Not in the way she had allowed him.

She let her eyes close as she sung the potent Christina Aguilera song. Every word, every syllable, every note flowing through her. If only Crow could hear them, understand what he meant to her. When her tattoo was done, she could only hope he might not want her to go. He might not want her to move on.

Possibly ask her to stay.

But then again, she shouldn't hold out that hope, because she could end up disappointed in the end.

No matter what, the last two weeks with him had made her stronger. Made her feel more like herself. Or how she used to be when she actually loved life. And now, because of him, she was once again looking toward her future, whether he was in it or not.

She hoped he was.

Because every night when he'd come home late from the shop, he'd climb into bed with her, wake her gently, then make love to her.

Every night.

Every night she lost another piece of her heart to him.

Every night their intimacy built a stronger connection between them...

Maybe she was fooling herself.

Maybe he was only doing her a favor by helping her move on. Following through on his promise to her.

But she didn't want to move on when it came to him.

She didn't want to cut those ties. She didn't want to be freed from those chains...

When she sang the last line of the song, declaring how she was bound to him, she let her fingers still and slowly opened her eyes.

And met his nearly black ones. He had a shoulder leaning against the doorway as he watched her. His expression made her heart skip a beat.

Without a word, he stalked toward the bed, lifted the guitar strap over her head and put the instrument aside.

Her thumping heart began to race as he tugged his T-shirt over his head and slipped out of his jeans.

Then he was on her, over her, kissing her, touching her. Lips, fingers, tongue. His body was hot and hard. For once there was no foreplay, no taking his time.

No assuring himself that she was ready.

No going painstakingly slow, which drove her out of her mind.

No, he only said her name once. Her full name.

Jasmine.

Then he took her.

Completely.

She wrapped her legs around his hips and encouraged him to keep his feverish pace. She cried out his name, scraping her nails down his back.

When she shattered around him, her only thought was...

They fit perfectly.

This was how it was meant to be.

This was where she belonged.

She.

Was.

Home.

J azz sat on the back deck at Crow's house, facing the woods as the sun lowered slowly behind the trees. To her right was a small table that held a glass of Jim Beam with a splash of pop. She was hoping it would dull the pain from the work Crow did two days ago on her tattoo.

He had retraced a lot of the lines that hadn't held the black the first time and started filling in the negative space with some color. He hadn't gotten as far as he would've liked because the pain had become unbearable and no matter how hard Jazz tried to hide it, she couldn't fool him.

Every few minutes he'd look up, assess her expression, then his dark eyebrows would knit together and a frown would mar those beautiful, full lips of his.

Lips she loved to have all over her body. Lips that kissed her with expertise. Lips that would make her orgasm when they sucked on her clit.

Heat rolled through her and landed in her core as she pictured that.

Clearing her head, she held the guitar carefully against her body, avoiding pressing too hard against the fresh ink.

She was picking at the strings and playing around with different chords, attempting to flesh out a song in her head she was writing, a song that had been disturbing her sleep.

She cleared her throat and dropped her chin to her neck, concentrating on the words that slipped from between her lips.

"Faith, hope and whiskey. Gotta have all three to get me through the day," she crooned, then laughed because what she was feeling and what was coming out were two different things. And what was coming out sounded like a really awful country song.

She paused, took another sip of her strong drink, letting that warmth slide into her stomach, and went back to plucking at the strings, trying to find the right words.

She started from the top a little more seriously this time, strumming along with the words that spilled from her. "Baby, spread your wings and fly. Take me on this journey through the sky. No matter where we land, as long as we're together, please understand..."

She drifted off. While she had taught herself how to play the guitar solely using YouTube videos, she certainly didn't learn how to write lyrics. Or apparently have the talent for it.

It would be best for her to stick with songs she knew.

She lifted her head, reached for the glass, and...

Screamed.

She pressed a palm to her chest to keep her heart from trying to escape.

How the fuck did he sneak up on her without her knowing?

"Never heard that one before." His deep voice resonated through her.

She finished reaching for the drink and downed half of it before placing it back on the table with shaky fingers.

"There's a reason for that," she told him, hoping the alcohol would get her blood pressure back down to normal.

"Your voice is beautiful."

Well, that certainly didn't help. Her heart was still beating like a runaway train as she responded, "Thank you." She tilted her head as she looked up... and up... at Mercy. He towered over her, the fading light making his face look more savage than ever. "What are you doing here?"

"Got something for you."

Oh, Jesus. Hopefully not more trophies of dead men.

"Mercy, I don't think that's a good idea." She glanced around quickly. "In fact, you being here isn't a good idea at all."

His eyes narrowed dangerously. "Why? He claim you yet?"

Her mouth dropped open. "Uh... no." She pulled the strap over her head and set her guitar carefully on the chair next to her. When she shifted, she winced. Her hand fluttered over her lower belly, even though she knew better than to touch it...

"What's wrong?" Mercy asked sharply.

She shook her head.

"You hurt?"

"No."

"Bullshit."

"It's nothing."

"Jazz, I know what they did to you there. I fuckin' saw it."

Heat crawled up into her cheeks and she grabbed her glass. As she lifted it to her lips, he snagged it from her fingers and set it back on the table. Before she could stop him, he pulled her to her feet by her elbow and lifted her shirt just enough to see the tattoo.

"Hey!" she shouted, trying to tug her tank top back down.

"Jesus," he murmured, rolling her black yoga pants down enough so he could see more of it.

"You can't just... touch me like that," she exclaimed, her pulse now pounding in her throat.

He released her quickly and stepped back. His eyes were dark and his face completely blank as he stared at the area, even though it was once again covered.

"Jazz..."

She lifted a hand. "Isn't any of your business." She shut her eyes for a moment, because that wasn't true. It was his business.

He'd seen everything that day. He settled the score with Squirrel and Black Jack. He'd wreaked havoc on that outlaw MC for her and the rest of their victims. She was one of a few reasons that D's crew did what they did.

She was one of those reasons why that room in that garage out in the middle of nowhere was full of Warrior cuts.

So, yeah, it was his business.

He might have the emotions of an iceberg, but deep down inside, everything that happened to her had affected him. Deep down in the center of that icy exterior burned an inferno that drove him to exact vengeance.

For her. For Kiki. For Jewel. For the club.

"Sorry," she whispered. She tugged down the waistband of her stretchy yoga pants and pulled up the hem of her shirt enough so he could clearly see Crow's in-progress work. "He's fixing me."

Something changed in Mercy's face at her words. A shift. It wasn't any warmer than his former expression, but it was different. "You don't need to be fixed."

"We all need to be fixed in one way or another." She wondered if the scar that marred his face bothered him. She was worried about a scar that she could easily cover with clothes. Unless he was wearing a ski mask, his would always be exposed. He couldn't hide it, not like her.

And while they both wore scars as reminders of what

happened to them, that wasn't all she meant when she said everyone needed to be fixed. It wasn't the actual physical scars that needed fixing, but the emotional ones.

"What we experience throughout our life makes us who we are. Good or bad. It shapes us. No one needs to be fixed. We just need to embrace who we are and how we ended up that way. Every situation we survive makes us stronger. It teaches us how to deal with the next one."

That was deeper than she ever expected to come out of his mouth.

He continued, "Need someone who will accept you as you are."

Did he think that was him? "Not someone. Myself. I need to accept me as I am. But not with this. I don't like seeing this reminder every damn day."

She needed to pull him from the deep and back to the surface. Because she wasn't willing to discuss with him just how deep her scars went.

He reached out and Jazz winced, fighting the instinct to step back out of his reach. She forced her feet to remain planted and her eyes to remain open. His long fingers curled around hers and he peeled them from both her tank top and her yoga pants and smoothed her clothes carefully back into place.

"You came back for that."

It wasn't a question and she really wasn't obligated to answer... "Yes. Among other things."

His gray eyes bore into her. "What other things?"

Jazz chewed on her bottom lip. Unfortunately, that little action told him everything. He was good at reading people, that was clear. But it made sense since he needed to be to do the jobs he did for D.

"You in his bed?"

"He only has one bed," she countered.

"He in it with you?"

Instead of answering, she deflected, though she was pretty

sure how he'd read that, too. "How did you get in? This neighborhood is secure."

His lips twitched at the word "secure." He pulled a small
remote out of the front pocket of his jeans and held it up.
"Bought a lot here. Not sure if I'm gonna do anything with it.
Not sure if I wanna live in a neighborhood, even though this isn't
the typical 'hood."

No, it certainly wasn't. It was exclusive for the DAMC, but it
would make sense that Diesel would offer his guys lots. Having
his men live there would up the security by probably a million
percent and that was a conservative estimate.

"Can't see you living in a house like this."

"D'you ever see Crow doing the same?"

Jazz turned her head and glanced at the house before
answering honestly, "No, I didn't. It surprised me."

"I understand why Z wanted his so-called compound. Can
understand why my boss wants us moving in. It's smart. Not only
is it safe, it's got nosy fuckin' neighbors who are looking out for
each other. An extended family who cares."

His eyes slid to the side and so did Jazz's.

She muttered a "fuck" under her breath when she saw
Diamond standing on the back deck of her own house, a cell
phone to her ear while she eyeballed them.

Jazz knew who was on the other end of that phone. The
woman was not only disturbing Crow at work, but was snitching
on her. She needed to get Mercy gone.

She tilted her head and studied the tall man before her. "So...
Why are you here?"

"Need you to come with me."

Ah, Jesus, not that shit again. She sighed. "Where?"

He, of course, didn't answer. She guessed he figured she'd just
jump into his vehicle and let him take her to some unknown
place. Like she didn't learn her lesson the first time.

"Where, Mercy?" she asked again, more firmly. "I can't just

disappear. Not like last time." Which caused a whole panic she didn't want to cause again.

"The warehouse."

"D's warehouse?"

"Yeah."

Well, that *should* be safe enough. Especially if Diesel was there. But what the hell would be there that she needed to see? A bazooka? A tank? The Batmobile?

Jazz glanced over her shoulder at the house next door. With what looked like narrowed eyes, Diamond shot her a frown while she kept talking into the phone.

"She's looking out for you."

"Sure she is," Jazz answered, shooting Diamond an answering frown.

"Why I don't live here. Too many eyes."

"Isn't that the truth," Jazz muttered. She turned her head toward her nosy club sister and shouted out, "Tell him the warehouse." She turned back to Mercy. "Guess you're driving. I'm sure my ride home will be following soon enough."

With a smile that didn't reach his winter gray eyes, he nodded and, after putting her guitar in the house and setting the alarm, she did something she'd never thought she'd do a second time.

She got into Mercy's monster SUV, so he could show her something she wasn't so sure she wanted to see.

I f Mercy was a house cat, he'd be the kind that kept bringing dead birds and rodents to his owner to make sure his human didn't starve.

Mercy's idea of gifts wasn't a normal one. No way, no how.

But then, she doubted that the man had a normal cell in his body. Otherwise, he couldn't to do what he did and not go off the deep end.

Or that's what she told herself.

Maybe insanity was his normal.

Maybe he wore his icy exterior as a cloak, a disguise to hide who he truly was. To deal with everything he's been through, everything he's done.

Sort of like she had with her hair and her clothes.

She could understand that. That's why she didn't hesitate too long to go with him to the warehouse. And this time, Crow knew where she was.

Thanks to Diamond.

But now she felt as frozen as Mercy appeared. Because what he wanted to show her was just...

Fucked up.

So fucked up.

She was trying desperately to wrap her head around what she was seeing and why it was important that Mercy show it to her.

Not *it*. Him.

A man, she had no idea who, was tied to a metal chair. A bright light was shining in the man's face or would be if his head wasn't hanging low.

She might not know his name, might not know what he had done to deserve what he had been through recently, from how fresh some of his wounds looked, and what he would go through in the near future. But she had a really good fucking idea on who he belonged to.

Or what.

Plastic sheeting was spread under the chair and covered a good perimeter of the floor around where he was restrained.

Easy clean-up. Which meant the two men who were standing in the open area of the warehouse with her expected things to get messy.

Mercy being one. The other, Mercy introduced as Steel. Steel had his knuckles wrapped in tape like a prize fighter. Or an MMA competitor. He was solid and had bulging muscles under a drab olive tank top that looked a bit snug on him. Jazz didn't expect that the man needed any weapons other than those fists to cause a lot of damage to the unfortunate receiver.

She had a feeling this Steel remembered her well. Though she didn't remember him at all. Just like she hadn't remembered Mercy.

She let her gaze slide from Steel, who stood with his bloody fists clenched by his sides, to the man in the chair.

"Why?" she whispered to Mercy. "Why am I here?"

"Think he's the last one."

The last one. Impossible. They were like roaches. Just when you thought there was only one, there were hundreds more hiding in the walls waiting to come out when the lights were off.

"How do you know?"

Mercy didn't answer her, instead just stared at the man bound to the metal chair with a look on his face that scared the shit out of her. She was glad it wasn't directed at her. As a shiver slid down her spine, she wrapped her arms around herself.

"Was he there?" As far as she knew it was only Squirrel and Black Jack that day. Though, maybe more Warriors showed up once she was floating in and out of consciousness?

Holy shit, if that was true...

"No."

Then this made no sense. For him to bring her here. For her to stand in judgement of the man before her. For her to witness what they might... no, *would*... do to him.

Was this display solely for her? "What did he do?"

Mercy's gray eyes dropped to her. "He didn't do shit."

"He didn't do shit? You're going to... whatever you're going to do... over nothing?"

"Baby."

She lost her breath when he called her that. Was this all a weird way he was trying to woo her?

Who in their right mind did things like this?

With a determined stride, Steel approached her, "He didn't do shit 'cause he didn't get a chance to do it," holding something in his red-tinged fingers. She recoiled back unsure on what it was.

Then it became clear. A cell phone.

Or was it a bomb that looked like a cell phone?

No, stupid. He wouldn't be holding it or offering it to her if it was.

"He's going to die because of the cut on his back and a phone?"

Steel hit the power button and jabbed at the screen a couple times. He began to swipe his finger across the phone and turned it after each swipe so she could see photos. And not just one, either. Horror clawed at her throat.

Even scarier, he didn't have to even say a fucking word. Not one.

Because every fucking one of those pictures was of a child. Taken from a distance. Clearly taken without them knowing.

In every single one of those photos was a DAMC kid.

Her mind began to spin.

Every member of the fourth generation had been photographed.

Violet. Indigo. Zeke. Zane. Ashton. Alexis. Lily. Emmalee.

Her blood turned to ice with each swipe of his finger. A chill skittered down her spine. "Why?" she whispered, staring up at Steel when he was done. "Why?" she repeated when he didn't answer. "Why?" She glanced at the man restrained to the chair. A man whose future had been already written the second he snapped those photos.

A man who had no qualms on doing something evil to children. *Babies.* Innocents to what started out as a turf war *decades* ago.

For what?

"Why?" she asked again as her feet carried her closer to that occupied chair. With every step she took, she began to scream, "Why?" over and over, her unnaturally shrill voice filling the large cavernous area. Echoing off the bare metal walls. Making her own ears ring.

"Why!" she screamed until her throat was sore. And she continued to scream it until her voice was raw and hoarse and her mind became numb.

Then she was on him. The Warrior tied to the chair. She was beating him with her fists about the head and shoulders. She couldn't stop herself, she couldn't stop asking her question. The only question she wanted an answer to.

Why?

Why did humans do this to each other?

Why did they have to hurt each other like that?

Why were they so evil?

Those children were innocent. Nothing but babies. They shouldn't be targets.

Shouldn't be involved in a grudge that should have died so long ago.

But they kept it alive all of these years. *Why?*

She kept striking out at the man until she could no longer feel anything. She couldn't feel her hands. She couldn't feel her heart. She couldn't feel her soul.

Then arms were around her. Tight. Pulling her away.

A mouth was to her ear. Murmuring.

She had no idea what.

She had no idea who.

She couldn't tear her eyes from the man in that chair. The man who wanted to hurt those kids.

The man who wanted to hurt the parents who loved them by doing something horrendous and unthinkable to their children.

The man who would do it with no regret.

She no longer cared what Mercy and Steel did to him.

Just like she didn't care what they had done to Squirrel and Black Jack.

By taking those photos, he had sealed his fate.

By taking her and Kiki, they had sealed their fate.

They made a choice and they had to live with the consequences.

She didn't get a choice; hers had been stripped from her
against her will.

Those children didn't get a choice. They didn't pose for those
pictures. They didn't decide to be a target.

Thank fuck they had found this man, who was now tied like
an animal to a metal chair surrounded by plastic in that big warehouse, before he could carry out his plan.

Thank fuck they had discovered his malicious intent before
it was unleashed.

And she only hoped to hell they were right. That the man
before her was the last of them.

May they all burn for eternity in a hell they created.

Her heels were being dragged along the floor as the distance
grew between her and the unnamed Warrior.

But she couldn't stop staring at him. She'd never forget what
evil looked like.

His head was no longer hanging low but was raised slightly,
blood trickling from scratches and cuts on his face, as he
watched her be hauled away. To a safe distance.

Safe for the Warrior who she wanted to kill with her own
hands. She would have broken every bone in those hands in an
attempt to end his life.

The arms around her were like a vice, squeezing the breath
from her. And she couldn't catch it. She could no longer breathe.
The low words in her ear were just white noise. She had no idea
what or who.

But then she heard one thing.

Diesel.

Roaring, "Office! Now!"

When she was picked up and carried, she looked up and her
haze cleared enough to see who it was.

The sharp angles of his hairless face, his broad nose, his onyx
eyes, the angry set of his jaw.

He was carrying her down a narrow hallway, and she jerked in his arms when he kicked a door open with a violent bang, before striding out into the warm night to a car in the parking lot. She numbly watched as Diamond scrambled out of her sports car and ran around to the passenger side, opening the door.

"Get 'er home. Stay with her 'til I get there. Got me?"

"Yeah."

Then she was being placed in the passenger seat, strapped in and the door slammed shut. The locks clicked loudly, breaking the silence before the noise of the Nissan's engine filled the compact space.

And if Diamond spoke to her on the way back to the compound, back to Crow's house, Jazz had no idea what she said.

All she could see was that man tied to the chair and those pictures on his phone.

CHAPTER THIRTEEN

F ury licked at him. Fueled him. He was a time bomb waiting to explode.

He felt the need to prowl the room, to burn off some energy. But he couldn't because Steel blocked his path.

The man stood like an impenetrable wall between him and Mercy.

Crow couldn't take Mercy, but he sure as fuck could try.

And win or lose, he was pretty fucking sure he'd feel better afterward.

He had gotten to the warehouse too late to shield Jazz from what she saw. But he had gotten there just in time to shove Mercy out of the way and to pull Jazz away from that Warrior during her meltdown before that motherfucker could.

Because, for fuck's sake, if he'd seen her wrapped in Mercy's arms, he would have...

He gritted his teeth, closed his eyes and filled his lungs deeply, attempting to tamp down his rage.

Because that's what it was. Pure fucking rage. Nothing more.

When Diamond called to tell him Mercy was on *his* deck, at *his* house, talking once again to *his* woman...

He got angry.

He had no business being jealous because she didn't belong to him. Truth was, she didn't owe him any kind of fucking explanation as to why she was talking to Mercy.

Mercy was simply making a play. Crow knew he wouldn't hurt her.

Or at least, he didn't think so until he walked into D's warehouse and witnessed what he did.

Then he knew, at that very moment, Mercy was out of his fucking mind.

There was no other explanation for bringing Jazz there, for bringing her in front of a Warrior.

There was no good excuse for any of it.

Diesel needed to get his men in order. Because what Mercy did was unacceptable.

Crow might be furious, but Diesel was like a raging bull, pounding his fist on his desk, causing the items on the top of it to go airborne. His face was a reddish-purple and his finger was pointing at them as he shouted at both Mercy and Steel. If that finger had been loaded, they'd both be on the floor bleeding out. Every jab of his index finger in their direction was accompanied by spit spraying all over his desk.

Crow had tuned all that shit out. He just hoped Diesel was firing their asses for doing something so goddamned stupid.

He couldn't get the picture of Jazz attacking that outlaw biker with her bare hands and screaming uncontrollably at the top of her lungs out of his head. Repeating "Why?" over and over.

It fucking broke Crow's heart, then that crack filled with anger.

He'd worked hard the last couple weeks on getting Jazz past some of her issues. And what Mercy pulled might have set her back.

Steel was watching Diesel lose his shit.

Now was his chance.

Shoving Steel aside was like trying to push a mountain, but he slipped around him and launched himself at Mercy.

Mercy took Crow to the ground with him when he lost his balance. Before Crow could get to his feet, a large hand had him by the throat and he found himself slammed into the wall.

Diesel's face was in his, his fury now directed at him.

"Out!" Diesel bellowed. "Get gone! Take that fuckin' trash with you an' fuckin' dispose of it. Out! Now! Before you both find yourselves un-fuckin'-employed."

Crow couldn't see past Diesel's bulk, and the brother remained in his face, almost nose to nose with nostrils flaring, until they both heard the door shut.

"Gonna release you. Need to keep your shit together. Fuckin' stupid to try to take on Mercy. Just motherfuckin' stupid. He'd have your fuckin' neck snapped in the span of a cunt hair. Ain't no good to Jazz dead. Got me?"

"Motherfucker needs a lesson."

"Yeah, an' that fuckin' lesson ain't comin' from you. *Got me?*" he roared in Crow's face. Diesel sucked in an audible breath through those flaring nostrils and then softened the grip on Crow's neck. "Ain't leavin' this room 'til I say so. Yeah?"

"Yeah."

Diesel finally let him go and stepped back, watching Crow carefully. "What the fuck, brother?" He shook his head and took one more step back but stayed between Crow and the door. "What he did was fuckin' stupid. Get that. But what you did was worse. Ain't doin' anyone any good by havin' Mercy take you out in self-defense."

"You see her?"

As Diesel's coloring returned to normal, his guarded expression slipped back into place. "Yeah. Saw her. Ain't good. Gonna have a word with 'im."

"That means you didn't approve of that fuckin' stunt."

"No," D grunted.

"D..."

"Said no. Ain't gonna say it again. Gonna have a word with 'im. More than one fuckin' word. Leave it at that."

He didn't want to "leave it at that," but he would for now. He needed to get home and check on Jazz.

"Says it's the last one. Couldn't be so fuckin' lucky," D muttered.

Crow's eyebrows shot up. "Yeah. How do they know?"

D lifted a heavy shoulder. "They got their ways. Not sure if it's true. Hope to fuck it is. Gotta get that monkey off my fuckin' back. The club's growin' like fuckin' crazy. Unless I hire personal bodyguards for every fuckin' ol' lady an' every kid..." He shook his head, moved behind his desk and settled into his oversized office chair with a grunt. He scrubbed a hand over his short dark hair. "Can't fuckin' watch everybody. Compound helps, but apparently not enough."

D's large paw shoved an object toward Crow. As it slid across his desk, he realized it was a cell phone.

"Check the pics. It's what Steel showed Jazz, so you know what the fuck you're dealin' with when you get back to your place."

Were they pics of that day? Of her in that abandoned house? Beat up and sliced open? Naked, bruised and bloodied?

His gut twisted. Because if they were, there was no fucking way he was looking at them. "D..."

"Just fuckin' look at 'em. Ain't of her."

Crow reluctantly picked up the cell and braced himself as he hit the power button and the screen lit up. He didn't have to open the photo gallery app to see the first one. Fuck no, he didn't. The first pic smacked him right in the fucking face.

His blood turned to ice.

Ashton. A shot of Kiki carrying her son to the SUV Hawk bought to haul the kid around. Wasn't hard to see that the photo was taken in front of their house, which was not within the compound. They still lived in Hawk's unsecure Cape Cod in town. He had a feeling that was going to change after today.

He forced himself to swipe left.

Dawg and Emma. The brother carrying his baby girl, Emmalee, while his wife held Lily's hand as they headed into a store, unaware they were being tracked.

Crow tried to swallow the lump in his throat, but it wouldn't budge.

He reluctantly swiped again.

Ivy with Alexis. The two with their heads together, making it difficult to tell where Ivy's red hair ended and Lexi's started. Mother and daughter so much alike. If Jag knew... *Fuck*, that brother would die a torturous death before letting anything happen to his girls.

Sophie with Zak's sons in a local park. Zane in a stroller next to Z's ol' lady as she pushed Zeke on a swing. She wore a huge smile as the sun shone down upon them, lighting up their faces.

Diamond. Clearly a recent shot since her stomach was rounded and she was obviously pregnant. She was exiting the club's gym, a hand to her belly. The belly he'd touched so many times, the one that housed her and Slade's unborn son.

And lastly, Diesel. Violet riding on her father's shoulders, one of his hands holding her steady, while Indie was tucked into the crook of his other bulky arm. Crow had no idea where it was taken, and it didn't matter.

What mattered was, it was all of them. The complete fourth generation of the DAMC.

Crow lifted his eyes from the phone and looked at D. His elbows were planted on his desk, his face hidden in his hands.

When Crow dropped the phone back onto the desk, D's words came muffled through his fingers. "Never wanted an ol' lady. Never wanted kids. This is exactly fuckin' why. Makes me weak. Makes me a target. Makes them a target." He slowly lifted his head. For once it was easy to read his expression. One he fought to hide but couldn't.

Vulnerability.

"Somethin' happens to them, I'll cease to exist."

Crow's chest tightened even more as he stared at the club's enforcer and his long-time brother. He didn't even bother to argue with what he said, because it was true. If anything happened to Jewel, Indie or Vi, Diesel would lose his fucking mind and the whole world would know it.

They were his life. His blood. His everything.

Crow understood it. Even though the women and children of the DAMC might be considered club property, they were anything but.

Fuck no. They were the heartbeat of the club. Every single one of them. The prior generation wanted to leave something better for the next. And the one after that.

Every living, breathing member of that club, whether patched or not, was a part of a family.

And the Warriors kept fucking with their family.

So, he had no qualms about Mercy and Steel, or any of D's crew, taking out the trash. He hoped that Warrior ended up at the bottom of the quarry where the fish could pick his bones clean like they probably had Pierce's.

The Shadow Warriors' biggest mistake was not letting the war go. Not walking away and accepting defeat. They let it fester throughout the decades. But holding on to that need for revenge was a fatal mistake for that MC, because in the end, that outlaw club would be annihilated.

And if more members popped up like roaches, Diesel would make sure those were squashed, as well. Even if he had to do it with his own big-ass biker boot.

D's voice was low and actually quiet for once when he said, "Know what Mercy did was fucked up. He don't see it as such. Tryin' to show Jazz he's doin' his fuckin' best to make all the women, all the kids, safe. We all are. Figured if Jazz saw the proof she'd rest easier."

"Wasn't good, D."

"Fuckin' saw it, so I know. Promise to have words with 'im.

Tell 'im to keep his distance from Jazz. He's encroachin' on your claim an' that ain't right."

"She ain't mine to claim," he said quickly.

"The fuck she ain't. She rolled back into town an' right to you, brother. Not her grandparents, not Hawk. Nobody. Right to you."

"For ink."

D shook his head. "No. That was her excuse. Only one reason. We all saw the real reason when she was up on the fuckin' stage singin' to you. You, brother. We saw it. You saw it. She came home to *you*."

No, she was using him for ink, using him to work through her issues. That was it. And he was allowing it.

Though, he was glad she came to him for what she needed. Because if she'd come back and he had to sit back and watch her with someone else...

"Brother, were a lucky fucker an' avoided gettin' stuck all these fuckin' years. No more avoidin' it."

There was no sticking to be had. "She's too young."

"Yeah. Agreed. She's too fuckin' young. She's too young for Mercy, too. But that didn't stop him from offerin' her a fucked-up prize for her attention. He'd never win, 'cause she only got eyes for you."

Crow opened his mouth to argue but D lifted a palm and stopped him.

"Need to get gone an' go take care of your woman. Go undo the damage Mercy did. He meant well but screwed the fuckin' pooch doin' it."

D was right. He needed to get gone.

While he trusted Diamond to take care of Jazz, she shouldn't be.

That was his job.

C row walked Diamond to the door. Before he opened it, he took her in his arms. Holding her always calmed him. And the same for her. No matter what Slade had thought, it was never sexual, they were just each other's rock. He had no idea when that happened, it just did.

"Thanks, baby doll," he whispered, lightly touching her stomach as his thoughts turned to the picture of her on that Warrior's cell phone...

He wondered if he should give Slade the heads-up or if D would. Someone needed to watch her carefully and the best person for the job would be her ol' man. Especially since he was a beast when it came to using his fists.

"She did a shot," she whispered back. "I made her do a second one. She was a mess until the whiskey went through her. She calmed down then. Wish I could've done more. Sorry, honey."

Diamond pulled out of his arms and reached for the door handle.

"Baby doll..."

She turned her head to look at him over her shoulder.

"You think she's mine?"

Diamond simply smiled, opened the door and left without a word.

Fuck.

Crow stood staring at the door for a minute, inhaled a few breaths to bolster himself, then headed upstairs, taking the steps two at a time.

Diamond had met him downstairs after he entered from the garage, so he knew Jazz was currently soaking in his jacuzzi tub. At least someone got some use out of it. He didn't have time to wallow around in a bunch of bubbles.

But if some whiskey and warm water worked to calm Jazz down, then whatever...

The door to the bathroom was cracked open and he pushed

it wider. She never heard him since the pulsing jets were loud enough to drown out his footsteps, but he didn't want to surprise her.

"*Kachina*," he said softly over the rumble of the tub.

Her head had been leaning back against the edge, the ends of her hair falling into the cloudy water, her eyes closed.

"*Kachina*," he said again, gently, as he stepped closer to the tub. Her head lifted, and she blinked open her eyes in what looked like slow motion.

"This is an awesome tub," she said so sluggishly that he thought she might be drunk.

"You have more than two shots?"

She shook her head, her hair dragging through the water as she did so. "No."

He blew out a relieved breath because he needed to discuss what happened with her and he didn't want to do it if she was wasted.

He knelt on the tile floor next to the jacuzzi, the knees of his jeans instantly becoming soaked, but he didn't give a fuck.

"Shouldn't you be at the shop?" Again, her question was lethargic, which worried him.

"Need to be here with you instead."

"I'm fine."

No, you're far from fuckin' fine.

"You need to run your business. This is the second time I've fucked that up for you."

While that was true, that shit didn't matter to him.

She did.

He reached into the tub and grabbed her hand, lifting it above the water. The tips of her fingers were already wrinkled from soaking too long. It also wasn't good that she was sitting in a tub when she had fresh ink. "*Kachina*, I'm strugglin' right now. I'm fuckin' pissed you went with him again." He lifted his other hand to stop her from interrupting him. "Let me fuckin' finish. Know that Diamond knew where you were headed. But if she hadn't been out there, no one woulda known. Again." He tried desperately to keep the anger from his words.

"I would have texted you."

"Well, that's a fuckin' relief," he muttered, not feeling relieved *at all*. "My point is, goin' off with Mercy... Nothin' good could come of that. Nothin'."

"He's persuasive."

Crow closed his eyes and tried not to snap out on her. "He's fucked in the head." When he opened his eyes, she was searching his face, so he did his best to hide the worry and anger.

"You said he wouldn't hurt me."

"An' that's true. He wouldn't." At least not physically. But emotionally? Maybe not intentionally, but what happened earlier was in no way good for Jazz.

"He asked if you claimed me," she said so quietly, he wondered if he heard her correctly above the noise of the jets.

"What?"

She focused her green eyes on him, her pupils bigger than they should be. "He asked if you claimed me."

This time there was no doubt about what he heard. "He's got a thing for you."

And for fuck's sake, that was something that ate at him even more than anything else. Diamond had given him a play-by-play of what occurred on his own fucking deck. Mercy had the fucking balls to come to *his* house, stand on *his* deck and make a fucking play.

"Yeah," she breathed.

He studied her, her pale skin barely visible under the cloudy water. Looking small and vulnerable in that tub, he could see why a man like Mercy would feel the urge to protect her. Or whatever the motive was in his fucked-up head.

The ends of her blonde hair were soaked, her small, tight nipples peeking just above the water's line. The rest of her exposed skin shined with whatever shit she had dumped into the tub to make the bubbles. He had no idea what, since he would never in his life buy bubble bath shit.

He released the hand he had intertwined with his and it dropped like a rock under the water, almost as if she had no control of her muscles. She frowned and peered at him from under her damp dark blonde lashes.

He thumbed a bead of water from the indentation above her lips. When they parted, he felt her warm breath against his fingers. He traced one over her top lip and then the curve of the bottom one, before brushing his knuckle across her damp cheek.

He hit the button to turn off the jets and waited until the water settled. Now he could see all of her beneath the water. Her long legs, that little patch of hair at the V. The bottom curves of her tits. He sat back on his heels and forced himself to say, "*Kachina*, if you're ready to move on, move on. I'm okay with that. That was the plan."

She sucked in a breath, but he continued before she could speak.

He kept his voice low and calm. He didn't want to sound like he was laying down the law, but he was laying down the law. "But what you will not do is move on with Mercy. He's not for you."

"He's not?" she asked in a whisper.

Fuck no, he's not. "No."

"Why not?"

Was she serious right now? Did he need to spell it out? "You need a man with a heart, a soul. Someone who's gonna love you completely. Someone who's gonna help you continue to heal, not drag you back down into the depths of hell. That ain't him."

"Someone like that might be hard to find."

He had to force his next words, too. "You'll find 'im."

"And who will you find?" she asked softly.

Nobody. He wasn't planning on finding anyone. He already found her. She was right in front of him.

"Stand up," he ordered softly.

She blinked those big eyes at him then she did as she was

told, the bath water sluicing down her still willow-like body. He offered his hand and she took it. He helped her step out of the high-sided tub and then ordered, "Start the shower."

Without a word, she moved to the large frosted-glass standup shower and leaned in to turn on the faucet.

Then she turned and watched him shed his clothes. First, his cut, what bound the DAMC together like family. He hung it carefully over the open bathroom door. Then his boots and socks. Followed by his jeans and tee.

She said nothing, just focused on his actions while he never let his gaze fall away from her.

His dick began to stir, but that wasn't what this was about.

His plan wasn't to take her in the bathroom or the shower, not after what happened earlier. His plan was to just take care of her.

He slipped the band from the bottom of his braid and his fingers moved along it, releasing the interlaced strands until his hair fell free along his bare back.

He avoided touching her as he reached through the open shower door and tested the temp of the water.

With a couple quick adjustments, he turned and guided her into the shower and under the spray with him.

He turned her to face the water, her hair clinging to her face and shoulders, becoming darker as it got wet. Reaching for her shampoo that was tucked on a corner shelf, he popped it open, squirted a generous amount onto his palm and began to wash her hair.

She groaned low as he took his time massaging her scalp, then made sure the length of it was completely clean before nudging her gently back under the spray. He rinsed her long strands until the water ran clear. Grabbing her body wash and her fluffy pink loofah, he soaped her up, then again rinsed her off.

When she was clean, he rinsed himself off quickly before shutting off the faucet. He assisted her back out and left her on the little rug she had placed in front of the shower opening. Something new she had spent his money on. He had no idea when, since he'd never paid attention until that very moment that she was decorating his house little by little.

It also hit him that the stuff she had picked out so far was perfect for him. Stuff, if he gave the smallest shit about decorating, he would've picked out for himself.

Earth tones. Masculine. Not one feminine thing to be seen.

He grabbed one of the new thick, clay-colored towels hanging from the nearby rack and carefully wrapped her up in it, gently patting her skin dry.

She went to take over the task, but he brushed her hands away and shook his head. "No, *Kachina*. Let me do this."

Another stark realization came over him. Without even planning it, he was showing her what kind of man she needed. Someone who would take care of her. Be gentle, understanding and be appreciative of everything that was Jasmine.

Not a man who would drag her ass in front of a Warrior about to die.

He was showing her what kind of man she needed.

But not him.

Not Mercy, either.

Someone good for her.

Someone right for her.

Someone who would love her like she should be loved.

Jazz sat on the bed, still wrapped up all snuggly in the towel. Crow had one of his own, barely hanging onto his lean hips, his black hair damp and shiny as it fell down his back.

After using his wide-toothed comb on his own hair, he quickly braided it back up and secured it with a black elastic band.

He sat on the edge of the bed, his legs as wide as they could go while wearing the towel and he had moved her to perch between his thighs. Taking his time, he combed carefully through her hair, even though hers wasn't nearly as long as his. Each knot, he untangled gently with his fingers, until he could smoothly run the comb through the length.

Then he braided hers, too, his fingers working swiftly, expertly, until her hair was neatly plaited and secured.

Besides those few words in the bathroom, they hadn't said much.

Now she sat in the center of his bed, her damp hair tightly braided, as he dropped his own towel and moved across the mattress on his hands and knees toward her.

He reminded her of a mountain lion stalking his prey. His movement fluid, his golden body lean and strong. His eyes dark and intensely focused as he moved up and over her.

The man had many sides. One moment soft and gentle, the next powerful and dominating. Though she had a feeling he kept the second part to a minimum with her. But she recognized it when his dominance would show itself, possibly when he didn't realize it.

She lost her breath, her heart beating rapidly in her chest as he loosened her towel and began to peel it from her as he pushed her down onto the bed. He trapped her nipple in his mouth and the pull of his lips shot lightning all the way to the center of her core. She moaned, her back bowing as he switched, sucking the other in deeply, tugging on it with his lips, scraping the tip with his teeth. Circling, flicking with his tongue.

Suddenly he was gone and rolling her off the towel and onto her belly. He tossed the towel off the bed and returned to press his smooth chest against her ass and that warm, wet tongue of his worked up her spine as he moved over her once again. Brushing her braid out of the way, he nipped at her shoulders and moved to the back of her neck, licking, sucking her heated skin.

She could feel the tingling, the need for him, between her

thighs. The more he cherished her body, the more the wetness grew.

Out of the blue, she wondered if she'd be this responsive to anyone else. Someone like Mercy. Any man other than Crow.

She trusted him.

But would she trust or be comfortable doing this with someone else?

If she wanted intimacy in the future, with a man other than Crow, she'd have to be accepting. Willing.

Because this was only temporary. He said so more than once. Just until her tattoo was finished. Just until she was comfortable in her own skin again.

So even though it was Crow's weight pressing down on her legs and hips, even though it was his mouth and fingers pulling the reactions from her, she closed her eyes and tried to imagine someone else. Anyone else above her.

Someone like Mercy. She tried to picture him doing the same things. But she could only see him standing in that warehouse. The same warehouse where that Warrior sat bound.

She tried to retreat from that image and return her concentration to the man who really was in the room with her. In this bed. It wasn't Mercy. It wasn't a stranger.

It was Crow.

But the image of the Warrior was seared into her brain. She no longer saw Mercy. She no longer saw the warehouse. She only saw that man wearing that Shadow Warrior MC cut streaked with his own blood.

SWMC.

So many surgeries she'd endured to try to remove those initials from her flesh. An attempt to remove them from her life.

Crow rolled her onto her back once more, stretched her arms straight over her head and, as he sucked at the skin of her neck, his cock pressed hard into her thigh.

Trailing his fingers lightly up her outstretched arms, she

arched her back again, encouraging him to take one of her aching nipples into his mouth once more.

He did.

His fingers continued to move until they got to her wrists, where he circled them... and tightened...

Every muscle in her body tightened, as well. Her eyes squeezed shut and she gasped when a flash of that nightmare blinded her.

Squirrel squeezing her wrists painfully, like a vise, pinning them to the dirty floor.

A flash.

Black Jack kneeling between her spread thighs.

A flash.

Excruciating pain.

Laughter.

Unbearable pressure.

Grunting.

Trying to fight.

A blow to her head.

Her face.

A kick to her ribs and the agonizing pain that followed.

Fingers digging into her thighs.

Something ripping her apart.

Blood.

Silence.

Then finally... darkness.

CHAPTER FOURTEEN

"*Kachina*."

The darkness began to recede, but not fast enough.

"*Kachina*, open your eyes."

She was trying to, but it wasn't working. Nothing was working. Every muscle in her body felt like lead. Or as if she was being pulled into quicksand.

Sinking deeper with each attempt to escape.

No, she couldn't let it swallow her up. She needed to fight to get back to the surface.

She hadn't been to this dark place in a long time.

And she shouldn't be there now. She was with Crow.

Crow.

Crow.

Crow.

"Yeah, baby, it's Crow. Open your eyes."

It's easy, Jazz. Just open your eyes. Open them so you can see.

This wasn't that house. He wasn't those men. He'd never be.

Somehow, she managed to unlock her jaws. "I can't."

"Yeah, you can, baby. You can. Just open 'em."

She inhaled deeply and willed her eyes to open.

His face, his familiar face, was only inches from hers. As it came into focus, she didn't like what she saw.

Fear. Deep-seated fear.

It marred his beautiful features. Though he tried to hide it, he couldn't.

She could see it so clearly. In the set of his jaw, in the thinning of his lips, in his eyes, in the creases of his forehead.

"*Kachina*," he whispered, cupping her cheek. "Sorry, baby. Didn't fuckin' think."

It wasn't his fault. None of it was his fault.

The men who caused this were long gone. Crow didn't deserve to deal with the mess they left behind.

She was curled up in his lap as he leaned back against the headboard. She turned her face until it pressed against his bare chest and his skin warmed her cheek. His steady breathing soothed her.

"They ruined my life. They ruined me."

"Not ruined, *Kachina*. Never."

It scared her that she might react in the future like she just did. No man would want to put up with that. Who'd want to be afraid that something they might do would trigger a reaction? Her parents had forced her to see a therapist for a while right after the incident and she had. The woman had told her the smallest thing may be a trigger. Or even something unexpected and unrelated at all to what happened to her.

Eventually she skipped out on her sessions because she was sick of revisiting that day over and over, and every time she walked into that office that's what happened. She'd live that nightmare again, even if they discussed nothing about that day. The sessions had turned into a trigger in itself.

Even though she didn't think it was fair that Crow be forced to deal with her issues, she couldn't let him go.

"You told me I could move on. But I can't. I can't, Crow. I can't be with anyone else. I tried."

His body jolted, then tensed. She could both hear and feel his heartbeat change against her ear. "He touched you?"

What?

"Mercy touch you?"

"No, when I say I tried, I meant imagining being with someone else. I was doing that when you touched my wrists..."

It probably was insulting when a man learned that the woman he was getting ready to have sex with was imaging someone else. But she needed to be honest. Especially with Crow.

"It triggered somethin'."

She didn't need to answer him. He knew.

"Fucked up by doin' that."

"It wasn't your fault. You couldn't know."

"Shoulda known." His low voice rumbled against her cheek through his chest. "Gonna find someone who'll be perfect for you. Promise. An' you'll fuckin' love him an' he'll treat you like you're priceless. An'—"

"I don't want anyone else."

"Baby..."

She shifted in his arms until she could look up into his face. "I don't want anyone else."

"Just sayin' that 'cause you feel safe with me."

The darkness that had remained on the edge of her consciousness vanished and there was nothing left but light. She could see everything clearly and he needed to see it, too. "No, I'm saying it because... I love you. I don't want anyone else. I want the man I love."

"*Kachina*," he breathed.

Now that light was turning into a flame as the anger licked at her. He was going to deny what she felt. Push it aside, like she was confused about what love was. Treat her as if she was still too young to know better. "Don't you dare tell me I don't. Or that I'm confused. Because I'm not. I might be screwed up about a lot of things, but not this. I love you, Crow. I don't give a shit that you're forty and I'm twenty-eight. Nobody else gives a shit, either."

"Jazz."

She shook her head, determined to get him to listen. "No. I know what I'm feeling. Don't tell me I don't. I knew it before I walked into your shop a couple weeks ago. I knew it not long after you startled me that day at Hawk's."

"Jazz, you couldn't—"

"Yes, I could. I did. I wasn't a little girl then. I'm not a little girl now. So when I tell you I love you, it's true. Just accept it."

J *ust accept it.*

Crow blinked. His mouth opened.

Only air came out.

Well, fuck.

No, she definitely wasn't a little girl back then. And she wasn't one now, either.

The woman in his lap, his arms, was anything but.

Her thighs were a little softer now than when she first returned. Between him and Momma Bear making her eat better, she'd already begun to fill out, making her curvier. The concave of her belly, gone. The line of her ribs, gone. The hollows of her cheeks, gone. Her hip bones, while still visible, not so bony. Healthier. She was looking so much more like her old self.

Not her old self like when she was fresh in town, when she was barely eighteen. But more like when she was twenty-two before everything happened. She was still thin back then, still becoming a woman. Becoming who she was meant to be.

Until those fuckers stole that all from her.

But even back then, he recognized something in her he knew he wanted.

What he desired.

He beat himself up about it because she was so young. Not to mention, under Hawk's care. *Fuck*, she was Grizz's granddaughter. A college student.

While he was a biker, twelve years older than her, who had no education other than a barely-earned high school diploma. His skills consisted of marking people's skin with permanent ink.

He was fine with that. Content.

While Jazz had the whole world ahead of her. Her whole life.

There was no way he was settling down back then, anyway. He wasn't ready, she certainly wasn't, either.

And it would've done her a great disservice. Or so he thought.

Maybe if he would have gone against his own conscious and claimed her, she wouldn't have been in Hawk's house when Keeks got nabbed.

But even so, it would have caused a lot of tension. Hawk would have fucking flipped his lid. Grizz and Momma Bear, too. They were proud when one of their grandchildren went to college, wanting to better themselves with an education.

Grizz grumbled about college being worthless. But Crow had watched the old man over the years when he talked about his grandkids. The look in his eye when he did so...

Yeah, the man was fucking more than proud.

And now, the woman he'd left alone for both of their sakes was in his arms. Dealing with shit. But dealing with it...

In. His. Arms.

She admitted she was messy. And she was. That didn't bother him. He could deal with mess if it was worth it.

Jazz was worth it.

Even though she was young in age, she'd already lived a lifetime of hurt. And that made her older than her years.

His own life had started with tragedy, losing his parents so violently when he was so young. She had dealt with tragedy herself. Not as a witness, but an unwilling participant. They could deal with that shit together.

Maybe they were meant to be. Maybe the spirit gods had put his *Kachina* in his path that day for a reason. Guided him to open Hawk's door, when he normally wouldn't just walk in.

He had forced himself to push her out of his mind so long ago and then when she left, it made it easier to leave that alone. But now, she was back, in his house, in his bed, in his arms.

He could no longer ignore it.

Especially now.

She loved him.

That's what she said. That's what she believed.

"You're not going to say anything? I know you don't love me, Crow. And I don't expect you to say it back. I don't. But I needed to get it out. You telling me that we're done when my tat is finished is wrong. You might be done with me, but I'll never be done with you."

This was not the way things were supposed to go. It certainly fucking wasn't. "Baby."

"You can push me away when that time comes, but I'll never push you out of my heart. Never."

Jesus fuckin' Christ. She was killing him. "Baby."

"I'm sorry how I reacted earlier—"

She was sorry? Like she had control over that? *Fuck that.* If anyone was sorry, it was him. "Never be sorry," he growled. "You didn't fuckin' choose to react that way. That wasn't your choice. I shoulda known better than to take it that far after today. After that shit with..." He let that drift off. No need to repeat the fuckery that happened earlier at the warehouse. "It affected you. Shoulda left you alone."

She shoved her face into his throat and curled her fingers around the back of his neck, holding onto him. "No, please don't leave me alone. I pushed myself because I was... I was trying to imagine my life without you. With someone else."

"*Kachina.*"

"Crow, I will leave when you ask me to. I promise I will. But just know I'll have to fight against every instinct to do so. But I don't want you to feel obligated. I don't want you to feel the need to stick to someone you don't want to be stuck to because of guilt. I only wanted to let you know I love you, that's all. I appreciate what you're doing for me. I appreciate your patience. I can't imagine anyone else would be as accepting as you."

"Baby." It wasn't that he was trying to interrupt her, he just didn't know what to say to everything she was revealing. No, that was fucking wrong, he did want to interrupt her because the more she said, the harder it was to deal with. The harder it was to admit to himself that he wouldn't be able to let her go, either.

Should he feel guilty he wanted to keep her? Claim her as his?

Make it so no other man would have the balls to walk onto his property and try to steal his woman.

Because *fuck that*.

He didn't like violence but the thought of losing *his* woman made him itch with it.

And he would lose her if he remained stubborn by telling himself it was for the best.

It wasn't.

Even so, her life stopped that day in that abandoned house and he wanted nothing more than for her to pick up where it left off and experience everything she should have from that point on. She was robbed of her twenties when she began to hide herself. Him claiming her might not let her experience everything she missed.

But that wasn't all that held him back. He also wasn't sure he wanted a life of domesticity. He was forty. Yeah, it wasn't ancient, but he was set in his ways. If he was going to have kids, he should've started ten years ago. While he was thrilled with every baby born to his brothers, at this point in his life he wasn't so sure that was for him.

If he claimed Jazz, he would have to consider all of that, too. Because he couldn't imagine the woman didn't want babies. Right?

Didn't most women want babies? Even Brooke had been considering Dex's plea. Though, so far it hadn't happened.

"Fuck. I'm sorry, I never should have told you," she whispered against his throat. Her lips were like silk against his skin.

Truth was, she didn't need to tell him.

He knew.

He'd been hoping it was just a crush held over from years ago. But when she actually said the words...

Now that she said them, it was hard to get them out of his head. And he wasn't sure if he wanted to.

No one had ever said those words to him before. He never stuck with anyone long enough for that to develop. Maybe he did it on purpose, who knew.

While he figured his parents might have told him, he didn't remember them saying it. He'd been way too young.

While he also knew his club brothers loved him like family and the feeling was mutual, they never said it. *Fuck*, that would just be weird. While he knew his club sisters loved him as family, it wasn't like they were going around declaring that shit, either.

So, yeah, his aunt, his mother's only sister, had told him a couple of times from what he could remember. At the time, he assumed it was only because they were blood. The poor woman had been stuck raising a nephew when she never planned on having kids of her own.

So, when it came to saying those words Jazz was the only person he ever heard them from.

Suddenly, he hoped like hell she meant it. Because words without real meaning were empty. Hollow.

"Tell me again," he murmured.

Jazz lifted her face from his neck, and before she could speak, he dug his fingers into both sides of her head, holding her so she couldn't avoid his gaze.

But she didn't even try. Fuck no, her eyes met his and, not even wavering for a second, she stated, "I love you."

He wanted to ask, "Are you sure? Is this really what you're feelin'?" But he didn't, because, *fuck him*, he could see it.

She fucking loved him.

"*Kachina*, I—"

"I said you didn't have to say it. So don't. I don't want you to say it if you don't mean it." Her eyes slid to the side.

A heartbeat later he said, "Again."

Her wide green eyes quickly came back to him and her mouth dropped open for a second. "I love you."

He dropped his head and said softly over her parted lips, "Yeah, me too, baby," before crushing his mouth against hers.

Sealing his lips to hers was his attempt to trap those words between them. So they could never be taken away.

But he didn't control the kiss. Not this time, he let her take it as far as she wanted. He had plenty of time to be the one in the driver's seat. And only when she was ready. The last couple of weeks, things had gone well. Today was just a hiccup.

He expected more in the future. And each one would be dealt with. Whether he needed to retreat just far enough before pushing forward again.

But, no matter what, they would be pushing forward. Together.

She loved him.

That changed everything.

CHAPTER FIFTEEN

The official meeting of the DAMC sisterhood had commenced on the second floor above Sophie's Sweet Treats. Z and Sophie's former apartment had been converted into a little sitting area, almost like a café, for people to enjoy Wi-Fi, coffee and, of course, tooth-aching, calorie-ridden, orgasm-worthy baked goods. Like Bella's to-die-for filled cupcakes.

Jazz was on cupcake number three and was feeling no shame about it. None at all. Crow was always encouraging her to eat more to put on some weight. While he preferred a woman with curves, she was pretty sure he'd be content no matter what she looked like.

But now, when she looked in a mirror, she saw *herself*. Not through her jaded eyes, but through his. She had to admit, she was liking the curves, too. Though, she'd gone up a whole size in clothes. Even her bras were now a little tight, the cups beginning to overflow slightly. That wasn't a bad thing, either.

Giving her a run for her money on a sugar overdose was Diamond, who was finishing her second cupcake moaning and groaning like she was having the best sex of her life.

"Hungry and horny. That describes pregnancy perfectly," she said between an eye-rolling bite of cake and lick of icing.

Sophie snorted. "Tell me about it. Zak definitely didn't mind the horny part. Especially when I would take charge and jump his bones—"

"Bah bah bah!" Jayde shouted, covering her ears with her hands. "I don't want to hear it. I don't want to picture it. Just no." She turned to look at Bella. "From you, either. I don't need to hear about my brothers' sex lives. Please and thank you."

Bella dropped her head and shook it, smiling.

"So, is sex better when you're pregnant?" Brooke, Dex's ol' lady asked, surprised. "I'm not sure sex with Dex could get any better."

"Really?" Jewel asked.

"No, because we like to... Uh... Never mind."

"Thank you," Bella said.

"Agreed," Ivy said. "We don't want to hear about our brother's capabilities in that department, either."

"How can we participate in women's talk without talking about sex?" Jewel complained.

"Some of us don't have male siblings," Ivy said.

All eyes turned to Jazz.

"Yeah," Sophie said, leaning toward Jazz. "Nobody in this room is going to stop you from talking about Crow in the sack."

Ivy laughed. "Oh no. In fact, we're going to encourage it."

"Ply you with the cupcake flavors of your choice," Bella added. "A lifetime supply, in fact." She turned to Emma. "You too, Emma. Watching Dawg with you makes us all quiver in our boots."

Emma popped the last bite of her first cupcake into her mouth and laughed. "You know that's not happening." She wiggled her eyebrows.

Suddenly all eyes turned back to her. "Linc and Jayde!" Jazz exclaimed, trying to get the attention off her.

"Meh. No. We want to hear about Crow," Kiki said.

"What do you mean 'meh?'" Jayde yelled. "Linc's got those sexy flexy hips. God, I hope he never gets arthritis or needs a hip replacement."

"Linc's in our office way too much," Kiki announced. "I don't think I can hear the nitty gritty details and still look at him the same afterward."

"But you can hear about Crow and you all can look at him the same afterward?" Jazz asked.

A loud resounding "Yes!" rose up from almost all of them.

Jazz turned her head to look at the one female in the room who hadn't agreed. "Diamond?"

Diamond smiled. "I'm not voting, but I'm also not closing my ears if you decide to spill."

"Nothing to spill," Jazz muttered. She was not talking about her and Crow's sex life. It probably didn't even compare to the rest of theirs. After that blackout episode, Crow was back to taking things as slow as molasses left outside in winter.

"Uh huh," Ivy muttered. "We've all wondered, you know. I mean, what hot-blooded straight woman hasn't wanted to test drive him at least once."

"He's not a car," Jazz muttered.

"No, he's a fucking Porsche," Bella murmured.

"Isn't that the truth," Sophie whispered, her expression becoming dreamy.

"You've got Z," Jazz reminded her.

"That's right. I love my ol' man, but I also have eyes in my head and working lady parts. Doesn't mean I can't look. Or fantasize." She sighed, tucking a fist under her chin. "I miss seeing D's naked ass, too."

All eyes turned to Jewel, who shrugged. "I missed it, too, until I made him put a mirror above the bed in the house." She glanced at Ivy. "Best decision your ol' man ever made, putting that mirror on the ceiling of the pawn shop apartment."

"Agreed," Jayde answered. "It freaked me out at first, until I completely saw the value of it."

"Problem is, you now have two babies because of those mirrors," Kiki reminded Jewel.

Jewel shrugged. "And that's it. No more. He didn't want one. Now we have two and I have to fight to spend time with babies that *I* grew in my belly. He gets the fun parts. I get the shitty parts. Literally."

"Z was no better," Sophie muttered.

"And there's where I'm lucky. Hawk doesn't mind doing all of that. Doesn't mind getting up in the middle of the night when Ash wakes up crying. Best dad ever."

"Hey! Dawson isn't chopped liver. He's great with Emmalee," Emma reminded them.

"And Lily," Bella added.

"Right. And Lily," Emma agreed with a sharp nod.

"Jag is awesome with Lexi," Ivy said, her lips curling at the corners, her expression becoming soft.

"That's because my brother worships every red hair on your head and Lexi is a mini-you," Diamond said.

Ivy gave Diamond a knowing smile. "Yeah, he's a good man."

"Took long enough for you to finally figure that out," Bella reminded her sister.

"Look who's talking," Sophie said. "Axel pined for you right here in this bakery. It was *sooooo* obvious. He'd come in here and tongue that icing, trying to get your attention like a peacock spreading his tail."

A few snorts and chuckles went around the table.

"Speaking of Axel, what's the latest on the road to adoption?" Diamond asked Bella.

Bella's eyes hit Sophie's and something unspoken was communicated between them. "We're looking at all the options. We have a few more steps to take."

After a few moments of silence and Bella not saying anymore, everyone left it at that. When Bella was ready to share, she would.

"So, we still haven't heard how Crow is in bed." Ivy nudged Jazz.

"And you won't, either," Jazz answered.

"Mercy back off?" Diamond asked, side-eyeing her.

Jewel answered before Jazz could. "D sent him off on a job out of state. In Vegas actually."

"Damn," Sophie whispered. "Since when does he give his men long distance jobs?"

"Since Mercy overstepped. And, anyway, D thinks the Warriors are no more."

"What do you mean?" Kiki asked, leaning forward, her eyes focused intently on Jewel.

Jewel shrugged. "A few weeks ago," she shot a quick glance at Jazz, "they nabbed who they think might be the last one."

"Are they sure?" Kiki asked. "Hawk hasn't said a word."

"Not a hundred percent. There could always be a couple hiding out. They're nomads for the most part, they don't have a permanent base."

No one said anything for a minute. Instead, they all considered what Jewel just revealed.

"Are you planning on staying in town now?"

Jazz turned to look at Kiki. The older woman now studied her. "My plans had nothing to do with the Warriors. Remember, I only came back to town to get my tattoo."

Ivy slammed her palm on the table, making everyone jump. "Holy fuck! I forgot about that. Let's see it!"

A murmur of agreement swept through the other women.

Jazz wasn't sure if she was ready to show anyone her scar cover-up. The only one who had seen it recently was Crow, of course. It wasn't meant to be seen by anyone else; it was only meant to be appreciated by her, to cover those letters that had haunted her.

But it would also be a shame if no one else ever saw the perfect piece of art that Crow had drawn for her. "I don't know," she whispered.

Kiki reached out and covered Jazz's hand that was fisted on the table. "If you're not comfortable..."

She could tell Kiki wasn't very comfortable, either. Maybe she didn't want to see it. She probably didn't want a reminder of that day since she had suffered as well.

Kiki then squeezed her hand. "I'd love to see it. But only if you're okay with it."

She loved Kiki. She was the best thing that ever happened to Hawk. She was the perfect woman for him. She was smart and sexy, and kept her husband on his toes. And now the woman gave that man, the man she loved with every breath she took, a son.

Jazz fucked up that day she ran out of Hawk's house. Her first instinct was to help Kiki. But looking back, she realized it would've been better for her to call 9-1-1 or Hawk. Or even Diesel. She could've given them descriptions of their kidnappers. A complete run-down on what they looked like, what they were driving, what direction they headed.

But instead, she ran outside with her cell phone and never even got a chance to call anyone before she was tackled and her phone destroyed.

Kiki blamed herself for Jazz being taken because she screamed out Jazz's name.

Jazz blamed herself because Kiki would've been found a lot sooner and possibly unharmed, if a witness had been left behind.

And she never would've had to get that tattoo. Because she never would've been carved up, left broken and battered...

Move on.

Move on.

Move on.

It was good advice to herself and she needed to listen to it. But in the meantime, the women were all waiting on her.

She was never part of the club sisterhood years ago. She didn't grow up DAMC. She wasn't born into the club. The only thing tying her to it was her grandparents. And eventually becoming Hawk's house mouse. So when Diamond invited her today to this "meeting," she had been floored. She almost turned her down. Now she was glad she didn't.

The women made her feel welcome, a part of their group. And when Crow had heard she'd been invited, he had just smiled and shook his head.

Whatever that meant.

When she looked around the table, she realized every single one of them was an ol' lady. Every single one.

Except for her.

She looked across the table at Diamond. "Did Crow ask you to invite me today?"

Diamond's eyes widened for a second but she quickly hid her surprise. "No. Why wouldn't we invite you? You're part of the sisterhood."

"I wasn't," Jazz said softly.

"Well, now you are," Kiki answered.

Maybe they thought her and Crow were going to remain together?

"But I'm not an ol' lady," Jazz murmured, staring at the coffee mug in front of her. She ran a finger around the lip of it.

"You don't need to be an ol' lady to be a part of the sisterhood, Jazz," Sophie reassured her.

"Has he talked about claiming you?" Diamond asked, her head tilted as she watched Jazz carefully.

Jazz bit her bottom lip. She wasn't sure if she wanted to talk about her relationship with Crow with any of them.

"Jazz—" Kiki started.

Jazz pushed her chair back with a squeal and stood up. She unfastened her shorts and pushed them down before yanking up her shirt with one hand.

All eyes landed on her lower belly.

No one said a word for a long moment. Then it was like the flood gates opened.

"Wow."

"Holy shit."

"That's beautiful."

"Stunning."

"His nicest work yet."

Jazz wasn't keeping track of who said what until Brooke asked, "Is he doing it in small sessions?"

She nodded. "Yes, because of the scar tissue and the pain."

"How many have you had so far?" Sophie asked.

"Four."

"He's been doing one every two weeks, right?" Diamond asked.

"Yes." They'd now been living together for over eight weeks. Sharing the same bed for almost the same amount of time. And it had been amazing. Even the nights where he did nothing other than hold her once he got home from work. But she wasn't sure how many more sessions he'd need to finish the tattoo. And once he did, she wasn't sure what would happen to them. She hadn't asked after that night she confessed her feelings. He also hadn't brought it up again, either.

"Well, it's perfect," Kiki whispered, suspiciously wiping a hand over her eyes.

Jazz's heart skipped a beat, if Kiki started crying...

She needed to quickly switch gears again. "When it's completed, he wants me to move on."

Fuck. She shouldn't have let that slip out. Because suddenly the warm group of women turned cold. Their spines snapped straight, their eyes narrowed, their mouths got tight.

"Why?" Jewel asked, a bit of anger tinging her question. "Don't tell me he's as stubborn as my beast?"

"He isn't going to make you his ol' lady?" Ivy asked.

"He hasn't brought it up. He thinks I should be with someone my own age."

"You're only about a year younger than me," Jayde announced. "That's bullshit. Crow acts like he's an ancient, wise old man. He's what?" She wiggled her fingers in the air, waiting for someone to answer.

Which Diamond did. "Forty."

"Forty!" Kiki spouted. "Hawk isn't far behind him. Jesus. If forty is old..." She shook her head. "What's wrong with him?"

"Doesn't he know forty is the new thirty? And, anyway, he's in his prime," Brooke exclaimed.

"Is he ever," Sophie mumbled under her breath.

"He's still plenty young enough to start a family," Kiki said.

Family?

Did he want a family? She hadn't even considered that. Maybe he wanted a family, but just not with her?

Everybody else was settling down and having kids. Hell, even Diesel! Being forty, maybe he wanted to get started soon and knew it would take a while for Jazz to completely recover? Especially if it took her six years to get this far. Maybe he thought it would take way too long for her to get to a point where she would be a good mother?

Was that possible?

Was she even mother material?

Holy shit, did she even want kids?

She glanced around the table. The only women who didn't have any yet were Brooke, Bella and Jayde. And Crow had said that Jayde miscarried but she and Linc planned on having some in the future once she passed the bar exam, which was soon. Plus, Bella and Axel were planning to adopt.

Brooke... Well, the little Jazz knew about Brooke—and only because Crow had told her when he'd given her the run-down on the sisterhood—was that she was a kickass, independent woman who challenged Dex at every turn. And the man had no complaints. Apparently, he ate that up.

Crow said Dex and Brooke were the perfect match. But then so was D and Jewel. Sophie and Z. Bella and Axel...

Hell, all of them were.

Crow and her were not perfect. They seemed to be the oddball couple. Their differences were obvious.

Maybe Crow was waiting for his perfect match like the rest of his brothers.

Apparently, she wasn't it.

Most likely, he wanted what they had. She didn't blame him. He saw with his own two eyes how his brothers, once they finally claimed their women, were happy.

He may never have what they had with her.

He was right. She needed to move on once her tattoo was done. Let him find his perfect ol' lady. One who wouldn't hold him back. One who would be willing to give him the family he wanted, since she wasn't sure.

But even so, maybe the two of them were so imperfect together that they were perfect? "I told him I love him."

Jazz didn't miss the collective sucking in of air around the table.

Shit. Did she say that out loud, too?

"Did he say it back?"

She turned her eyes to Sophie, who was wearing a soft smile. "I... I think so. Though, he hasn't come right out and said it."

"What did he say?" Ivy asked.

"When I first told him, he said 'me, too.'"

Jewel threw her hands up. "Well, there you go."

"I'm not sure... He hasn't said anything since."

Jewel lifted her coffee to her lips, saying, "Oh, please. If you expect any of these guys to say it like a normal man... Forget it. Take what you can get."

All eyes turned to Jewel. While they were all thinking it, it was Brooke who was brave enough to ask, "Has D said it to you?"

Jewel swallowed her coffee, then smiled. "He's D."

"That doesn't answer the question."

"That's my answer," Jewel said saucily.

"Does it bother you that he doesn't?" Emma asked her.

"Who said he doesn't?" Jewel shot back.

"We all know D is coo coo for Cocoa Puffs over Jewelee," Jayde announced. "Let's leave them alone."

"True. Actions speak louder than words," Sophie murmured. "All those weeks that Zak snuck over here in the dead of night to win me over..."

"And it worked," Ivy said.

"It did," Sophie agreed. "Just like Jag never gave up on you. Axel never gave up on Bella. Shit..." She shook her head. "These men..."

"When they know what they want, they go hard and heavy," Bella said.

"It's not only the men..." Ivy drifted off, looking at Jewel.

Jewel shrugged. "Who wouldn't want the Eighth Wonder of the World in their bed?"

"Me. Nice to look at. Frustrating as hell to deal with," Diamond said.

"Well, you and D have always butted heads," Jewel reminded her sister.

"Okay, so now what?" Kiki tried to bring them back on track. "Jazz is in love with Crow. We assume Crow feels the same. He's being stubborn about his age for some dumb reason. What can we do about it?"

"Oh, I don't know, Kiki. I don't think it's a good idea if we get involved," Sophie said, a worried look on her face.

"Why not?" Kiki asked, a determined look on hers. "Look, we all love Crow. We want what's best for him."

"I'm not so sure I'm what's best for him," Jazz said. And that was true.

"Diamond?" Ivy asked.

Diamond studied Jazz for a moment before confirming, "Yes, I think she's best for him."

"So there you go. Crow's 'baby doll' has given her seal of approval," Jewel said with a laugh.

Brooke lifted a palm, her eyebrows high on her forehead. "Wait. If he calls Di 'baby doll' what the hell does he call you?"

"*Kachina*," Jazz answered.

"What does that mean?" Brooke's brows dropped, knitting together.

"Spirit."

Brooke pursed her lips. "He only just started calling you that?"

"No. Since the day I met him."

Brooke sat back in her chair and it was easy to see the wheels spinning in her head. "And how old were you when he met you?"

"Eighteen."

"That's young," she said softly.

"Right. I think he still sees me like the first day we met."

"And how long have you loved him?"

Jazz thought back before she answered Brooke. "Eighteen." Okay, maybe it was more like a crush that turned into lust which turned into love. Not that she was keeping track.

"Damn," Brooke whispered.

"I don't think he still sees you as eighteen," Diamond murmured. "Otherwise, you wouldn't be in his bed."

"He's just helping me."

Jayde snorted. "*Helping* you. Right. Crow isn't a dog. He doesn't just grab some where ever he can get it. He's pretty selective."

"Well, he has just grabbed some in the past, but they've never stuck," Diamond corrected her. She raised a finger. "Though, it's true, he is pretty selective even for that."

"You've been back two months now. That's the longest he's stuck with any woman," Ivy said.

"Because my tattoo isn't finished."

Ivy mumbled, "Uh huh."

"So back to what I said, how are we going to help?" Kiki asked. "Even if he expects her to move on once the tat is finished, or even move out of his house... We need to keep her in town. Keep her close. Let him see the error of his ways."

"I doubt he'll want me to stay as his house mouse forever."

"Right. So come work with Jayde and me. We desperately need help managing the office now, since Jayde is taking on more official duties and close to taking the bar exam. It'll give you a good reason to stick in Shadow Valley and let things develop as they need to. Plus, no one sitting at this table wants you to go."

Head bobs and *mmm-hmm's* went around the table.

"If you don't want to do that, come work for me in my interior design business," Brooke encouraged her. "I definitely need the help since business has been booming. I'm overwhelmed and good help is hard to find."

"You have Kelsea, don't you?" Jazz asked her. That's what Crow had told her.

Brooke rolled her eyes. "I wish I had Kelsea. I'm not sure who it is I have. Half the time she doesn't even bother to show up. And when she does..." She shook her head, frowning. "She's way too unreliable."

"Still?" Kiki asked, concern crossing her face.

"Yes, I keep threatening to fire her, but Dex keeps begging me not to."

"She's not on a good path," Jewel said after taking another bite of her cupcake. "D has his guys pulling her out of jams time and time again. He won't do it himself because if he does, he might strangle the shit out of her. But, honestly, we're both afraid she's going to end up... *fuck*... dead. Or..." She let that drift off.

They all knew what she was thinking. Kelsea could end up in a bad situation like Kiki and Jazz. Or even Bella. Something that would fuck her up for the rest of her life.

"The woman needs some sense shaken back into her," Kiki murmured.

"I wouldn't call her a woman. She's acting like a brat," Brooke said. "I love my sister but I'm scared to death for her. I just recently found her and I don't want to lose her."

"So you have two job offers, Jazz," Sophie said. "No reason for you not to stay in town. With us. With your family."

"And if you're not interested in those two offers, we always need help at the gym," Diamond added. "Especially with me being pregnant."

"Or here at the bakery," Sophie offered.

"Or even at the body shop. Since Diamond left, they haven't found anyone reliable there, either."

Ivy nodded. "Jag's always bitching about how no outsider lasts more than a few weeks."

"Well, yeah," Diamond laughed. "It's like being a kindergarten teacher over there."

"Isn't that the fucking truth," Jewel grumbled.

"Oh, and working with D's men is better?" Ivy asked, one eyebrow cocked.

Jewel grinned. "Fuck yes. You've seen them. If I didn't have D..." She sighed.

"But you do. And two baby girls. So you're very fertile. Don't even breathe all that feral hotness in," Jayde warned her cousin.

"But, fuck, I can't help but inhale all those masculine pheromones." Jewel laughed. "When D isn't paying attention, that is. When my ol' man calls them all in for a meeting... I pretend I need to be in there to take notes."

"And do you?"

Jewel snorted. "Hell no. I'm just sitting there with my ovaries exploding, my mouth watering, my eyes not knowing where to look first. My notes end up being a whole bunch of dick doodles."

Jazz covered her mouth to keep from giggling.

"Fuck! I'm so jealous," Jayde said with a laugh.

"Mmm hmm. You should be," Jewel said, also laughing.

"*Aaaaand* on that note..." Kiki brought them all back to reality. "Jazz, you have plenty of offers, so think about it. You still have time before your tattoo is done, right? At least another month?"

"Yes, he thinks two more sessions will do it."

"Well, now you know your options."

Ivy leaned in. "And, if you need it, the apartment above the pawn shop is once again empty. So you have a place to settle, if you need it. I'm sure Ace won't mind."

Jazz nodded and thought about it. She never lived on her own in her whole life. So maybe that would be a good thing. Become independent, get a good job within one of the club businesses. Prove to Crow she could be responsible and independent. That she wasn't just clinging to him because he was "safe" like he had suggested.

Maybe that's just what she needed to do. Talk to Ace about the apartment. Pick a place to work and settle into the sisterhood, like she belonged there.

She did.

As Crow's ol' lady.

He just hadn't realized it yet.

CHAPTER SIXTEEN

Crow left a trail of clothes as he moved across the bedroom floor. Wherever he pulled them off, he just left them where they fell. He'd pick them up in the morning. Right now, he was not in the mood to be neat.

No, he was in the mood for something else.

Three months it had taken to finish her tattoo. And tomorrow would be the last time she'd need to sit for it.

Three months Jazz had spent in his bed. Soaked in his tub. Cooked and cleaned for him. Decorated his fucking house and turned it into a home.

A home. Instead of just a roof over his head with a bed, a couch and an overpriced coffeemaker.

Three months of her burrowing herself under his skin.

Because at this point, he couldn't imagine her not being in his kitchen, in his tub, in his bed.

He'd always wanted her, even back then. Now he had her, but three months later he was still wondering if it was right.

He had told her they were done after her piece was finished and he never told her otherwise, even after her telling him she loved him.

In fact, after that, she never said it again.

That was most likely his fault. While a "me, too" had automatically slipped out of his mouth, he'd left it at that.

Because he wasn't sure.

Not about him loving her. If what he felt was love, then he did love her. He'd never told anyone in his life those words, not even his Lakota aunt who had so generously taken him in.

But was what he felt actual love? Or just a deep caring?

Every night when he came home and saw her curled up in his bed, he'd sit on the edge and watch her sleep. Her face was peaceful, not haunted like when she first showed up. Her body had filled out and she wasn't starving herself any more. Wasn't trying to be someone she wasn't.

Her hair was getting longer, and he could tell where her natural blonde ended, and the dyed part started. She said once the natural part grew longer, she'd have the salon-dyed ends cut off.

He didn't give a shit. As long as it wasn't the depressing black, he was fine with it.

The sex was good. Every week it got even better. He let her decide when she wanted to take it further. To experiment. To push her limits.

So far, so good.

He hadn't had one complaint in that department. Because every time he got to sink into her wet heat, he felt like that was exactly where he belonged.

She belonged in his bed, in his life, his house and on the back of his bike.

Both Grizz and Momma Bear kept asking when he was going to claim her.

He didn't have an answer.

Because he wasn't sure.

His instinct was to claim her. Take her. Keep her.

But he couldn't think about what was best for him, he had to think about what was best for her.

Though he got the blessing from her grandparents, Hawk still wasn't happy, thinking Crow was taking advantage of her.

He wasn't.

He'd never do that to Jazz. Or any woman.

The club VP was just looking out for Jazz like an overprotective father and Crow understood it. So he tolerated it.

By the time he got to the bed, he was naked and like he did every night, he lifted the sheet and slid in.

Like she did every night, she rolled into him, curling herself around him, throwing one of her thighs over his.

Claiming him.

He combed his fingers through her hair as he stared up through the dark to the ceiling and waited.

Because also every night, it didn't take long for her to wake up and want to explore.

And since her tattoo would be finished tomorrow, he didn't want to miss out on this one last time being with her.

"Hey," she said softly, her warm breath sweeping over his bare chest making his nipples pebble, probably as hard as hers were pressed against him.

"Hey," he answered just as softly.

"How long have you been home?"

"Just a few minutes."

She snuggled deeper into his side. She was naked. She went to bed naked every night and in the morning, she'd pick up his abandoned clothes and slip into the T-shirt he'd worn the previous day to make him breakfast.

He loved every fucking second of that.

Because when that first started, he told her that she could grab one of his clean tees from his drawer and she refused. She insisted she wanted to wear the one that smelled like him.

And he loved hearing that, too.

"*Kachina*," he whispered.

She lifted her head from his chest. "Yeah?"

He forced himself to say, "Think tomorrow will be the last one. Just gotta do some touch-ups, then it'll be done."

He didn't mean just the tattoo and she knew that because her muscles tightened around him. She didn't like hearing that.

But it had to be said.

He didn't want her to feel obligated to stay. She needed to live her life, pick up where it left off, before she settled down. Not live in a biker's house being his house mouse.

She was much better than that. She deserved more.

She melted against him again and her hand trailed along his belly to his dick, which was now hard, laying along his hip.

Tonight needed to be the best time between them. He had to make sure she never forgot it. A positive experience for her to build upon for when she found someone else.

Her fingertips traced his hard-on and she kept moving until she cupped his balls. She gave them a light squeeze, then traced his length again.

Her little hot mouth sucked at the nipple closest to her face and she used her nails to lightly scrape along his skin from his sternum to his thighs.

He always let her set the pace, no matter how much he wanted it otherwise. He didn't want a repeat of what happened all those weeks ago that last time Mercy made a move.

He closed his eyes and let the breath escape his lungs slowly as she shifted over him, giving him all her weight.

He loved that, too. While she had filled out somewhat, she was still light. He let his hand drift over the smooth skin of her back, the indentation at the base of her spine, then over the round curves of her ass.

She had a great ass.

Maybe someday she'd be ready to let the right man take it. But tonight was not the time. And it would probably be a long time before she was comfortable enough for that. If ever.

Especially since that was another place those motherfuckers violated.

That usually took time and attention, but they'd just taken what they wanted. They took something that could be beautiful and special and made it ugly. So if she ever allowed that, it would be a man she would need to trust one hundred percent and who would have the patience of a Saint.

For now, Crow just wanted her anyway she was willing to give herself to him.

Whatever she was comfortable with, he gladly accepted. And everything she offered was like a gift.

Because she trusted him. She felt safe with him.

She loved him.

He hadn't realized he'd closed his eyes until they popped opened when her mouth wrapped around his throbbing dick. She had settled between his thighs with two fingers circling the root of his hard-on and with her fingers playing along his sac, she began to suck him hard and deep.

They'd spent many nights doing this very same thing. She would lick, flick, suck and then pause to ask him what his preference was. Ask him what he liked and disliked.

She had no idea that she was doing it, but what she was doing was edging. Nor did she realize he got off on that since edging made his orgasms even more intense. He didn't tell her because he just wanted her to do what came naturally and not get self-conscious about it.

Even so, it was like he was training her for some other man.

Fuck.

His fingers dug into her hair and he grasped the silky strands tightly. He managed to get out, "Lemme know if it gets to be too much, baby."

Because the urge to fist his fingers in her hair, hold her in place and fuck her face was overwhelming, but he was always cautious about how rough he could get.

How demanding.

Time and time again he'd have to fight to remain in control, especially when she'd take him to that very steep edge and then pull back.

And, *fuck*, he loved it because when he finally got a chance to let loose, it was the best fucking come ever.

But this time, she wasn't stopping to ask questions, or pausing to gauge his reactions. No, she was sucking him almost desperately.

Like she was trying to fucking prove something to him. Or to herself. Or maybe because this was the last time.

Once the tattoo was done tomorrow, he was setting her free.

She could head home to Buffalo or anywhere she desired. Just not back in his bed.

Because he was going to do the right thing.

Even if it fucking killed him.

The club had let him go when his mother's family showed up to claim him because in their eyes it was the best thing for him. It was the right thing.

He had taken a life. Because in his eyes it was the right thing.

Now he needed to do the right thing with his *Kachina*.

His spirit.

He had helped her get ready to fly. Now he needed to let her do just that.

To keep her would be selfish.

Her mouth was gone and, while he missed it, he realized she was hovering above his hips. With one hand on his dick, she was sliding the head between her own slick soft folds.

When he started to reach for the drawer, she grabbed his arm to stop him. "No."

"*Kachina*, need a wrap."

"No. I'm covered. It's covered."

"What's covered?" He lifted his head off the pillow and tried to see her in the darkness of the room. He could only make out her silhouette.

"I went on birth control over a month ago. The doctor said it would be safe now."

She did what? And didn't tell him until now? "You sure?"

"Yeah, he said a month. It's been over a month."

Jesus Christ. That meant there would be nothing between them during their last time. He'd never taken a woman in his life without a wrap. Not once.

And here, Jazz was giving him this gift, too.

Why was she making this shit more difficult for him?

But that question quickly disintegrated as she lowered herself on him and when that tight wetness surrounded him, squeezed him, his head fell back onto the pillow, and the air rushed from him.

She was most comfortable on top and he didn't complain about that, either.

She was getting so good at that, too. She knew just how to move her hips to drive him to that edge, then pull back and leave him wanting more.

She'd do it again and again until he was half out of his mind.

He'd be torn between wanting to thrust up and come deep inside her, or trying to hold off to make it last longer.

By allowing her to take her time and the lead, she'd learn exactly what she loved, too. What movements, positions, made her orgasm.

He'd paid attention as well. He certainly had. Because the second she unleashed him and allowed him to take over, he did exactly what she needed. And once she pulsated around him intensely and that rush of wet slid over his dick and down his balls, he lost himself within her.

Since this was their last time, he could only hope that once she was done taking her time with him, she'd hand over the control to him.

Because not only did he want her to remember tonight. He did, too.

With her hands planted on his chest, her thumbs brushed back and forth over the pebbled tips of his nipples. While she had discovered things about herself in the last three months, he did, too. He loved her playing with his nipples just as much as she loved him playing with hers.

She began weeks ago by mirroring his actions, whatever he did with hers, she did in return. He learned the more attention he gave her tits, the more she'd clenched tightly around him, urging him on with whispers and whimpers.

Reaching around her hips, he spread her ass cheeks and slipped his fingers low enough to where they were connected to gather some of her slickness, then used her natural lube to slide his index finger up and down her crease.

She gasped and dropped her head, her hair a silky curtain sliding along the heated skin of his chest.

He gently circled and stroked, making her groan his name.

"*Kachina*," he struggled to get out. "Tell me when."

His body was tight, his breathing as ragged as hers, and he was doing his best not to flip her over before she said it was okay. But tonight he wanted to be between her thighs while he was deep inside her. When he finally let go.

He needed to turn on the light because he wanted to watch her face, her unfocused green eyes, her parted lips, her reaction to each movement of his hips.

But right now on his back, he remained still, except for his finger carefully teasing her in a place he avoided all these weeks. A sensitive area that she might grow to love touches, licks and more...

The thought of getting her to the point of begging for him there made his hips buck up uncontrollably.

"Baby, hit the light," he urged.

"Crow..." she breathed.

"The light. Gotta see you."

She lifted up enough where he was almost completely free of her, but he tilted his hips so they could remain connected as she leaned over to turn on the small nightstand lamp.

Then she shifted her weight again and impaled herself back on him as she straightened up.

"Better?" she asked.

So much fucking better. He let his gaze wander over her face, which was flushed, her bottom lip slightly swollen, probably from biting it. To her nipples which were pointed and puckered. Down the slight swell of her belly. Over her hips and landed on the trimmed, dark blonde hair which pointed to the spot where they were connected.

He flexed his dick deep inside her and her eyelids dropped a little lower. She caught her lower lip within her teeth and stared down at him as she explored him just as thoroughly with her own gaze.

"So fuckin' beautiful, baby."

She released her bottom lip and smiled. "I should be telling you that."

"You just did."

"We fit," she murmured, sliding her palms up his ribcage, her eyes following the same path. She skipped his nipples this time and traced his collarbones with her fingers. They trailed up his cheek and then she explored his face softly with her fingertips. Over his chin, jaw, his lips, the curve of his nose, his eyebrows, his forehead.

Then she leaned forward and took his mouth.

Fuck. She tasted so good.

She deepened the kiss for a moment, then pulled away, her breath mingling with his.

"We fit," she whispered again, staring down into his eyes.

"Yeah, baby, we fit." But he couldn't let that change anything.

When he agreed with her, he expected her eyes to light up like they did when she was happy, but they didn't. Instead, sadness crossed her face and her eyes slid down, breaking their gaze.

She began to move again. Rolling her hips, circling them. Rising and falling at an excruciatingly slow pace.

He blew out a breath and cursed himself as a lone tear rolled from the corner of her eye down her cheek.

Another quickly followed, landing on his stomach. She dropped her head, covering her face with her hair and she swiped at her cheeks.

"I... I'm sorry," she mumbled with a sniff.

For fuck's sake, she might as well be stabbing him in the heart right now.

This was one time in the last few weeks that he didn't wait until she was ready. He rolled his body and took her with him until his weight pressed her into the mattress.

He watched a few more tears escape and disappear into her hair.

"We fit," she stated softly, her voice thick.

"Yeah, baby, we fit, but that doesn't... It doesn't..." He closed his eyes and gritted his teeth, trying to keep his shit together.

It would be easy to say... *Stay.*

But life wasn't about doing what was easy. It was about doing what was right.

So he kept his mouth shut, he held back what he wanted to tell her and he began to move instead.

This was their last night together and it wasn't supposed to be about sadness and tears. It was supposed to be special. Something to remember each other by if she decided to leave the Valley.

He hoped she did. Because he wasn't sure if he could watch her move on to someone else. He'd be too worried they weren't treating her right.

And he didn't want to think of any other man being right where he was at that very moment.

He didn't want to imagine her wearing any other man's T-shirt while she made him breakfast and sipped on coffee.

Even though her pace had been slow, he began to move just as slowly. He knew that exact moment her tears stopped and a determined look crossed her face.

She was a fighter. A survivor.

She wasn't going to give up so easily.

Whether she knew it or not, she was strong as fuck.

"I love you, Crow."

His rhythm hiccuped.

Jesus fucking Christ. She was pulling out the big guns. She knew what she was doing, and she knew how to do it well.

But he knew what he was doing, too.

He took slow, long, deep thrusts, each time he hit the end of her she gasped. Her set jaw went soft and her mouth went slack. As her eyelids began to lower lazily, he shook his head and grabbed her chin. "No, *Kachina*, look at me."

Her eyes widened for a split second. Then she did as was told, locking her gaze with his.

He wanted to take her hard and fast and he would only do that when he was absolutely sure that he was the only one in the room with her, when he was sure she was concentrating on him and him alone.

No ghosts. No hidden memories. Nothing but the two of them.

"Baby, you ready?"

"Yes," hissed from between her lips and while he wanted to kiss her, he also wanted to watch her come.

He planted his palms into the mattress, kneed her thighs wider and then drove it home, tilting his hips up at the end of each stroke. He knew she loved it because, not only had she told him so, her body rippled around him. Her heat, her wetness became almost unbearable for him and he had to fight to keep his own eyes open.

He wanted nothing more than to get lost within her.

He couldn't do that. He couldn't.

He needed to be smart.

But *fuuuck...*

When those ripples turned into pulses and her body bowed and jerked beneath him, he watched her reaction. Her mouth working open, a long wail escaping, her nails digging sharply into his back, her heels digging into his thighs, her head rolling back, her eyes fluttering. But she did it. She did what he demanded.

She kept them open and focused on him.

Unfortunately, that was his complete undoing.

He was going to unravel. Completely come apart.

He forced her to keep his eyes on him, but he couldn't do the same.

This was the last time they'd ever be together and the only time without a wrap. Every wave of orgasm that swept through her, he felt.

Her heat was like warm honey, smooth and slick surrounding him.

So, because he wasn't as strong as her, he dropped his face into her neck and grunted as nothing held him back from coming deep inside her, giving her a piece of him to hold onto.

Even if temporary.

CHAPTER SEVENTEEN

The hardest session she sat through was this morning. Her tattoo was now completed.

They were done.

With the tattoo. With each other.

That's what he wanted. That's what she had agreed to.

The two hours she'd sat in the tattoo chair with him working so intently over her belly, making sure everything was perfect, was pure torture.

Not because of the pain.

Because she had to make herself not beg. Not cry. Not plead with him.

They fit.

He'd agreed with that.

But that didn't matter.

He wasn't letting go of the foolish notion that she needed someone more appropriate for her. Younger, living a different lifestyle.

She disagreed, but she couldn't convince him.

Bikers were nothing if not stubborn as fuck. Even Crow. He

might not be the typical biker, but he was still a biker down to his roots. Down to his very soul.

She was accepted into the sisterhood.

But that wasn't enough.

She had come a long way with finding herself again and getting comfortable in her own skin.

But that wasn't enough.

She had worked hard to turn his house into a home.

But that wasn't enough.

She had told him she loved him.

But still... that was not enough.

They simply fit.

Apparently, that wasn't enough.

So, there was no point in fighting it anymore.

She came to Shadow Valley for two reasons. Hoping Crow would help her with her emotional scars and intimacy issues.

He did.

Hoping Crow would cover her physical scar. Her visible reminder.

He did.

He was done.

And so was she.

Lately, she had spent many sleepless nights wondering where to go from here. Should she return to Buffalo? Back to her parents and her dead-end job? Should she stay in Shadow Valley and take one of the many jobs she'd been offered?

Or should she just move on and start fresh elsewhere? Somewhere no one knew her past.

In the end, her decision was to stay. For now.

She didn't tell Crow because she wasn't sure how he'd feel about it, but Ace had offered her the apartment above the pawn shop. She was family and he told her he only rented to family.

She'd also accepted the job running the front office of the club's law firm with Kiki and Jayde.

She hadn't told Crow that, either.

Mostly because she'd only decided what she was going to do during her session this morning. As she watched his dark head with the long, black braid bent over her lower body, she knew she couldn't leave. So, on her way back to his house, she'd called both Ace and Kiki and accepted their offers.

She couldn't give up.

He thought they were over. She knew better.

He might be stubborn, but so was she.

She'd leave him alone and, like six years ago, if she had to, she'd watch him from afar. But she'd be close enough for him to reach out.

When he was ready.

When he finally realized age was nothing but a number and their age difference didn't define them.

They fit.

She went into his walk-in closet which was mostly empty. He wore jeans, short- and long-sleeved tees, thermals and sometimes Henleys. He had nothing to hang up. Her clothes only took up a tiny portion of the oversized space. She grabbed her overnight bag which was on the floor next to his single pair of spare boots. It took no more than a minute to pull her stuff from the hangers and tuck it into her bag.

She dumped the hamper, dropped to her knees, and sorted through the clothes, pulling her items from the pile and throwing her dirty clothes into a plastic grocery bag. As she threw his stuff back into the hamper, she hesitated on the T-shirt he'd worn the day before. She had only thrown it in there this morning before they'd left for the shop.

Her fingers smoothed out the worn, soft cotton, then she lifted it to her face and inhaled. When her eyes closed, she lost her balance and landed on her ass, the tee still clutched tightly in her hands.

She dropped her head and let the tears fall. Though she tried to stop it, a sob bubbled up anyway. And once one escaped, she couldn't fight the rest. If she was going to feel sorry for herself, she needed to just do it and get it over with.

Then move on.

Like he said.

When she had no more tears and his shirt was soaked, she shoved it into her bag.

She slowly got to her feet, sucked in a breath to bolster herself, threw the strap of her bag over her shoulder and left the closet.

Without a backward glance, she exited his bedroom, headed down the steps, grabbed her guitar, which was leaning against the wall by the front door and walked out.

The hardest session he'd ever done in his career was this morning. Her tattoo was now completed.

Her tattoo was done. They were done.

That's what he wanted. That's what she had agreed to.

Crow hit the remote and the garage door lifted, giving him a clear view of a very empty space.

His heart squeezed painfully in his chest. This was the first time in over three months that he'd come home after a long fucking day at the shop and Jazz's vehicle wasn't parked on the right side of the two-car garage.

He pulled his sled in, shut it down, and hit the remote once more. As the door rumbled to a close behind him, he stared at the oil spot left behind on the concrete floor where her piece of shit had been parked.

She needed a better vehicle. He should have seen to that before she left. He had no idea where she went, where she was headed. How far of a drive she had ahead of her.

He didn't ask.

He should've done that, too.

Instead, earlier, he'd put his head down and concentrated on finishing her tattoo and making sure it was perfect. He hadn't wanted to think about anything else while he was touching her, breathing in her scent, feeling her heat as he worked. Otherwise, he might have asked her to stay. And he had to remind himself a few times that would've been fucking selfish of him to do.

He walked down the hall from the garage to the kitchen, the house quiet, the rooms dark. He knew the way, so he didn't bother to hit the lights. Without thinking about it, he found himself standing in front of his fridge, staring into the lit interior. He eyeballed the beer she had stacked neatly on the middle shelf.

He didn't want a fucking beer.

He slammed the refrigerator door shut and went to the cabinet next to it instead. He grabbed an unopened bottle of Jack that was tucked behind an almost empty bottle of Jim Beam and he cracked it open.

Lifting it to his lips, he let the whiskey slide down his throat and warm his gut. He lifted it several more times before turning on his heel, bottle in hand.

He stopped when he noticed something on the center island. He moved over to the switch and reluctantly turned on the recessed lights.

On the counter were the remotes for both the compound gate and the garage door. Sitting next to them was his house key on top of a note handwritten in a feminine scrawl.

Thanks for everything.

His nostrils flared as he sucked in a breath and closed his eyes, but he could still see the words on that scrap of paper clearly in his head.

You're so fuckin' welcome, Kachina. Thank you for trustin' me.

He shrugged out of his cut and slipped it over the back of one of the kitchen chairs, then he took himself and his buddy Jack into the living room.

With a grunt, he dropped onto the couch, took another long

swallow before putting the bottle on the floor next to him as he unlaced his boots and kicked them off.

Then he and Jack crashed on the couch for the night.

Because there was no fucking way he was going upstairs to sleep in his cold, empty bed.

B etween one of his so-called customers tapping out halfway through the first hour of a sitting, because he was a fucking pussy, and then his last client of the night being a no-show, he'd closed up shop early and headed over to church.

Drinking alone in the dark last night had completely sucked ass.

At least if no one was drinking at church, he could head into The Iron Horse to maybe shoot a game of pool and drink with other living, breathing beings.

The talking and the typical bar sounds would fill his brain matter, fill the emptiness, unlike his silent home that now reminded him of a tomb.

Maybe he needed to move back into his room at church. There was no good reason one person needed a house like he had. None.

And church was safe enough.

Walking through the back door, he saw a couple of fresh prospects shooting pool at one of the tables. His gaze slid through them to one of the couches that lined the walls where Rig sat with one of the newer sweet butts grinding her crotch on his lap.

Rig's attention went from Cherry, who surprisingly still had on all her clothes—though probably not for long—to Crow as he strode across the common area. Rig gave him a grin and a chin lift. "Brother."

Crow returned the chin lift and answered, "Brother," but didn't slow his roll. With disappointment, he passed the deserted private bar and kept moving through the swinging doors, the large commercial kitchen, then ended up on the public side of the building, The Iron Horse Roadhouse.

For a weeknight, it wasn't real busy, but then, it was late. A couple of stragglers sat at the bar and a few more were scattered at the tables that lined the outer reinforced walls. Reinforced only after those fucking Warriors shot up the bar during their club Christmas party a few years ago.

His gaze landed on Linc, who was moving behind the bar with a draft beer in his hand. Once the younger brother slid the pint glass in front of his customer, he headed back in Crow's direction, his surprised expression on his face easy to read.

Linc stopped on the other side of the bar from him and said, "What the fuck you doin' here? You're never in here."

"Need a drink." He added "need company" silently.

Linc cocked a brow, but after a moment, just nodded and asked, "Beer?"

Crow shook his head. "Gimme the strong shit. Straight. Neat."

Linc's brow cocked again. "Aren't you on your sled?"

"Yep. Still got a room upstairs, though." He'd kept the room because on the occasions he needed pussy, that's where he'd take them. He never brought any of them home and no one but Jazz had ever been in his bed there.

Only her.

Linc stared at him for another long moment, then moved away, grabbing a glass and a bottle off the top shelf. Jack Daniel's Single Barrel. The good shit.

Crow watched Linc pour him three fingers-worth. Then, before putting the bottle back up, he grabbed a second glass and poured another three.

When Linc was done he moved back to Crow, who'd settled his ass onto one of the bar stools.

Crow jerked his chin toward both glasses. Linc shrugged.

"Said you needed a drink. I'll join you since the crowd's light right now. Jester's in the back taking inventory if I need him."

Crow lifted his glass and took a mouthful, appreciating the heat when it hit his gut. Linc did the same but watched Crow carefully as he did so.

"Have a feeling I know why you're here," Linc said, after swiping the back of his hand over his mouth and setting his glass on the bar top.

"Yeah, why's that?" Crow asked his whiskey.

"'Cause you pushed your fuckin' woman away and it's fuckin' killing you."

"She ain't—"

"The fuck she isn't. Remember all those words you had for me about Jayde? All that shit you said, telling me to get my head outta my ass?"

"I didn't—"

Linc shook his head. "The fuck you didn't." He grunted and finished swallowing the amber liquid in his glass before slamming it onto the bar. "Brother, can't believe I'm giving you advice this time. Usually it's the other way around."

"Ain't here for advice," Crow grumbled, then downed half his whiskey before meeting Linc's gaze head-on. "I'm older than you—"

Linc interrupted him again. "Yeah, no shit, you're older. Who fuckin' cares? But you're also a fuckin' fool."

Crow's spine snapped straight, and he pulled back his shoulders as he glanced at the man he'd put forward as a prospect for the club what seemed like forever ago.

"Mister *I'm-older-and-wiser* did something stupid," Linc continued. He planted both palms on the bar and leaned toward Crow. "That woman fuckin' loves you."

Hold up. How the fuck did Linc know that? "She told you?"

"Brother, she told the sisterhood. You instantly went from the most loved to the most hated. They're all royally pissed that your ass didn't change your mind about your little deal. You go touching my woman or any of them, don't be surprised if they knee you right in the fuckin' nuts."

Crow's hand automatically dropped to his balls, but he managed not to wince. After a second, he muttered, "Want what's best for 'er."

"Doesn't that sound fuckin' familiar," Linc grumbled, grabbing the bottle from the upper shelf again and pouring himself another double and adding another couple of fingers-worth to Crow's half-empty glass.

"For such a wise soul, never heard you be so fuckin' stupid. But then that seems to be a pattern for us when we find the right one. Brother, *you* are what's best for her. We all saw her when she rolled back into town. And we've all seen her recently. Two fuckin' totally different people."

Crow tilted his head to stare at Linc. "When d'you last see 'er?"

"Today. When I went to bring them their order of Bangin' Burgers."

"Them who?"

Linc rolled his eyes and crossed his muscular arms over his equally muscular chest. Slade wasn't the only one who'd been working out a lot recently. "My ol' lady, Keeks and Jazz."

Crow's head snapped up. "What the fuck are you talkin' about?"

Linc did a slow blink and something crossed his face that Crow didn't like.

He leaned over the bar toward Linc and growled, "What the fuck are you talkin' about?" again.

"She didn't tell you?"

"Tell me what?"

"She took Jayde's old job at Keeks' law firm."

Jesus. He assumed she'd left town. "When did that happen?"

"Today."

"No. When did she take the fuckin' job?"

"Jayde said she finally called Kiki yesterday to let her know."

"Keeks offered her a job?"

"A while ago. Jayde said just about everyone offered her a damn job. Everyone wants her to stay in the Valley." He frowned. "Think you're the only stupid fuck who wanted Jazz to go."

He didn't *want* her to go.

He stared at his full glass. Instead of picking it up, he pushed it away. She took a job with Kiki. That meant she planned on staying in town.

That was not good.

No, that was fucking bullshit.

That meant she'd be nearby, within reach. Most likely attending club activities and hanging with the DAMC women.

How the fuck was he supposed to resist her when she was so fucking close?

"Assuming she didn't tell you she moved above the pawn shop, either."

Fuck no, she didn't.

It was like everyone in the club was conspiring against him. Ace. Kiki. Linc.

Who knew who else?

Probably even Diamond. Goddamn it.

Crow slowly lifted his gaze from his untouched whiskey and frowned at Linc.

"Not sure why your fuckin' ass is still on that stool. But I know what the hell you'd say if our positions were switched," Linc grumbled.

When Crow reached for his glass, Linc was faster, snagging it and putting it below the bar.

"On your sled," Linc reminded him. "Not doing your woman any good if you dump your bike and crack your noggin open on your way over to get her ass and take her home."

"Sometimes you just need a fuckin' pop in the mouth," Crow muttered.

Linc grinned. "Yeah, and it ain't gonna be from you. You

know what the fuck is right. Known you long enough that you only wanna do what's right."

"Leavin' her be is what's right."

Linc shook his head, still wearing that grin that Crow wanted to wipe off his face. "I fuckin' swear, that's the first time I've ever heard you be wrong." Linc was brave enough to lean over the bar toward him again. He got right in Crow's face. "Think that woman cares you're fuckin' forty? Nobody gives a shit. She certainly doesn't. You're just dealing with a fuckin' number, while I had to deal with Axel, Z and, for fuck's sake, Mitch of all fuckin' people. Coulda ended up dead with a bullet between my eyes. The only thing you're gonna be dealing with is gray hairs on your wrinkled-assed balls. Here's an easy fuckin' solution: shave 'em."

"Kids," Crow muttered.

Linc tilted his head. "What about 'em?"

"She might want 'em."

Linc shrugged. "Gray hairs on your nut sac ain't gonna make you shoot blanks."

Crow gritted his teeth before saying, "Not sure if I want 'em."

Linc snorted. "Right. Every time one of our women becomes knocked up, you're all over that shit. Touching them, feeling the kid move. Driving all the brothers crazy with that touchy-feely shit."

That wasn't a lie.

He pictured Jazz pregnant with his kid. Her belly with that newly finished tattoo he designed special for her rounded with his future.

An invisible band tightened around his chest as he slid off the stool to his feet.

"See? The good thing about her being younger is she can give you a dozen before you croak of old age. So there you go."

A dozen. *Fuck.*

He'd be happy with one.

Hell, maybe two. A boy and a girl.

What the fuck was he thinking?

Why the fuck was he still standing there?

Linc glanced at the clock that was hidden under the bar. "Well, look at the fuckin' time."

"What time is it?"

"Time for you to get your ass over to her apartment and go claim your woman."

"Asshole," Crow grumbled as he spun on his heels and headed back through the bar, listening to Linc laugh his ass off behind him.

CHAPTER EIGHTEEN

J azz jerked upright in bed. She heard weird noises again which she suspected was because it was only her second night in her new apartment. She figured it would take a while before she got used to them, especially since she never lived alone before.

She heard another noise, louder this time.

That wasn't the automatic ice maker or the air conditioning kicking on. Hell no, it wasn't.

Her heart began to pound as loudly as the pounding on the front door.

With her hand at her throat, she grabbed her cell phone and looked at the time. 11:47. Why would someone be beating on her door at that hour?

With trembling fingers, she clutched the phone to her chest and climbed out of bed, listening carefully.

There it was again. More pounding.

Then a voice.

Male.

Holy shit.

Taking her phone with her, she moved quickly through the

small furnished apartment, but hesitated at the front door. Stepping on tiptoes, she looked through the peephole, dropped back to her heels, then spun around and leaned against the door, trying to catch her breath.

Why was he out there?

"*Kachina*," he yelled through the door before pounding once more.

Shit. Was he mad she moved out leaving only a note?

She wasn't going to find out until she opened the damn door. She blew out a shaky breath and turned to slide the chain open, then twist the deadbolt.

Before she was even done, the door burst open, making her quickly step back.

He pushed inside and took his time redoing what she had just undone. When he turned, he glanced around the dark apartment, then his eyes landed on her. "What are you doin' here?"

"Doing what you wanted me to do. Moving on." She had to bite her bottom lip so she wouldn't add "duh" to the end of that.

"No."

"Yes, Crow. You said we were done when my tattoo was finished. *You* said that I needed to move on."

"Not here."

She frowned. "Are you saying this isn't far enough away?"

"No."

No, she wasn't far enough away? Or no, that wasn't what he was saying? She went with the second option. "Then what?"

"It's too far."

Jazz blinked and stepped back from him. "Unlike the rest of the brothers, you usually know how to use your words. Will you please use them to explain what the fuck you're talking about?" When he took a step forward, she took another one back.

"It's not safe for you here."

He took another step forward and she took a third one back. "What do you mean? The Warriors are done."

"An' that might be true, but still not safe."

What was he getting at? Her eyebrows knitted together. Did he know something she didn't? "Why?"

"Never know who's out there."

Her eyes slid to the closed and now locked door, then back to him. Since it was still dark in the apartment, she couldn't see his eyes clearly, but she felt them on her. "Where will I be safe?" The question came out in a whisper because she knew the answer. She just wanted to hear it come from him.

"In the compound."

Was he going to resist the truth to the very end? "I can't afford a place there."

"Not your own place."

Holy shit, she was about to pull her hair out. Or his. Which if she did the second one, the DAMC women would probably stone her to death. "Then whose?"

"Mine."

Her pulse began to race. If he wasn't going to make this whole thing easy, then neither was she. No fucking way. "You wanted me to move on. I told you I would."

"You also told me you loved me."

She smiled. "Yeah?"

She could see his grin, even in the limited light when he said, "Yeah."

Nope. Not making it easy. "And that changed what?"

"That changed everything, *Kachina*."

Instead of stepping back, this time she stepped forward. "Just those three words?"

He stayed in place, planting his feet. "No. Not the words."

She took another step forward. "Then what?"

"We fit."

Her smile widened. "Sounds familiar."

"Was fuckin' stupid."

"Yep," she agreed, trying not to let her smile get too big as she stepped even closer, until her body was pressed to his. She slipped a hand under his cut and fisted his T-shirt.

His long fingers traced her jawline, then he cupped her cheek. "When I said 'me, too,' I meant it."

"I know you did, but that's not the way to tell me."

His lips twitched. "It ain't?"

"No, there are much better ways."

His mouth twitched again. "You got a list?"

"I can make one if you need it."

"Pretty sure I can figure it out on my own."

"Good."

"No, baby, it's gonna be a whole helluvalot better than good."

"So glad you finally see that."

She squealed when he squatted just enough to scoop her up in his arms. Then she laughed as she wrapped her arms around his neck as he took determined strides down the short hallway to the only bedroom in the apartment.

As he carried her into the room, she reached out and hit the light, then squealed again when he threw her on the bed.

She was still bouncing as he began stripping himself of his boots. When he straightened, he froze. "You steal my shirt?"

She ran a hand over his pilfered T-shirt. "It was only fair."

"Why?"

"Because you stole my heart."

It took him about thirty seconds flat to yank off the rest of his clothes, then he was on the bed, naked, stalking toward her on his hands and knees, his golden skin gleaming under the light, his almost-black eyes heated.

"No, baby, you got that backwards."

"I do?" She laughed as he climbed up her body, until his lips were just above hers.

"Fuck yeah. You stole mine the second I saw you dancin' an' singin' across Hawk's living room. Shoulda known I was fucked that very second."

"Just like I'll be fucked in the next few?"

Suddenly, the air changed, his smile disappeared and his dark eyes became serious. "Love you, *Kachina*. You're my fuckin' heart an' soul."

Took him long enough to realize it, but she kept that to herself. Instead she said, "Love you, too, Crow. You're my everything. Now stop talking and show me how much you love me."

He did.

And she got to watch it all in that mirror above the bed.

She'd have to recommend them getting one of their own.

EPILOGUE

"Baby."

Crow glanced over his shoulder. He had a three o'clock appointment with a new client, but he'd been in the back taking inventory for a while now, so maybe he'd lost track of time.

He placed the clipboard on the shelf. He'd finish inventory later. Turning, he let his eyes travel over Jazz's hair, which was now completely back to her own natural color and also long enough to sweep over her shoulders. Then his gaze wandered lower.

She had a lot more curves than a year ago. And there was a good reason for it.

Her hand was pressed to her belly and he smiled. "You okay?"

"Yeah, he's a bit active today."

He moved across the storeroom floor and when he reached where she was leaning against the door frame, he dropped to one knee, lifted her maternity blouse and pressed his lips to her tattoo which was now stretched across her tight skin.

After laying a line of kisses along her belly, he stood and dropped one more kiss on Jazz's parted lips.

"You scare me every time you go down on one knee."

He tilted his head, pretending he didn't know why. "Why?"

"Because I keep thinking you're going to pull out a ring."

Little did she know, he did have a ring. But the last place he was going to give it to her was in his shop. He was also waiting for the perfect time. He just wasn't sure when that would be. Though, preferably before the birth of their first child who was due in about two months. No matter what, it wasn't today.

No, today he had a client that not only wanted a big piece done, Crow had no idea what that piece was.

If the guy thought he was going to start it today, he was dead wrong. Crow didn't rush any of his work. He was meticulous and a perfectionist. That's why he was one of the best ink slingers in the state.

"You wanna ring?"

She shook her head. "I don't need one. I have you." Her hand dropped to her belly again. "And soon, him. Plus, you claimed me as your ol' lady. If it's good enough for some of the sisters, it's good enough for me."

"You sure?"

When her eyes slid to the side to avoid his, he knew she was lying.

He shrugged. "Okay. Good enough for you. Good enough for me."

Her lips flattened out and he fought to keep his from tipping upward.

He reached out, curled his fingers around the back of her neck and pulled her into him before dropping a kiss on her forehead. "So, are you horny or hungry?"

"Both. But that's not why I came to find you."

"Damn," he whispered.

"There's a... a *guy* out front waiting for you."

"Probably my three o'clock."

"Yeah, maybe. But..." She pursed her lips, then shot a glance over her shoulder.

He tilted his head again as he stared down into her conflicted expression. "But what?"

"I think he's a biker."

"Okay?"

"He's wearing colors."

Crow lifted his head and looked over Jazz toward the front of the shop with a frown. "Did he say anything to you?"

"Only that he was looking for you."

With a nod, Crow released her and pushed past her to head out of the storeroom. When he hit the brightly lit shop, there was no doubt his three o'clock was a biker.

But he was wearing colors Crow never saw before.

Since he was staring out of the front picture window, Crow could clearly read the back of his cut.

The top rocker said: BLOOD FURY

The bottom said: PENNSYLVANIA

The center insignia was of a skull and crossbones, with red blood dripping out of the eye sockets and mouth. To the right of that was "MC" in a smaller square patch.

The man turned when he noticed Crow's reflection in the glass.

Crow's eyes dropped to the worn and discolored rectangular patch that read "President." Below that was the patch stating the biker wearing the cut's name was "Buck."

The man noticed what Crow was staring at and covered the patch with his hand. "No. Ain't me. Name's Trip."

Was he a wanna-be biker and bought an old cut at a yard sale or some such shit? "Who's Buck?"

"Was my pop."

"Why you wearin' his colors?"

Trip tucked his thumbs into his front jeans' pockets and just that little movement pushed his cut back enough that Crow noticed a semi-automatic handgun tucked in his waistband. "They're mine now."

Crow watched the man cautiously as he asked, "You take him out?"

"No, took himself out. Long time ago, doing somethin' stupid."

Crow wanted to check where Jazz was, but he refused to unglue his eyes from the stranger in front of him. "Whataya here for?'

"Want my colors inked on my back. Everyone says you're the best. 'Specially at that."

"Yeah, but it's gonna take more than one sittin'."

Trip shrugged his broad shoulders. "Got plenty of time."

"Where'd the rest of your brothers get theirs done?"

"No others. Just me." Trip pursed his lips. "For now. Club's been disbanded for more than a couple decades. Time to resurrect it."

"Club's just gotta start with one."

"True. An' that one is me. So you willin' to do a brother a solid?"

"Long as you ain't comin' to encroach on our territory, then yeah. But gotta draw up a sketch first."

"Whatever you draw up, you need to keep on hand. 'Cause there's gonna be more of us."

Crow stared at the man in front of him. He seemed decent enough but never judge a biker by his fucking looks.

They just rid themselves of the Warriors, last thing the DAMC needed was another outlaw club trying to shoulder in on their town. Or their businesses. Or their fucking women.

That decades-long war was over, nobody was ready for another one.

Crow lifted his chin toward a bench he had along one of the walls. "Need your cut so I can start drawin'. Have a seat an' relax while I get shit to do that."

Trip nodded, shrugged out of his cut, handing it to Crow and then headed to the bench.

Once the stranger was sitting, Crow relaxed a bit and turned to see Jazz standing behind his counter. He headed back toward the storeroom, the man's cut in his hand and jerked his head when he approached Jazz, indicating she needed to follow him into the back.

She did. One good thing about his ol' lady was she did not give him a bunch of shit like the rest of the women did with their ol' men. And thank fuck for that.

Once they hit the back, Crow lowered his voice. "*Kachina*, call Z. Have him an' Diesel stop over here. Yeah?"

"Okaaaay," Jazz drew out, then placed her palm on his gut, looking up at him with eyes full of concern. "You sure he's safe?"

"Yeah, think so. He's a fuckin' MC of one. Unless he's lyin'. Want you to head home, too."

"Crow," she said, shaking her head.

"*Kachina*, gotta make sure you an' the kid are safe. Got me?"

"And what about you? I don't want to leave you here alone. Can I wait until Z and D show up?"

Crow glanced back toward the shop. "No. Want you to go home as soon as you call Z. Don't give me lip about it."

Jazz frowned.

He gave her a reassuring smile and touched his lips lightly to hers. "Love you, baby. And one of the reasons is, you don't give me shit. Yeah?"

Jazz nodded. "Yeah." She sighed. "Fine. I'll call them and then head home. Can you check in with me, please?"

Crow gave her a smile. "Promise." He placed his hand over her stomach. "Go home an' take care of the hungry part, an' when I get home, I'll take care of the horny part."

"Promise?"

He dropped his head and gave her a longer kiss this time. He pulled away just enough to say, "Fuck yeah, I promise."

"Okay," she breathed. As she headed toward the back door to where her new SUV was parked, she threw over her shoulder, "Love you."

"Love you, too, *Kachina*."

Crow waited until the back door shut then headed back out
into the shop.

———

Forty-five minutes later, Crow paused while filling his ink
cups. He had the outline drawn up for the piece and had
applied the pattern to Trip's back. The man now lay face down
on the tattoo chair. Crow had blocked out four hours for this
appointment so he figured he'd at least get the outline started
while the man was in town.

He glanced over his shoulder as he heard a couple sleds with
straight pipes pull up out front. Through the large window he
saw Z and Slade dismounting from their Harleys and coming
into the shop, their bodies tight, their eyes wary.

Both sets of eyes landed on Crow, slid to the man in the
chair, then to the cut that had been left on the bench, colors
facing out.

Zak's smooth swagger hitched a little as he read the back of
the vest. And Slade came to a complete stop.

Slade's dark brown eyes landed on Trip once more. "For
fuck's sake," he shouted.

Crow froze as Trip planted his palms on the chair and pushed
up into a seated position, facing the three of them.

"Holy motherfuckin' shit," Trip responded, then got to
his feet.

Crow rolled his stool back, giving the man some space, not
sure what the fuck was going on.

Trip jerked his chin up. "You an Angel?"

A huge smile crossed Slade's face. "Fuck yeah. You still a big
piece of shit?"

Trip's smile matched Slade's. "Fuck yeah. Never thought
you'd land anywhere other than underground."

Slade laughed. "Nope. Still fuckin' standin' on two feet with
my dick in my hand." They moved toward each other, clasped

palms and bumped shoulders. As soon as they separated, Slade
went over to the man's cut and picked it up to turn it around.
"Buck?"

"Yeah," Trip answered.

Zak stood to the side observing both men with a deep frown
on his face and a hand on his hip, but said nothing, letting shit
play out. Which was smart. It was a good way to find out info
without having to ask a lot of questions.

"Why you carryin' around your old man's cut?" Slade asked,
his brows dropping low.

"Mine now."

Slade's expression got serious. "What the fuck you talkin'
'bout?"

"Gonna get the club rollin' again."

Slade's mouth turned down even farther. "Club's got bad
blood, brother. Bad fuckin' luck. You sure you wanna do that?
You wanna be in a club, we're always acceptin' good prospects."
Slade turned to Z to explain, "Trip an' I served together."

Now it made sense how they knew each other. Not because
Slade's pop was a Warrior. Thank fuck. It was the Marines
which connected them, not both being born from outlaw
blood.

"Woulda recruited your ass to join me, but looks like you're
settled here?"

It should have been a statement, and Crow didn't like the
way Trip ended it as a question instead. Almost as if he was
hoping Slade wasn't settled. That made the hair on the back of
his neck stand up.

Slade's gaze slid through Crow then landed on Zak, when he
said, "Yeah. Got it good." He turned his attention back to Trip.
"Got an ol' lady an' a fuckin' son now."

Trip's eyebrows rose. "No fuckin' way."

"Yeah. Hudson. Future fuckin' Angel. Not plannin' on goin'
anywhere any time soon."

"Or ever," Crow muttered.

Slade's eyes slid back to Crow, but Diamond's ol' man didn't say anything.

Slade needed to stick in the Valley where he now belonged. There was no way he was taking Crow's godson and Diamond anywhere.

The brother came into the Valley as a rolling stone, but he settled nicely. The DAMC was his family now. He had his woman, his kid and ran a successful business, Shadow Valley Fitness, with Diamond. Crow had also inked their club colors into the skin of his back.

He was fucking going nowhere.

Zak stepped closer to the two of them. "My brother mentioned your club had bad blood. Sure you want to resurrect it? Like Slade said, we're always lookin' for quality prospects. Our club's financially stable. Got good businesses. Good things happenin' all 'round. The DAMC's solid as fuck."

"Appreciate the offer. But wanna give it a go."

"Whatcha got left to work with, Trip?" Slade asked. "Got any members? A clubhouse?"

Trip shook his head, his long dark blonde hair brushing his bare shoulders. While he was muscled, he wasn't as heavily muscled as Slade. But then a lot of men weren't. The man also had no tattoos Crow could see with just his shirt off. That first one Crow was going to ink into his skin was going to be one fucking rude awakening when they finally got down to business.

"Got nothin' but my granddaddy's place, a fuckin' barn full of farm equipment that I have no fuckin' clue how to work, and a run-down warehouse just outside of Manning Grove."

Slade nodded. "Out of the ashes rises the Phoenix. You wanna be that Phoenix."

"Fuck yeah," Trip murmured. "Need something to call my own."

"How you gonna support this fuckin' club?" Z asked. "Sounds like you're startin' from scratch."

Trip eyeballed Z's front patches, then he lifted his gaze and met Zak's directly. "Didn't come down here just for the ink. You got a good rep. Was hopin' you got some worthy advice for a fucker like me."

Zak tilted his head and studied the man for a long minute before saying, "Could carve out some time for a little sit-down."

"Would appreciate it."

Z nodded. "Will call my executive committee an' set up a meet. Got a spare room above church if you wanna crash for the night once you're done here with Crow."

Crow watched the surprise cross Trip's face at the offer. "He's trustin' you only 'cause of Slade. Don't fuckin' do anythin' to break that trust," Crow warned him. "Got me?"

Trip stared at Crow for only a few seconds before nodding. "Yeah. Got you." He turned to Z. "Thanks, brother. Appreciate it an' will take you up on your offer."

Slade turned to their club prez. "I'll stick here an' then take him over to The Iron Horse for a drink an' set 'im up at church for the night. Yeah?"

"Yeah. I'll set the meetin' up in the meantime. Meet you at church later." With that, Z turned and headed back toward the exit. Just before walking out of the door, he flicked two fingers over his shoulder.

When the door shut behind Zak, Crow smiled. No matter what Z endured over the years—prison, the Warriors, Pierce being a traitor, even his own blood turning on him—their president's goal had always been to make the DAMC prosperous, keep the club above board (for the most part) and turn it into a big fucking family that had each other's support and loyalty.

Crow had to admit, the man had been successful at all of that.

Even if their "family" was dysfunctional as fuck.

But, hell, they could all live with that. And they happily did.

As Crow turned back to look at Trip, The Blood Fury MC's current president and sole member, he sure hoped like hell that the man heeded Z's advice.

If not... Crow shook his head and silently wished him fucking luck.

**Turn the page to read a special note from the author and
a sneak peek of
Guts & Glory: Mercy
(In the Shadows Security, Book 1)**

AUTHOR'S NOTE

Thank you, readers, for coming along on this journey with me. Crow's book is the last book in the Down & Dirty: Dirty Angels MC series. It's been a helluva ride and I never expected the members of this MC to be so loved.

However, don't despair, you'll see more of the DAMC in the near future. Diesel and Jewel will appear the upcoming Guts & Glory series. The first book in that series will feature Mercy and then the rest of D's Shadows will each have their own book. Expect cameos of the DAMC members in those books, too.

After that, Trip's story will be the first book in my all-new MC series: Blood & Bones: Blood Fury MC! That club will be based just outside of Manning Grove, PA, where my Brothers in Blue series was based. So expect to see the Bryson brothers (Max, Marc and Matt) as well as TEDDY showing up in that series. And I will also have a few more surprises for not only you, but for my characters!

Once again, thank you for being a part of this family and loving my boys (as well as their women) as much as I do. I hope you'll come along for the next journey. Happy reading!

I also have to do a BIG shout-out to all of my peeps in my FB readers group: Jeanne St. James' Down & Dirty Book Crew. They are all supportive and we have a lot of fun. Come join us!

Turn the page to read a sneak peek of Guts & Glory: Mercy (In the Shadows Security, Book 1)

GUTS & GLORY: MERCY

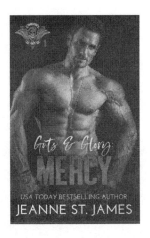

**Turn the page for a sneak peek of
Guts & Glory: Mercy
(In the Shadows Security, Book 1)**

SNEAK PEAK OF GUTS & GLORY: MERCY (UNEDITED)

"Justice is for those who deserve it; mercy is for those who don't." -
Woodrow Kroll

Chapter One

With his fingers curled around her delicate skin and the fragile frame of her neck, he increased the pressure.

"Harder! Do it harder," she hissed at him.

Mercy had a feeling she wasn't talking about fucking her. Fuck no, she was one of "those."

His grip twitched but he didn't do as she demanded, instead he pretended to misunderstand her and slammed his cock deeper. His pounding rhythm became mindless. Because that's what she was, just another mindless fuck.

One that had a freaky side, though.

He seemed to attract those types of bitches.

Random snatch he picked up at the bar. A woman who saw him as a freak and had someone like him on her sexual bucket list.

Or one who thought they could bring the life back to his eyes. They saw him as a challenge.

Those he tried to avoid since they became the challenge. Scraping them off at the end of the night.

But nights like this were typical for him. Him doing the using, and him being used.

Just busting a nut into some—what the DAMC brothers called—"strange."

No numbers exchanged.

No after-fuck cuddling.

No deep conversation.

Hell, he didn't even bother to ask their names.

And if they asked him, he just told them his name was John.

It didn't matter if he was John, Joe or Jack. They just wanted to fuck a cold-hearted, dead-eyed, scarred freak.

They got off on that shit. And he let them for the moments it took for him to get off.

Then it was over.

A few nights later it would happen again. New night, new woman.

Rinse. Repeat.

But the one he was sliding his dick into now?

Fuck. Total fucking freak.

He realized she was still talking. Why didn't she shut the fuck up?

"C'mon. Show me what you got! Don't be a pussy. You look like you'd like it rough. Squeeze harder."

Mercy adjusted his grip on her neck, his fingers curling tighter into her flesh, and he pumped his hips faster and harder.

She was just a "her" to him because if she had told him her name at the bar earlier, he hadn't listened. Or even fucking cared.

"Pretend I'm the enemy, soldier, and your life's on the line."

Yeah, bitch, if you were, you wouldn't be breathing or yapping those flapping gums.

"That's it, fucker. Give it to me like you mean it."

He did his best not to sigh out loud.

"Fuck me while you tell me how you got those nasty scars. I want to hear every detail."

Since she could still talk, he apparently wasn't squeezing quite hard enough.

But choking her out or telling her about his past was never going to happen. Just like he was never going to end up in this bitch's bed again.

Suddenly, out of nowhere, she just out and out clocked him right in the face.

His head jerked back, and his body went solid. His hips stilled, and his eyes met hers.

Her blue eyes surrounded in thick mascara widened, and her red lipsticked mouth became slack. He dropped his gaze to his fingers and realized he'd finally done what she asked for. Only now, he could see the fear in her expression.

Total fucking panic.

A gurgle bubbled up. He willed his fingers to release her and, luckily for her, his brain was still connected to his digits. He pulled out, rolled away from her, yanked off the condom and threw it on her now heaving stomach. He sat on the edge of the bed, a chill sweeping through him at how close she came to dying.

He would have killed her and not had a second thought about it.

Her voice was raspy when she demanded, "What are you doing? We didn't finish!"

Mercy scrubbed a hand over his short hair.

"I'm not done, you... you monster!"

"You're done," he growled without looking at her.

"No, I'm not."

He pushed to his feet, found his pile of clothes and methodically pulled them on, making sure his knife was still in the back pocket of his jeans and his .38 still tucked in his boot.

He strapped on the ankle holster after yanking his jeans up over his hips.

Mercy ignored her sitting up in bed, glaring at him.

"Are you seriously leaving?"

He ignored that, too.

"Why are you taking what I said personal?"

He concentrated on lacing up his boots.

"Hey! I can have any guy I want!" She screamed as he straightened and focused on the door to his freedom. "Asshole! You ugly-ass freak! It was only a pity fuck!"

A few strides later, he was out her apartment door and jogging down the steps. At the bottom of the stairs he hooked a right and saw his true love waiting for him under the halogen light.

His Harley. A Jag Jamison custom he paid a fortune for. But his sled was more steadfast and loyal than any female.

The only thing he appreciated more than his bike was his Terradyne Gurkha RPV. Every time he drove that sweet bitch, he got a hard-on.

And so did other men just looking at it.

He had needed to relieve some tension tonight. Forget another female he'd had on the brain lately. One who would never be his.

Normally, there'd be two ways to relieve his pent-up frustration.

A round with the punching bag or fucking. Tonight, the fucking didn't work since his balls were still heavy and in need of some relief. So, he now had only one other option.

His fists.

———

With a grunt, he struck the well-used, patched-up heavy bag that hung in a dark corner of the warehouse as hard as he could.

He adjusted his stance and punched it again. Sweat dripped

off his brow, soaked his sleeveless tee both front and back, and spotted the concrete floor beneath him.

The exertion was just what he needed to get that bitch's face and words out of his head. He needed to stop picking up females in bars and start looking elsewhere.

He just didn't know where.

He thought of Jazz and how he would've stopped his midnight trolling for her. But Crow had claimed her before he could, and the brother wasn't giving her up without a fight.

Not that Mercy blamed him.

He had that in his bed, he wouldn't give her up without a fight, either. Fuck the fight, there would be total devastation before Mercy'd let anyone else have her.

But Crow won her. Crow deserved her.

Crow was right for her.

He saw it clearly now.

Not that he liked the outcome.

His lip curled, and, with a grunt, he pounded the bag with a quick jab right, quickly followed by a left uppercut.

One of the overhead halogens lit up and Mercy winced at the sudden brightness until his eyes adjusted. Once they did, he saw his boss lumbering in his direction. And like normal, he wasn't alone.

His newest baby, Indigo, was tucked within his arms. That man did not go anywhere without one of his two baby girls glued to him. He took their safety to the extreme.

He pitied any guy wanting to date them when they got old enough.

"Brother," D's deep grumble was low, probably so he wouldn't wake Indie up. His dark eyes slid to the bag, then to Mercy's hands.

Mercy glanced down at his clenched fists. He hadn't bother to wrap them and now his knuckles were raw and bloody. Even a bit swollen.

He looked over his shoulder. The bag had blood smeared on it.

"I'll clean it up, boss," he muttered.

"Ain't out here to talk about that." He adjusted Indie in his arms. "Got a job for you."

Thank fuck.

"Need to stay busy, D. This down time's getting me torqued."

"Know it. Know why. Got it."

"Right. So, what is it?" When Diesel hesitated, Mercy frowned. "Don't tell me it's another douchebag football player. I'm not a fuckin' babysitter."

"No."

"An entitled celeb who shits out gold turds and has an assistant who wipes his ass?"

"No."

Mercy's buzz of getting an assignment quickly turned to shit. "I'm not liking this."

"Got a package for you to move."

"From where?"

"Vegas."

His jaw tightened. He fucking hated Vegas. A city of greed and overindulge. Too many damn people, the press of bodies, the lights, the noise, the non-stop action. Good place to blend in. Bad place for his head.

"Delivered to where?"

"Safe house."

His brows raised. "We don't have a safe house."

"Not ours."

"Whose?'

"Rich fucker. Got one set up. Get the package, deliver her to the house, an' then go from there."

"Her?" *Fuck.* "Send Steel."

D shook his head. "Sendin' you."

"He's up for the next babysitting job."

"It's yours."

Mercy's jaw got even tighter. He forced himself to ask, "This have to do with the shit that went down with Jazz?"

D cocked a brow at him.

Fuck. It was.

"Is she the rich fucker's piece?"

"Don't know. Don't fuckin' care. Payin' big. Just gotta keep her safe 'til he handles the threat."

He handles the threat? "So, we don't even get a piece of the fun?'

"Ain't getting' paid for that. They wanna pay for that, you get a piece of it."

"What's the threat?"

"Soon as I get that shit, gonna email it to you."

Mercy snorted and cocked a brow at D.

"Jewelee's gonna email it to you."

That was more like it.

But even so, he wasn't liking this at all. Walking into a job without all the details prior?

"When?"

"Soon as she gets it."

"No, when do I have to fly out?"

"Tomorrow, first thing. Gonna set you up at one of his casinos for the night 'til we get the details an' further instructions. Got me?"

He was liking this job less and less. "Fucker owns casinos?"

"Fucker owns a lot of shit. Sure a lot of his businesses ain't legit."

"So, this job is a possible dirty side piece?"

"Or main piece. Who fuckin' knows. Who fuckin' cares? Keep her ass safe. Bonus in it for you at the end if you keep it 'er in one piece. You don't, we still get paid. But the bonus might be worth you keepin' her breathin'."

"I can do whatever I need to to protect her, right?"

D smiled. "Yep."

Mercy smiled, too. Maybe this job wouldn't be so bad. How

hard was it to watch one female and deliver her breathing at the end of the job?

Diesel's nostrils suddenly flared, then his face twisted. "Fuck," he muttered, staring down at his daughter.

A second later, Mercy caught a whiff of what he was smelling. "Fuck," he agreed.

"Gotta find Jewelee."

Mercy pinned his lips together as he watched D, his biker boss and the Sergeant at Arms for the Dirty Angel MC, lumber back toward where he came from.

Then he realized he never asked how long this job was going to take.

Fuck.

GUTS & GLORY SERIES

COMING SOON!

Want to read more about Diesel's "Shadows?"

Keep an eye out in 2019 for the spin-off series starring the hard-core former special ops crew of
In the Shadows Security:

Mercy
Ryder
Walker
Hunter
Steel
Brick

And learn how they earned their call names.
More information coming soon!
www.jeannestjames.com

IF YOU ENJOYED THIS BOOK

Thank you for reading Down & Dirty: Crow. If you enjoyed Crow and Jayde's story, please consider leaving a review at your favorite retailer and/or Goodreads to let other readers know. Reviews are always appreciated and just a few words can help an independent author like me tremendously!

Want to read a sample of my work? Download a sampler book here: BookHip.com/MTQQKK

ALSO BY JEANNE ST. JAMES

Made Maleen: A Modern Twist on a Fairy Tale

Damaged

Rip Cord: The Complete Trilogy

Brothers in Blue Series:

(Can be read as standalones)

Brothers in Blue: Max

Brothers in Blue: Marc

Brothers in Blue: Matt

Teddy: A Brothers in Blue Novelette

The Dare Ménage Series:

(Can be read as standalones)

Double Dare

Daring Proposal

Dare to Be Three

A Daring Desire

Dare to Surrender

The Obsessed Novellas:

(All the novellas in this series are standalones)

Forever Him

Only Him

Needing Him

Loving Her

Temping Him

AUDIO BOOKS BY JEANNE ST. JAMES

The following books are available in audio!
Down & Dirty: Zak (Dirty Angels MC, bk 1)
Down & Dirty: Jag (Dirty Angels MC, bk 2)
Down & Dirty: Hawk (Dirty Angels MC, bk 3)
Down & Dirty: Diesel (Dirty Angels MC, bk 4)
Down & Dirty: Axel (Dirty Angels MC, bk 5)
Down & Dirty: Slade (Dirty Angels MC, bk 6)
Forever Him (An Obsessed Novella)
Rip Cord: The Complete Trilogy
Damaged
Double Dare (The Dare Menage Series, bk 1)
Daring Proposal (The Dare Menage Series, bk 2)

Coming soon:
Dare to be Three (The Dare Menage Series, bk 3)
The Brothers in Blue Series
Down & Dirty: Dawg (Dirty Angels MC, Bk 7)

ABOUT THE AUTHOR

JEANNE ST. JAMES is a USA Today bestselling romance author who loves an alpha male (or two). She was only thirteen when she started writing and her first paid published piece was an erotic story in Playgirl magazine. Her first erotic romance novel, Banged Up, was published in 2009. She is happily owned by farting French bulldogs. She writes M/F, M/M, and M/M/F ménages.

Want to read a sample of her work? Download a sampler book here: BookHip.com/MTQQKK

To keep up with her busy release schedule check her website at www.jeannestjames.com or sign up for her newsletter: http://www.jeannestjames.com/newslettersignup

www.jeannestjames.com
jeanne@jeannestjames.com

Blog: http://jeannestjames.blogspot.com
Newsletter: http://www.jeannestjames.com/newslettersignup
Jeanne's Down & Dirty Book Crew:
https://www.facebook.com/groups/JeannesReviewCrew/

facebook.com/JeanneStJamesAuthor

twitter.com/JeanneStJames

amazon.com/author/jeannestjames

instagram.com/JeanneStJames

bookbub.com/authors/jeanne-st-james

goodreads.com/JeanneStJames

pinterest.com/JeanneStJames

BEAR'S FAMILY TREE

		ZAK Jamison DAMC (President) b. 1985
	MITCH Jamison Blue Avengers MC b. 1967	**AXEL Jamison** Blue Avengers MC b.1987
BEAR Jamison DAMC Founder Murdered 1986		**JAYDE Jamison** b. 1993
	ROCKY Jamison DAMC b. 1964	**JEWEL Jamison** b. 1989
		DIAMOND Jamison b. 1988
		JAG Jamison DAMC (Road Captain) b. 1987

DOC'S FAMILY TREE

DOC Dougherty
DAMC Founder
b. 1943

ACE Dougherty
DAMC (Treasurer)
b. 1963

ALLIE Dougherty
b. 1968

ANNIE Dougherty
b. 1971

DIESEL Dougherty
DAMC (Enforcer)
b. 1985

HAWK Dougherty
DAMC (Vice President)
b. 1987

DEX Dougherty
DAMC (Secretary)
b 1986

IVY Doughtery
b. 1988

ISABELLA McBride
b. 1987

KELSEA Dougherty
b. 1991

Get a FREE Erotic Romance Sampler Book

This book contains the first chapter of a variety of my books. This will give you a taste of the type of books I write and if you enjoy the first chapter, I hope you'll be interested in reading the rest of the book.

Each book I list in the sampler will include the description of the book, the genre, and the first chapter, along with links to find out more. I hope you find a book you will enjoy curling up with!

Get it here: BookHip.com/MTQQKK

31251146R00182

Made in the USA
Lexington, KY
17 February 2019